MICHAEL LINDLEY

THE SISTER TAKEN

Book #4 in the Amazon #1 bestselling "Hanna and Alex" Low Country mystery and suspense series.

As always, thank you to the many book retailers, publishing and marketing partners, fellow authors, and, of course, my family for their continued support in the pursuit of these stories.

"You may be as different as the sun and the moon, but the same blood flows through both your hearts. You need her, as she needs you."

George R.R. Martin

Also by Michael Lindley

A missing twin. A wayward sister. A "jaw-dropping" twist.

The shocking disappearance of a young woman and a suspicious death put Hanna and Alex back in the crosshairs of the ruthless Dellahousaye crime family.

Hanna and Alex again find themselves in the troubled waters of love and commitment. Alex returns to South Carolina with the promise of a new start but with strings attached that Hanna may never be able to live with.

Here's what Goodreads and Amazon readers are saying in over 1300 Five Star reviews for *THE SISTER TAKEN* (4.5 Stars overall)

☆☆☆☆☆

"A real page-turner with many twists and turns."
"You can't wait to get to the end, but then wish it hadn't ended."
"I STILL cannot believe how it all unfolded!"
"Totally loved this book!"
"Engrossing, thrilling, mind-blowing!"

If you love mystery and suspense with twisting plots, compelling characters and settings that will sweep you away, find out why readers are raving about *The Sister Taken*.

Chapter One

Ida Dellahousaye stood in the loose sand, rising embers from the beach fire seeming to follow her every move. A billion stars flooded the inky black sky of night above, and the first trace of a new moon rose over the trees beyond the dunes. The smoke from the fire burned her eyes and mixed with the scents of the salt air and fish washed up on the shore. *What am I doing here?*

Her group of college friends barely noticed her stepping away. They kept on laughing and talking over each other between long pulls from the beers in their hands. A familiar country music song played on someone's phone. Her boyfriend, Jordan, seemed least interested, the cute little *Jennifer* beside him keeping his attention with the low cut of her swimsuit and incessant chatter about how drunk she was.

Ida had to steady herself, reaching her arms out for balance, suddenly feeling light-headed from the beer and standing so quickly. She continued to back away from the fire, her toes taking purchase in the cool sand of the Atlantic shore. A fresh breath of wind blew her short brown hair into her eyes and she pulled it back behind both ears. She zipped the orange *Clemson* sweatshirt she had put on earlier higher up on her neck as the night chilled. Her bare legs prickled with goosebumps as she got further from the fire.

She turned and looked for the path up into the dunes. *I need to get away, clear my head.*

Her eyes began to adjust to the growing darkness away from the fire and she saw the lighter gap in the dune grass ahead, the path back to the parking area where they had left their cars much earlier in the day.

It was the last day of their spring break. They would all be checking out of the beach house they had rented here on the shore north of Charleston in the morning. School started on Monday. She thought about the stress of her last term ahead and then med school in the fall, as she walked unsteadily up the narrow path between the dunes.

She felt her cell phone vibrate in the pocket of her sweatshirt. She pulled it out and saw her mother's name and number on the screen. "Oh no," she muttered under her breath. *Why's she calling so late?* She pushed the call to voice mail, thinking this was the last person she wanted to talk to.

A sudden rush of movement in the darkness beside her caused her to flinch. A large hand grabbed her face, covering her mouth and pulling her off her feet. She felt herself falling and reached out to catch herself as a strong arm pulled her down. She could smell the breath of her attacker close to her face, but she couldn't see him.

She landed hard on the sand and beach grass. She felt the wind knocked out of her and gasped for air. She saw the man now, looming over her, still holding his hand on her face to muffle her scream. He was dressed in a dark shirt with a ball cap pulled low over his eyes. He was only a shadow above her against the night sky and sparkling stars.

Then she felt the tip of a knife on her cheek. In a low whisper, the man hissed, "Do not make a sound."

Her body was trembling, and she struggled to get air through the tight clench of his hand pressing her head down into the sand. He was on top of her, his legs pinning her arms to the side. Her chest heaved, struggling to get air. A cold chill of fear raced through her brain, thinking of the worst to come.

The hand and knife pulled away from Ida's face and just as she started to scream out into the night, she felt the heavy push of tape stretched tight across her mouth. As she tried to get air through her nose, she struggled to pull away from the man who still held her down with his heavy body. The knife pricked at her cheek again.

"Do not make me cut you," the man said, leaning in close.

He stood suddenly and pulled her to her feet. She stumbled and fell. He pulled her up again and then down the path away from the beach. She felt the vice grip of his big hand on her left arm and the cold edge of the knife against the right side of her neck. She was still struggling to get her wind back and panic swirled in her head.

Up ahead she saw the cars they had parked earlier through the gloom of the dark night, a sandy pull-off to the beach on a remote part of the island. There was another car there now. The prick of the knife left her neck and a moment later she heard the low tone of a key fob as the trunk popped open ahead with no light coming on.

The man lifted her from behind and then dropped her into the trunk. Her head hit something hard and she winced in pain, dazed now as the fear and panic were overwhelming. Her arms were pinned behind her and she felt the bite of a plastic zip tie pulled tight around her wrists and then her ankles. She felt him reaching into her pants pockets and then her sweatshirt. She watched as he took her cell phone, turned it off and threw it up into the dunes behind the cars.

Ida screamed a muffled cry out into the night with little hope her friends at the beach would hear. The tape and her heaving breath made the sound barely a whisper. As she saw the trunk lid coming quickly down on top of her, enveloping her in total darkness, she thought she might never see the stars again.

Chapter Two

Hanna Walsh stood alone in the far corner of the deck in front of her house on the shore of Pawleys Island. She leaned against the weathered wooden rail and took a sip from a cold glass of white wine. A small crowd of friends and family were gathered around a bar and food table at the other end. The day had recently slipped away into a night filled with stars and the first slice of moon in the month of April. A soft breeze cut the heat from earlier in the day.

A flock of at least a hundred seagulls had gathered down on the long expanse of sand from the low ebb tide in front of the house, chattering among themselves and drowning out the soft rumble of low waves washing up on the shore.

She was throwing a party for the return of her *significant other*, Alex Frank. He had been away in Virginia for several months finishing his training to join the Federal Bureau of Investigation. They had seen each other just twice on short weekends when he was able to get back to South Carolina. She looked over and saw Alex talking with her son, Jonathan, both with beers in theirs hands as they stood beside his father, Skipper Frank and his new wife, Ella.

Standing near them in another conversation group was their friend, Dugganville Sheriff Pepper Stokes, and two FBI agents who were now Alex's colleagues. Special Agents Will Foster and Sharron Fairfield had also become friends and unfortunately, too often involved in her life. First, there was the kidnapping of her son two years earlier and more recently, on a dangerous case she and Alex had found themselves in with the gangster, Asa Dellahousaye.

She looked back at Alex and her son, Jonathan. The two men in her life were back and together which was a rare occasion. She was comforted in knowing Alex and Jonathan got along quite well. It had been almost three years since Jonathan's father had been killed and slowly, her son had been able to accept the loss and begin to deal with his grief. Alex had been a great refuge for Jonathan through those difficult years having dealt with tragedy in his own family growing up.

Hanna knew she should get back to her family and guests, but she needed a moment alone. The joy and excitement of having both Alex and Jonathan back, at least for a short time, was tempered with thoughts she couldn't put aside. Since Alex had left for Quantico months earlier, she had rarely been able to sleep and when she did, nightmares and images of her abduction by the crime boss, Asa Dellahousaye and run-ins with his hired assassin, Caine, continued to haunt her. She had been seeing a psychotherapist for six months, but it was having little effect. She was overwhelmed with guilt at the impact this was all having on her law practice and the free clinic she ran in Charleston. She was also still taking on clients for a firm here on Pawleys Island. She knew things were slipping, and she seemed powerless to get the daily events of her life under control.

She took another long sip from her glass of wine and then felt a hand on her shoulder. There was a soft kiss on her neck.

"Thank you for the nice homecoming," she heard Alex whisper behind her.

She turned and put her arms around him, pulling him in close and kissing him, tentatively, then looking away.

"What's wrong?" Alex asked.

"I'm sorry. I shouldn't be thinking about work."

"No, you shouldn't."

Hanna forced a smile and pulled him close again, her mouth close to his ear. "I'm so glad you're back."

Alex pulled away and moved beside her, looking out across the dark expanse of beach and ocean.

"How long can you stay?" she asked.

Alex hesitated, turning back to her. She could see the concern on his face even in the dim light of the porch. "I got a call earlier. I need to be back in DC on Monday. I thought I had it cleared to stay for a few more days, but..."

Hanna took another drink from her wine, staring back at him.

"I'm sorry." He reached for her free hand, squeezing it softly.

She tried to push the disappointment aside. "Well, let's just enjoy the time we have."

"We always do," he said, leaning in to kiss her again on the cheek. When he pulled back, he said, "I need to talk to you about something."

She could sense the nervousness in his tone.

"My new supervisor talked to me yesterday about my assignment now that I'm through with training."

"And what would that be?" She placed her glass on the rail.

"They want me to stay on in DC, assigned to a special unit on organized crime."

Hanna had been concerned for months their separation may be extended. "How long?"

He didn't answer right away.

"You're not coming back to Charleston?" Hanna said before he could answer, not trying to hide her disappointment.

"Not for a while it seems."

She turned away, looking off into the night.

"Hanna..."

"No really," she said, too quickly, pulling her hand away. "Let's just enjoy the time we have."

They stood side-by-side, each with one hand on the rail, the other holding their drinks.

Alex broke the silence. "I've been thinking about asking you to come with me."

Hanna turned quickly, both surprised and even stunned at his tentative invitation. "Thinking about it?"

"I don't know how long I'll be assigned up there. I don't want us to be apart."

Hanna's thoughts were swirling about the implications of leaving her home in South Carolina and all that was part of her life here. "I can't just pick up and leave, Alex."

"Hanna, please just..."

She tried to hold her growing anger back. "No, you can't ask me that."

"I know...."

"No, you don't know!"

Alex reached out for her and pulled her in close, his arms around her back. She stood there for a moment, then rested her face on his shoulder, taking long slow breaths and trying to calm her emotions.

"I love you, Hanna. I want us to be together."

"I guess I've known all along the chances of you getting assigned down here were slim."

"Can you just think about it? It wouldn't be forever. They know this is my home and I want to get back here as soon as possible."

Hanna paused, trying to clear her thoughts. "I can't just close down the clinic. And what about Jonathan? I don't want to be that far away. I'll never see him."

"I know. I've been thinking about all that."

She sighed as she sensed their often tenuous and troubled relationship edging toward a steep cliff again. Alex Frank had become an important part of her new life. The two of them had built a strong bond despite numerous roadblocks and challenges. Alex's ex-wife had tried her best to win him back and Hanna's college boyfriend who suddenly resurfaced had also tried to rekindle old feelings. The thought made her cringe as she remembered the final moments on Sam Collin's boat and the deadly aftermath. She looked up when Alex stepped away.

"There's something else I've been meaning to get to," he said.

She watched as he reached in his pocket and fumbled for something. In the dark light she saw him pull a small object out but couldn't see what it was. Her eyes opened wide as he bent down on one knee and held a small black box out between them. He opened it and the dim light caught the reflection of the stone on a silver ring.

"Really," she said, pulling her hands up through her loose hair and then to the sides of her face. Alex was staring up at her.

"I want you to marry me, Hanna Walsh."

She couldn't find words to respond.

"I want us to be together... as man and wife. Will you marry me, Hanna?"

He stood and took the ring from the box and reached for her hand. She felt the cool hardness of the ring slip onto her finger. A flood of thoughts raced through her brain... *surprise, exhilaration... doubt.*

She looked down at the ring on her finger and touched it with her other hand. When she looked back up at Alex, he stood there in anticipation, the look on his face so endearing she felt tears start to build at the corners of her eyes.

"I asked you to marry me, Hanna," he said quietly. "Usually that means you have to say *yes* or *no*."

She pushed all her crashing thoughts and emotions aside and slid into his arms, holding him close.

"You know, we haven't had the best luck at this," she said, images of Alex's crazy ex-wife and her own unfaithful and now long-dead husband clouding her thoughts.

"I think we've moved past all that."

A heavy silence lingered. She felt him pull her even closer in his arms. "We can work through all this other stuff, Hanna. I want us to be together."

She sighed and looked up into his eyes. "I hope you're right."

Chapter Three

Ida tried with all her will to control the violent trembling in her body as the car she was entombed in bumped along in the dark night. She had no concept of time and how long she had been in the dank smelling trunk. The edges of the plastic ties cut into her wrists and ankles, and her muscles ached from the tight position she was confined in. Her mind raced with the frightening images of her abduction and the feel of the razor-sharp knife on her skin.

The motion of the car was causing her to feel nauseous and she was terrified she might choke on her own vomit with the tape tight across her mouth. *Where is he taking me? Why is he doing this?*

She shuddered again, thinking about what this man might have planned for her. *How will anyone ever find me?*

Over the loud roar of the tires against the road and the rush of wind outside the trunk, she thought she could hear the man talking. His words were low and muted. She couldn't make out what he was saying. *Was someone else in the car? Is he talking on a phone?*

With all her will, she tried to regain some sense of calm. She knew she had to keep her wits to have any chance of escape.

She woke with a start as the trunk lid above her popped open. The night was still dark and there seemed to be no lights nearby as the black shadow of the man loomed above her again. Ida realized she must have fallen asleep or passed out. She had no idea how much time had elapsed since she'd been taken from the beach. She felt his arms reach under her, lifting her out of the car. Her feet touched the ground, but she stumbled as her legs failed to respond after such a long time of tight confinement. He leaned her back against the side of the car, and she felt the zip tie on her ankles cut away.

She watched as the man stood beside her. She still couldn't make out the features of his face under the shadows of his cap in the low light.

He leaned in and said, "I won't hurt you if you do everything I say." His voice was a low raspy hiss of a sound, his breath sour. There was the slightest sense of an accent she couldn't place. Another shudder of fear shot through her and she willed herself again not to throw-up. Tentatively, she nodded.

He took her arm and pulled her away from the car. Looking around now, she could see the dark shadows of large trees against the night sky, no lights visible in any direction. Her bare feet sensed cool loose sand and she struggled not to fall as her legs prickled with blood rushing back into her extremities. The large man continued on ahead of her, pulling on her arm, still secured to her other behind her back.

Just beyond, Ida now saw the outline of a house set up on stilts, a shadow against the trees and night sky. She stumbled on the first stair and he picked her up again in his arms as if she were weightless. They climbed the steps up to a wooden deck. He placed her down, standing next to a screen door that he pulled open, then pushed her in ahead of him. She stumbled on the door jam and fell helplessly forward, turning to break her fall with her shoulder rather than her face. A shock of pain laced through her shoulder and arm and she cried out a desperate scream.

He picked her up violently and the lightning bolts of pain flared again. He pushed her roughly ahead of him into a small room. Even in the dark, she could see a bed against one wall but no other furniture. The outline of one window was covered with a dark shade. He pushed her down on the bed and then reached behind to cut the tie holding her wrists. As her arms came free, she winced at the pain in her shoulder.

She couldn't stop from shaking as thoughts of what he might be planning to do to her flashed through her mind. *Is he going to rape me, kill me? Oh God, please no!*

Ida gasped as the man tore the tape from her mouth. His right hand came down hard across her face as she started to scream out into the night.

10

"No one can hear you," he growled. "No one will find you." He pulled his hand away and sat beside her on the bed.

"Please don't..." she pleaded, painfully trying to pull away against the wall.

"There's no way out of here," the man said, standing now. "If you do what I say, this will go much easier for you."

Chapter Four

Hanna reached for her son's arm from behind. The tall young man with the sandy brown hair and striking looks of his father turned and smiled back. He was standing and talking with some of their neighbors from the beach who Hanna had invited to the party. Alex stood beside her with a hand on her back.

She leaned in to whisper in her son's ear. "Let's take a walk."

"What's up?" Jonathan asked, turning to face them and taking a long swig from his beer.

Alex said, "We have something we need to talk to you about."

A look of confusion came over Jonathan's face. "Okay, what did I do this time?"

"You didn't do anything, honey," Hanna said. "Let's go down to the beach."

Jonathan walked beside Hanna and she felt the comforting hand of her suddenly new fiancé, Alex Frank, in hers. The gulls spooked and flew away as they walked through them down to the shore. The wind was soft from behind and only a slow cadence of low waves touched the cool hard sand. They headed south along the water; the thin reflection of the moon broken across the ripples on the black surface of the ocean.

"So, what's up?" Jonathan asked.

Hanna began, "Alex has been assigned to the DC office."

Jonathan turned to face them as they kept on. "So, you won't be able to get back down to Charleston?"

"Not right away," Alex said.

"Alex has asked me to move up there with him."

Jonathan stopped and they all stood together, looking out over the water. Hanna could see her son contemplating all the issues she was already trying to process.

"There's something else," Hanna said. She reached over with her left hand and took her son's hand. Holding it up, Jonathan saw the ring on her finger.

"You're kidding me!" he said.

"I've asked your mother to marry me. I'd like your blessing."

Hanna couldn't read the expression on her son's face in the dim light. She took a deep breath, anticipating his first reaction. He surprised her by moving quickly to give her a tight hug.

"That's so great, mom. I'm really happy for you."

She savored the warm embrace of the boy she had raised and been through many wonderful but occasionally dark times. She was pleased he was moving on so well with his life in school and with a career he was hoping to build practicing law, following in the steps of his parents and his grandfather. He had already expressed interest in applying to law school at UNC. His girlfriend, Elizabeth Hanley, who couldn't come down for the weekend, had practically become part of their family and Hanna had grown to love her dearly.

"I'm sorry this will take us to DC for a while, but..." Alex said.

"It's not so far," Jonathan said. "I've got my key to the beach house here," he said, smiling back.

Hanna turned to Alex. "Don't jump ahead on this moving thing," she said, a bit irritated he was taking it for granted.

A school of dolphin breached just offshore and took their attention away for the moment. They all watched the dark shadows rise and slip away again and again, effortlessly across the surface.

"When is all this happening?" Jonathan asked.

"We haven't talked about a date," Hanna said, thinking again about all the changes and new events ahead.

"I'd like you to be my *best man*," Alex said.

Jonathan reached over and shook his hand firmly, then pulled him close in a man hug. "My pleasure. I'm so happy for you guys."

Hanna felt a strong sense of relief and joy in the easy way her son had accepted their sudden plans. "I hadn't really thought about it," she said, "but wouldn't it be wonderful to have Elizabeth stand with us as *maid of honor?*"

"She'd love that," Jonathan said, then hesitated before continuing. "I don't want you to freak out, but Liz and I are talking about taking a break from school."

"Taking a break?" Hanna repeated.

"Just this next term. We both need a break."

"What's going on?" Alex asked.

"This last term just took its toll. I don't know how we both got so far behind, but we barely passed a couple of our classes."

"Why didn't you tell me about this?" Hanna asked, taking him by the shoulders and peering into his dark face in the low light of the beach.

"I guess we thought we could pull it out at the end of the term, but we both bombed our finals. We're burned out. We need a break."

"What are you going to do?" Hanna asked, not letting him pull away.

"We want to stay out here on the island, get jobs, make some money... recharge."

"Recharge?" Hanna said.

"It's only one term, Mom."

Hanna shook her head, trying to remain calm. Her son had always been a very good student. He was on track to be able to get into a good law school, maybe even UNC. She thought it was something he had always wanted. "What about law school?"

"We'll catch up," he said, though Hanna felt little reassurance in his tone.

"Look, we can talk about this later," Jonathan said. "I don't want to spoil your big night. I'm really happy for both of you."

"Thank you," Alex said, reaching for Hanna's arm.

She stepped away from her son. "Can we at least talk about this in the morning?"

"Sure," he replied, hesitantly. "Look, I'm gonna head back."

"We'll see you later," Hanna said as he moved away down the beach.

"How about you and I take a walk," Alex said, whispering in her ear.

They had walked for several minutes along the shoreline, holding hands and taking occasional sips from their drinks. Alex broke the stillness of the night. "I'm looking forward to calling you *Mrs. Hanna Frank*."

"I'm thinking Hanna *Walsh* Frank. I want to keep my son's name."

"Of course."

"I can't believe Jonathan wants to walk away from school, even for just a term. It's just not like him."

"Maybe they really do need some time. You know how stressful school can be for kids these days."

"I'm afraid he'll never go back."

"Your son is an amazing young man. He's smart and strong."

"This doesn't seem so smart."

"Look, I don't want to get between you two here, but maybe we should at least hear him out in the morning."

She nodded and leaned into him and he pulled her along with his arm. "This has been quite an evening," she said.

"Just a little excitement... a new husband, a new home."

Hanna hesitated and she knew Alex could feel her trepidation as her body stiffened.

"We'll work this all out, Hanna. I know how much this place means to you and all you've built down here... what you've come back from. We'll work it out."

Hanna listened but couldn't reassure herself there was an easy solution. "So, when do you want to do this?"

"What?"

She punched him softly on the arm. "Set a date!"

"As soon as possible." He paused. "Do you want a big wedding? I'll do whatever you like."

"I've had a big wedding. No need to go down that path again. Let's do something small and casual, just family and a few friends. Have you told the Skipper yet?" she asked, referring to Alex's father who owned and operated a shrimp boat down in Dugganville, just north of Charleston.

"Not until I knew you'd say *yes*."

"You had your doubts?"

"After all we've been through these past few years, I wouldn't have been surprised if you told me to go to hell!" He smiled back at her and pulled her in to kiss her.

They held each other close, the warmth of the ocean swells washing over their feet. Alex said, "Not many lights on around here," looking up into the dunes.

"What did you have in mind?"

He took her hand and they walked up through the loose sand between two low dunes. He held her tight and they kissed deeply. Hanna felt a warm gust of wind on her cheek. Alex sat down in the sand and she moved with him and pushed him back, lying to his side and kissing him again. "I think we could go to jail for this," she said quietly.

"I have friends in high places."

She reached for the top button on his shirt.

Chapter 5

Chapter Five

The call to the Sheriff's office in Dugganville, South Carolina came in at 2:20 that morning. The boyfriend of a college girl was frantic she was missing, walking away from a bonfire at a beach near town and never coming back. The dispatcher sent a patrol car to the scene to meet with the boy. He decided not to alert Sheriff Pepper Stokes until they had more information.

When Deputy Sam Mills arrived at the small parking pull-off near the beach, there were three cars and a dozen young people milling about. Most were on their cell phones. One of the women was sitting in a car sobbing. A boy who looked to be in his early twenties came forward and extended his hand. Mills got out of his car and put his hat on.

"Officer, I'm Jordan Hayes. I'm the one who called. We can't find Ida."

"Hayes? You the senator's son?"

"Grandson."

"And who is Ida?" the deputy asked.

"My girlfriend, Ida Dellahousaye."

Mills shook his head, then said, "She wouldn't be part of *the* Dellahousaye family?"

Jordan Hayes nodded. "Remy is her father."

"Asa's son?"

"That's right," Hayes said. "We've looked all over. We thought she might have passed out or fallen asleep in the dunes, but we can't find her anywhere."

"When is the last time you saw her?"

"She got up and walked away from our fire down there on the beach around

18

midnight, I guess."

"You guess?"

"Officer, we've been drinking. We're legal age. It's our last night of spring break. We're all renting a house down the beach."

"So, you don't know exactly when she left?"

"Right."

"And did she say anything before she left?"

One of the girls walked up and put her arm around Jordan's waist. She was dressed in only a thin white bikini that stood out in the glare of the patrol car's lights. "Jordan, this is freaking me out. Where could she be?"

"And what's your name, miss?" the deputy asked.

"Jennifer. Ida is my friend and sorority sister."

"And you've been back to the house to check?" Mills asked.

"Robby just got back," Hayes said, motioning to another boy in the crowd by the other cars.

"Do you have any other cars?

"No, this is it."

"And how much did Miss Dellahousaye have to drink tonight?"

Jennifer jumped in. "She doesn't drink much. She definitely wasn't drunk."

"No reason you can think of she might have just walked away?"

The deputy watched as Jordan Hayes and the girl named Jennifer, still clutching him closely, looked at each other.

Hayes finally said, "No, officer. She seemed fine and then she was just gone."

Deputy Mills sat in his patrol car. His radio mic was in one hand while he booted up the mounted laptop beside him. The dispatcher acknowledged his call. Mills responded, "Who can I get out here tonight to help with this missing person's search?"

"We've got two units nearby. I'll get them over to you."

"Roger that." Mills thought for a moment, then said, "Better wake up the sheriff. This missing girl is a Dellahousaye and the shit is gonna hit the fan in no time. Hopefully, she's just passed out down the beach somewhere, but let's prepare for the worst."

Sheriff Pepper Stokes shook himself awake as his cell phone ringing on the nightstand beside him finally brought him out of a deep sleep. As he reached for the phone, he looked over at the woman sleeping beside him. The noise hadn't roused her. *What was her name? Marjorie? I need to stop hanging out at Gilly's so late.*

He answered the call, "Sheriff Stokes".

He listened as the dispatcher brought him quickly up to speed on the missing girl. He ended the call and slammed the phone down. "Shit!"

Forty minutes later, Sheriff Stokes pulled into the parking area along the beach where two patrol cars sat with their lights flashing. He got out and found his deputy talking with two college-aged kids. The other was in his car on the radio.

"Morning, Sheriff," Deputy Mills said, walking away from the kids. "Sorry to wake you." He motioned for the sheriff to follow him over behind his car away from the others. "We got a senator's grandson here, Jordan Hayes, and the missing girl is from the Dellahousaye family."

"You're shittin' me?" Stokes said. "You mean *ex-senator*. Sonofabitch should be in prison after what he pulled last year in the Asa D case."

"Thought you'd wanna know."

"Right. What's happening?"

"Got an officer with two of the college kids walking the beach in each direction with flashlights looking for the girl. One unit has already been over to the beach house they're all renting. No sign there."

How long's she been gone?" Stokes asked.

Mills looked at his watch. "Least three hours. The kids say she wasn't drunk, so not likely she passed out. Maybe fell asleep somewhere to get away from the fire, but we've covered a lot of ground already."

"You've tried her cell?"

"No answer and it must be turned off, or the battery is dead. Can't track it."

Stokes senses went on full alert. "Why in hell would she turn her phone off?"

"Don't know, Pepper."

Stokes walked into his office just past six a.m. and grabbed a cup of stale coffee from the kitchen before going in to sit behind his desk. He threw his hat on a chair in the corner and rubbed his eyes. They had found no sign of the missing Dellahousaye girl, though he had sent two more deputies from the day shift out to help with the search now that the sun was coming up. He grimaced as his sour stomach churned. He thought about the woman, *Marjorie*, he had just dropped off at her trailer outside of town. *Jesus, I need to get a life!*

His mind raced with the implications of a missing girl linked to two prominent people. He knew he had to check all the right boxes and protocols to keep his ass out of a sling. He'd already called the State Police duty officer on his way back to the office. They were mobilizing to help with the search. As far as he knew, there was no indication this was an abduction, so he decided to wait on calling in the Feds.

He took a sip from the coffee and spit it back into the cup. "Goddamit!" he yelled out. "Can't anybody make a damn fresh pot of coffee around here?"

Chapter Six

The sound of the gulls caused her to stir. Hanna opened her eyes and then put her arm over her face as the bright morning sun blared through the window looking out over the ocean. A dull and familiar ache in her brain greeted her as it had so many mornings lately after too much wine and too little sleep. Pushing her sandy brown hair away from her face, she reached for a glass of water on the nightstand and felt the welcome relief in her dry mouth as she took a sip. When she turned, Alex was still asleep beside her, facing away, his bare back rising and falling slowly. The scars from two past bullet wounds always made her wince.

Memories of the previous night's events began coming back to her and she looked down at the new ring on her left hand. She inched herself up and propped pillows behind her, pulling the sheet up to cover her breasts.

The light from the windows caught the edges of the new diamond on her finger. She smiled as she thought about Alex's proposal. These past years together with Alex Frank had been some of the happiest of her life, unfortunately edged with several extremely difficult incidents that had come close to ending all they had hoped to have together. Now they would be moving forward as husband and wife, and as her head continued to clear from the past night's excesses, she knew this was truly the right time and the right man for her to build the rest of her life with.

Hanna reached to take another sip from the water glass and looked out over the expanse of beach and ocean outside her bedroom window. Thoughts of her distant great grandmother, Amanda Paltierre Atwell, came back to her and she imagined similar mornings Amanda would have awoken to this same view, with her first husband, Captain Jeremy Atwell, who died tragically in a battle fought weeks after the end of the Civil War; and then years later when she wed the mysterious Colonel Robert Morgan who returned to tell her the truth about Jeremy's death. *So much history. So much shared fate. Such cherished memories here in the old house on Pawleys Island.*

She frowned and looked away from the spectacular morning out beyond the window as she thought about leaving this place to be with Alex in D.C., with his first assignment with the FBI. Of course, they would be able to get back occasionally, but she would have to walk away from her work in Charleston at her legal clinic and the work she did for the firm here on the island. She didn't know anyone in Washington. She had only been there on two occasions with her family when Jonathan was just a boy. She had no idea what she would do professionally or personally when she got there, other than be the new wife of Special Agent Alex Frank. Then, she remembered her son's sudden decision to leave school with his girlfriend, Elizabeth. How could she walk away and not be here to help him through this rough patch?

Alex stirred beside her, groaning softly and then turned to face her. His face was flushed from sleep and he squinted at the bright early morning light, his short black hair, edged in gray, all askew. He reached under the sheet and put his arm across her bare belly, pulling her closer. "Good morning, Mrs. Frank," he whispered in a throaty voice.

"Not so fast, mister," Hanna said, managing a smile and then scrunching down to nestle into his arms.

"Looks like a beautiful morning out there," Alex said.

"We should go for a walk."

"There's a great view from the dunes down the beach," he said and smiled back at her.

She remembered their celebratory tryst on the beach under the stars the previous night. "I hope we didn't wake the neighbors."

"They'll get over it."

Hanna pulled her left hand up in front of their faces and the ring sparkled in the sunlight. "It's beautiful, thank you."

"I should have done this so long ago, but...."

"No, this is perfect..." She didn't finish the thought and pulled her hand back to push a scattering of hair she was letting grow longer behind her ear.

Alex said, "I know you're worried about moving, but there's no rush. We'll do this all when we're ready, okay?"

Hanna pressed her face down into his neck and felt the scrape of his morning's beard on her forehead. "I know we will... thank you."

"What about that walk?" he asked.

She lifted her face to his and kissed him softly. Their eyes met and she saw him smile back at her. She kissed him again and pulled him closer. "There's no hurry."

Chapter Seven

Ida Dellahousaye woke to the sound of crows squawking outside her window. She squinted at the morning light. It took only a moment for all the terrifying events of the past night to come racing back. She sat up and pain shot through her shoulder where she had fallen earlier. She also felt her wrist held fast to the metal frame of the bed by a hard steel grip. She looked over and saw a pair of handcuffs holding her captive. The features of the dank room were just coming into focus. There was no other furniture and a small window behind her had shades pulled down shadowing the light. The walls were paneled in dark wood. The air smelled of mold and... death, *probably some dead animal in the walls*, she thought. The door across from her was closed and she assumed locked.

She remembered the shaded face of her captor and shivered again. Taking inventory of her clothes and body, apparently the monster hadn't done anything to her after she fell asleep from exhaustion.

She heard movement out beyond the closed door, then the muffled sound of two voices. One was clearly female. She felt some relief in the presence of another woman, though she wasn't entirely sure why.

She pushed back against the wall when the knob turned. The door pushed open into the room. The large man came in, his face covered with a ghoulish Halloween mask. He wore black jeans and a tight black t-shirt stretched tight over a large chest and arms. He came across the room and handed her a bottle of water.

"Drink this."

She hesitated and then he turned the lid of the bottle, breaking the seal to open it, showing it was a fresh bottle of water. This small gesture of concern gave her some comfort they weren't planning to hurt her, *at least for now.*

Remy Dellahousaye was sitting in the office in his home along the Battery in Charleston. A wall of windows looked out across a large wooded park down to the waterfront of the harbor. He was always up early to begin the day's work, sorting through the many details of his extensive network of business interests around the world. Just past his 50th birthday, the man was still trim and fit, running several times per week and keeping track of his diet to maintain the fitness and energy required to keep on top of all he controlled in his life. His face was a younger version of his deceased father, former head of the Dellahousaye crime syndicate, deeply tanned with only a tint of gray in his black hair. He was dressed in running gear and would be out soon to get the six miles required in his workout regimen.

His father, Asa Dellahousaye, had died the previous year in a deadly shoot-out with police at a cabin in the South Carolina woods, along with two of his men. Remy had gone to great lengths in his adult life to stay above the fray of his father's questionable business pursuits. It was a never-ending challenge, particularly after his father's passing. The authorities descended on anything related to Asa D and his businesses. His own holdings also came under extreme scrutiny and several lawsuits were still active with courts trying to dig deeper into the structure of the Dellahousaye empire.

Remy took a sip from the energy drink sitting on his desk and looked at his watch... 7:02. As he stood to go out for his run with his bodyguard, Vincent, his cell phone buzzed on the desk. He didn't recognize the number other than the South Carolina area code. He pressed the speaker button to answer the call.

"Yes."

"Mr. Dellahousaye?"

"Who is this?"

"Sir, this is Jordan Hayes, Ida's friend."

Dellahousaye grimaced and looked outside across the park, boats passing slowly in the harbor, bikers and joggers on the path along the water. "What is it, son?"

"I don't know how to tell you this..." Hayes began, then paused.

Dellahousaye immediately felt a flush of apprehension. "What the hell's going on?"

"Sir, Ida is missing..."

"What!"

"She was with us up at the beach last night. She walked away up into the dunes around midnight and never came back. We've had the local Sheriff's patrol and the State Police out here all night helping us look for her..."

"Why the hell didn't you call me earlier?"

"We thought... we were hoping she just fell asleep somewhere down the beach, but..."

"Where are you?"

"The beach just north of Dugganville. A bunch of us have a house rented for the break. We're supposed to head back to school today."

"Is there a cop there I can talk to?" Dellahousaye asked.

"The deputy gave me the sheriff's number to call. He's not here right now."

"Why the hell not?"

"I don't know, sir..."

After calling Vincent to have his car brought around, Remy Dellahousaye dialed the number for the Sheriff's Department he'd been given. After a few moments, he was put through.

"This is Stokes."

"Sheriff Stokes?"

"Yes, who is this?"

"My name is Remy Dellahousaye. I just received a call from a friend of my daughter that she may be missing."

There was a brief pause, then, "Sir, all I can tell you right now is we have all of our available resources on this as well as the State Police."

Remy tried to control the panic he was feeling, standing and walking to the window. "And there's no sign of my daughter?"

"Not yet, sir."

He watched the traffic and a few walkers passing by his house, trying to remain calm and come up with some plan of action. "I want to come up there. Where can I meet you?"

"There's not much you can do at this point, sir," he heard the sheriff say.

"Dammit! I'm not going to sit here..."

"Mr. Dellahousaye, I would suggest it's best for you to stay where anyone involved with this can reach you."

"You think she's been kidnapped?"

"We have no reason to believe that yet, but it's certainly one scenario we're considering..."

He heard a knock on the door, then Vincent stuck his head in. "Car's ready, sir."

"I'm coming up, Sheriff. I want to see where Ida was last night. I want to talk to her friends. Where can I meet you?"

"Mr. Dellahousaye..."

"No! I'm coming now and if you won't cooperate, my next call is to the Governor!"

Chapter Eight

When Hanna came downstairs into her kitchen, her soon-to-be father-in-law, Skipper Frank, was fussing over the coffee pot, muttering to himself.

"Morning, Skipper," she said, startling the man. "Here, let me help you with that."

"Damned new contraptions! Used to be, you push a button and you get a pot of coffee."

"They're K-Cups, Skipper," she said, shaking her head at him. "One cup at a time."

"One cup! I need a whole damn pot for this hangover I'm nursing."

"You can have as many as you want. Hanna opened a drawer and showed him a selection of different flavors. "Take your pick."

His wife, Ella, walked in, her bathrobe pulled tight around her neck. Her face was puffy and flushed from sleep and her dyed red hair was all askew.

Hanna turned and gave the woman a hug, noticing the smell of whiskey and cigarettes still hanging on her. "Good morning, Ella."

Her future mother-in-law was also the mother of Alex's ex-wife, Adrienne, though she and Hanna had grown close over the past months.

Ella Frank said in a hoarse whisper, "Where's the *Motrin*?"

Hanna reached into a cabinet and handed her the bottle, then poured her a glass of water.

"Hanna," Skipper cut in, "would you pick me one that's a decent cup of black coffee?"

She walked over and put a K-cup of *Starbucks French Roast* in the machine. "Looks like you two had a rough night."

Skipper Frank just muttered something she couldn't understand. Ella was gulping down the glass of water.

"Well, I'm glad you could both be here this weekend."

Ella finished drinking and said, "Congratulations, honey. You and Alex, I mean."

"Thank you, Ella." Hanna held her new engagement ring up in the morning light coming in through the kitchen windows.

"Helluva nice rock," Skipper sputtered. He leaned in and gave Hanna a hug. "Welcome to the family, Hanna."

"Well, it's official now, anyway," Hanna answered. "I feel like you've been my second family all along now." She thought about her other house guests, still upstairs, and breakfast she needed to prepare. Her son would likely sleep late. *We definitely need to talk! Quitting school!*

She had no idea when Alex or his two FBI associates, Foster and Fairfield would come down. She had given Will and Sharron their own rooms, of course, but she always had a sense the two of them were more than just professional partners.

An hour later, everyone was seated around the long dining table, passing plates and sharing stories from the party the night before. Hanna looked around the room and smiled at the presence of so many friends and family members to celebrate Alex's return and now her unexpected engagement. Alex was at the other end of the table and she noticed he was staring at her even though Ella was bending his ear about something. He smiled back at her.

A phone could be heard buzzing and Will Foster reached into his pocket, standing and walking back into the kitchen. He was gone for about a minute. Hanna could hear his muffled conversation in the other room. She was talking with her son when Foster came back into the room. He had a concerned look on his face.

"Sharron, Alex, I need a word," Foster said.

The three of them went back into the kitchen and didn't return for a few minutes. When they came back, Alex walked around the table and whispered,

"Sorry, we have to go to work."

"It's Sunday!" Hanna said, looking up with a pleading expression.

"There appears to be an abduction, prominent family. Governor's involved. They want the FBI to step in."

Sharron Fairfield said, "Hanna, thanks so much for including us and putting us up last night."

"I'm glad you could join us. Sorry you can't stay."

"Duty calls," Foster said.

Alex leaned close. "I'll keep you posted. Hopefully, I'll be back soon."

Hanna watched the three of them leave to go upstairs. *Welcome to the FBI,* she thought.

Chapter Nine

Ophelia Dellahousaye was in a deep, still drug and alcohol-induced sleep when the buzz of her phone on the nightstand finally brought her back to consciousness. She sat up groggily and saw her two friends, Josh and Susanna, still asleep beside her, parts of their bare bodies sticking out from the covers.

"Hello?" she said, her strained voice barely a whisper."

"O? Is that you?"

"Daddy?"

"Where are you?"

"At home, what's the matter?" The other Dellahousaye twin lived in a condo her father had bought her in downtown Charleston. She had lived there over a year since dropping out of college, most recently with her new *love couple*, as she called them. She knew her father was not happy about the situation.

"I'm driving up to the beach near Dugganville," she heard her father say. A dull ache in her brain was distracting her from the conversation. "We think your sister has gone missing."

This got her full attention. "What!"

"The boyfriend, Hayes, called just a while ago. Ida walked away from a beach party last night and she's still missing."

She felt a shock of panic sweep through her dulled senses. *Her sister was missing!*

Ophelia pulled her feet around to the floor and leaned forward, her face in her hands. Her mind was racing, trying to sort through the fog from the past night. "They can't find her?"

"*I don't know what's going on,*" she heard her father say. "*I'll call when I talk to the police up there.*"

She started to reply, then sat upright, her eyes wide with fright. She was taken suddenly with an overwhelming sense of fear. It was a terror like none she had ever experienced or imagined. *Sister!*

Chapter Ten

Alex rode in the back seat and directed fellow agents, Foster and Fairfield, as they drove through his small hometown of Dugganville on their way to the beach at Isle of Palms. The familiar storefronts greeted him, and memories of his youth flashed back. They drove by *Gilly's Bar* and thoughts of earlier and almost deadly encounters there came back to him.

The morning sun was just coming up above the tall oaks and a breeze across the marshes pushed the hanging moss in a slow graceful rhythm. A flock of ducks flew in low and flared their wings to land on a still pond beside the road. They passed the old chapel, tucked into the shadowed trees, and the cemetery next to it where his mother was buried. He looked away as he tried to block the memories of her tragic car accident many years earlier.

Will Foster broke the silence in the car. "So, you thought you were through with the Dellahousaye family, Alex?"

Alex saw Foster's face in the rear-view mirror and nodded back. Images of the night in the old fishing shack when the crime boss, Asa Dellahousaye, had taken Hanna hostage came back to him. Asa D, as he was known, had not left the place alive. Alex took a deep breath as he recalled the violent assault on Dellahousaye and his men to free Hanna. It was an event he would never be able to reconcile with his conscience, despite the desperate situation they faced. Killing a man, if necessary, was part of the work he signed up for. He knew that and accepted it, but it didn't make the memories any easier to deal with.

"What do you know about the son, Remy?" Sharron Fairfield asked.

"Not much," Alex responded. "As deep as we dug into his father's affairs, the son seemed far removed from any of the illegal enterprises. Seems he took a different path to distance himself from his old man."

Foster said, "We came to the same conclusion when we wrapped up the Asa D files last year."

"So, he's got twin daughters and one goes missing," Fairfield said absently, looking out the window as her partner drove.

"A little early to call in the Feds, don't you think?" Alex asked.

"Things have a way of getting mobilized when you have a prominent family involved," Foster said. "They usually have connections in high places that light the fuse."

Foster added, "The father, Remy, is becoming a *who's who* on Wall Street. His string of companies and successful new acquisitions are substantial."

Fairfield was looking down at her phone reading notes on an email that had just come in.

As she read the message on her phone, Alex looked at the back of her head, her wavy blonde hair familiar from the time the two of them had been a couple. They had met during the investigation into the death of Ben Walsh and the abduction of Hanna's son. Their friendship turned more serious and intimate in the months that followed. It was over before he began seeing Hanna Walsh as more than just detective and crime victim. For whatever reason, he had not told Hanna about his relationship with Sharron Fairchild, nor had either of them shared all the details of their past before they became a couple. It seemed even more difficult for him to address this with Hanna now that he and Sharron were colleagues and would be working closely together. He didn't feel like he was trying to hide anything from her, it just seemed a complication that was best left in the past. *It's not like I was unfaithful to Hanna*, he thought.

"Looks like we have another *VIP* family to deal with," Sharron said, throwing her cell up on the dash.

"Who's that?" Alex asked.

"The scumbag Senator, Jordan Hayes, has a grandson and namesake. Apparently, he's the missing girl's boyfriend. He called it in last night."

"How the hell did Hayes stay out of prison last year?" Foster said with disgust clear in his voice.

"What'd you all say about *friends in high places?*" Alex responded, returning Foster's glance in the mirror.

Just before 11 a.m., Alex watched as their car pulled off the main road down a narrow sandy two-track trail. Within a minute, the road widened out into a sandy parking area with two County Sheriff's patrol cars parked and one with State Police markings. He saw his friend, Sheriff Pepper Stokes, climb out of one of the cars with a cell phone to his ear.

The parking area was surrounded by low sand dunes crested in grasses and low scrub. The sky was a deep blue without a trace of clouds. Alex heard the sound of waves rolling up on shore to the east. He got out of the car with the other two agents. He watched as Pepper Stokes noticed him and came over, ending his call.

"Morning Pepper."

"Thought I'd seen the last of you last night at Hanna's party," Stokes said, smiling.

"You left a little early," Alex said. "All work and no play?"

"No, had a date waiting down at *Gilly's.*"

"Should have brought her out to Hanna's."

The old sheriff smiled back. "A little soon for that. Got the cavalry called in early I see." He nodded to both Foster and Fairfield, who he had come to know quite well over the past couple of years.

"Where we at, Sheriff?" Fairfield asked.

"We been up and down this beach for miles and not a trace. Nothing at the house the kids are staying at that gives us anything to go on either."

Alex asked, "Assume no contact from a kidnapper or ransom request, or we would have heard about it on the way out?"

"Nothing yet," Stokes said, "but it's lookin' more and more like someone took her. We did find her cell phone up in the dunes over there." He gestured off to the north. "It was turned off. The last messages the girl responded to or sent out were just past midnight. Nothing suspicious, although her mother did try to reach her about that time."

"Anything else here around the cars?" Alex asked.

Stokes shook his head. "Too many tracks coming and going. Hard to say how many cars have been in here recently and no way to get tire impressions in this loose sand."

"Can we see the beach area, Pepper?" Foster asked.

"Yeah, follow me."

Alex trailed behind them all out through a narrow path between the dunes. The sun was getting hot and he wiped at his forehead to mop away the sweat. Over the last crest, the Atlantic Ocean came into view, low rolling blue waves rumbling up on the brown shoreline. They gathered around a fire pit hole dug into the sand and eight beach chairs circled randomly around it. Two coolers were set up against the last dune and a few towels and sweatshirts were strewn across some of the chairs. Crime scene tape was staked out in a wide perimeter. The fire was mostly out, but a thin stream of smoke still rose into the sky.

Alex left his colleagues talking to the sheriff and walked out onto the beach. The sand grew firm as he reached the shore. He looked in both directions. Only a few beach sunbathers were out yet further south. He took a deep breath and thought about Remy Dellahousaye and his missing daughter. He knew how much panic the man must be facing, and the girl as well if she had indeed been abducted. He said a silent prayer that Ida Dellahousaye was still alive.

He looked back when he heard someone approaching. Sharron Fairfield walked up beside him and stood staring out at the ocean for a moment. "Beautiful place," she finally said.

"Not your typical crime scene."

"By the way, congratulations on your engagement. I didn't get a chance to talk to you and Hanna personally before we left this morning."

"Thank you."

"Hanna is great. You're a lucky man."

Alex turned and looked at his new colleague... and former lover. She continued to look out over the ocean.

Chapter Eleven

The steel cuff on her wrist holding Ida to the bed frame had rubbed the skin raw. Her shoulder ached from her fall the past night. She fell back on the hard mattress and tried to find sleep. She was exhausted, but the terror of her abduction kept her senses racing. Through the shaded and dirty window and her clouded sense of time, she thought it was somewhere near midday.

She kept retracing the events of the last hours. *Does anyone know I'm missing? What do they think happened when I didn't come back to the fire? Has anyone called my father... and my sister?*

Ida remembered her last glimpse of her boyfriend, Jordan, as she backed away from her group of *so-called friends.* He had his arm around her sorority sister, Jennifer Wallace, spilling his beer in her lap and then trying to dry her off with his towel. She knew he was drunk, but Ida had been sitting right there beside him. It wasn't the first time his interests had strayed, she knew, but for some reason she had stayed with him, despite numerous hook-ups with other girls at school. *What was I thinking?*

She thought again about her sister. How would she react to news of her disappearance? As with most twins, they had been extremely close throughout their lives. They had been nearly inseparable until just a year ago, then O had left school, transferred to community college in Charleston, now living there with her two *friends.*

Their father had set Ophelia up with a lavish condo and bought her an art gallery to run a few blocks away. *The woman is a train wreck!* she thought.

Floorboards creaked in the room beyond the door. Ida sat up and pressed her back painfully up against the wall. In her mind, her captors were just biding their time until they played out their sick plans for her. She had imagined every disgusting form of abuse, torture and assault. The door opened and the man came in again, the grotesque mask hiding his features. There was something about his voice from earlier that had suddenly seemed familiar to her. He had a plate of food in one hand, a sandwich of some kind and a bottle of water in the other. He placed them on the bed beside her.

"You need to eat," he said in the low voice she tried again to recognize.

"Who are you!" Ida yelled out. "Why are you doing this?"

He didn't answer, looming over her, his hands clenched at his sides. He had heavy black hair on his exposed arms and hands. Strands of black hair also pushed out from behind the mask.

Chapter Twelve

Ophelia Dellahousaye sat at the granite-covered island in the kitchen of her condo. Windows looked out over the rooftops of other buildings in the historic downtown of Charleston. She sipped at a cup of coffee and took two more pills to ease the pain in her head.

Her sister was missing!

The thought of her abducted, kidnapped... dead, made her feel sick and she braced herself not to throw up, holding tight with both hands on the edge of the cold countertop. She was waiting for her father to call back with any news. Her cell phone lay next to her coffee cup. She heard shuffling feet behind her and turned to see one of her roommates coming into the kitchen.

Susanna Tolles was wearing a white tank top with a Hilton Head logo on the front, barely covering her lime green panties. She was tall, thin and deeply tanned. Her short brown hair was off at all angles, her face drawn and eyes swollen, smeared with yesterday's make-up. She came up to Ophelia and kissed her on the neck.

"Morning, O. I feel like shit. How 'bout you?"

Ophelia didn't answer, pulling back and again, trying to quell a wave of nausea. She looked out on the balcony of the condo and saw three mostly empty bottles of wine, two glasses and an ashtray full of what was left of the weed they'd been smoking last night.

"What's wrong?" Susanna asked, walking around to the coffee pot and pulling a cup down from a cupboard.

As she watched the woman pour, Ophelia said, "My sister is gone."

Susanna turned, her eyes squinting in the morning light. "What?"

"Ida is gone."

"Gone where?"

"I don't know, goddamit!" Ophelia yelled out and then clutched at the side of her head as the pain flared.

Susanna came back over and sat next to her on a stool.

Their third friend, Josh Gaines, walked in, bare-chested with only a pair of plaid boxer shorts on. His tall frame was muscled and taut. A white tan line showed above his shorts. His sun-bleached blond hair was held back in a short ponytail. He came between the two women and kissed each on the cheek, then pulled them close in his arms. "Why are you both up so early. Let's go back to bed and get the morning off to a good start."

He tried to kiss Ophelia again, but she pushed him away. She stood and walked around the counter to the sink. She found a glass and poured water, then took a long drink. She turned and said. "My dad called just a while ago. Ida disappeared last night. There's no sign of her." She watched the expression on Josh's face change quickly from lust to concern.

"You're shitting me?" he said, coming around to join her at the sink. He stood beside her and wrapped an arm around her back. "They really can't find her?"

"That's what I said!"

"What happened?" Susanna asked.

"We don't know yet. She was out at a beach party last night... spring break from school. She just walked away."

"Man, that's crazy," Josh said, leaving her side and walking over to the refrigerator. He opened the door and pulled out a bottle of orange juice, taking a long drink before offering it to Ophelia.

She shook her head *no*.

"What's your old man doing?" Josh asked.

"He's on his way out to the beach to meet with the police. He said he'd call me."

Susanna came over and hugged her close. "I'm so sorry, honey."

Ophelia rested her face in the woman's neck and leaned in close. Tears formed in her eyes and she felt the wetness on the skin between them.

"I'm sure they'll find her," Josh said. "Probably off in the dunes some-where passed out."

Ophelia pulled away, anger on her face. "God, I hope so."

"What can we do, sweetie?" Susanna asked.

"There's nothing we can do until I hear back from my father."

"So, let's go back to bed," Josh said, the look in his eyes very clear on his intent.

Ophelia looked away in disgust. She looked at the time on the clock on the far wall. "I need to get down to the gallery. I told Emma I'd open this morning."

"I'll go," Susanna offered.

She looked across at the two friends, the *love couple* she'd met three months ago on a trip to Jamaica. They'd hooked-up down on the island for several days, then she'd invited them back to the States to stay with her here in Charleston. The two of them had been *"seeing the world"* and working odd jobs as they moved from country to country. *They seem quite content now here in South Carolina*, she thought. Her father's money and the big condo seemed to have dampened their travel lust. She looked out across the skyline again, a sick feeling swelling through her as she thought about her sister.

A shock of pain in her right wrist surprised her and she looked down, rubbing it to ease what felt like a wire tightening and digging into her skin. There was nothing there, but the pain kept on. *What is happening?*

Chapter Thirteen

Alex's first thought when he saw Remy Dellahousaye get out of the passenger door of his long black Mercedes, was he looked much older than the pictures he'd seen in the police and FBI files. He was wearing a crisply pressed white dress shirt, open at the neck, with well-tailored tan slacks and shined black loafers. From the distance across the sandy parking area at the beach, Alex could certainly see the resemblance to the man's father.

He had never met the son and wondered now how he would react when he discovered the cop who had killed his father was now working on the team to find his daughter. He wasn't sure if Dellahousaye even knew who he was.

Another larger man got out of the driver's seat of the car. His dark black-on-black clothes had *"bodyguard"* written all over them. Alex couldn't tell if he was carrying a weapon under the black sports coat he was wearing. The two men came toward them. As Dellahousaye approached, his eyes locked on Alex's for a moment, then noticing the uniform of the Sheriff's Department, he turned to Pepper Stokes.

"Who's in charge here?" His voice was deep and edged subtly with a Cajun accent.

"Mr. Dellahousaye?" Pepper Stokes asked.

"Yes, are you Stokes?"

"Yes sir." The sheriff reached out his hand. "Sorry about your daughter, sir. We're doing..."

Dellahousaye cut him off. "Do you have any idea yet what's happened to Ida?"

Stokes took off his hat and held it at his side, looking out across the dunes.

"Afraid not, Mr. Dellahousaye. Seems your daughter just walked away without a trace."

Alex watched the emotions of fear and then anger sweep across Della-housaye's face. "You still have nothing!"

Agent Fairfield stepped forward. "I'm Special Agent Sharron Fairfield with the FBI, Mr. Dellahousaye." She extended her hand and they shook. "We were called in early this morning."

"So, you think she's been abducted?"

"We don't know yet," Fairfield said. "These are my colleagues, Agents Foster and Frank.

Alex watched Dellahousaye turn to him and a look of recognition came into his eyes.

Dellahousaye stared back for a moment, then said, "You're Alex Frank?"

"That's right," Alex responded, noticing his heartbeat rising.

"I thought you were with Charleston PD."

"I was."

Dellahousaye kept staring back at him and then shook his head, looking back to Stokes. "So, you really have nothing at this point?"

The sheriff said, "We're doing all we can..."

Alex's thoughts were spinning. *Your father kidnapped Hanna Walsh and Amelia Richards and would likely have killed them if Pepper Stokes and I hadn't come into the old fishing camp with guns blazing.*

Alex listened as Stokes brought the man up to date on the scope of their search and efforts to find Ida Dellahousaye. He ended with, "Your daughter's cell phone was found over in the dunes," pointing to a spot beyond the cars. "We have it on its way down to the crime lab in Charleston to see if we can find any prints or if any content on the phone can help us."

"How many people do you have on this?" Dellahousaye asked.

Stokes said, "I've got most of my department out now. The State Police have mobilized their investigative teams..."

Agent Foster cut in, "And the bureau is organizing a full response. We're taking the lead here on the ground but we're working now with our Charleston field office and DC to coordinate efforts to find your daughter."

Remy Dellahousaye absorbed their response, then looked over at his man standing behind him for a moment before turning back to Sheriff Stokes. "What can we do to help at this point?"

Fairfield responded first. "We'd like to spend some time talking to you about your daughter, what you know about her friends, anything happening in her life that would raise questions."

"Whatever you need."

Stokes said, "We should get back over to my office. Not much more we can do here now."

Fairfield stepped forward. The gathering wind blew her hair across her face and she swept it back. "We need to be thinking about a media response. We want to control the message and not let this leak out from some other source."

"It's only a matter of time until this gets out," Foster said.

"I want to put up a reward, whatever it takes," Dellahousaye said, with a hint of panic behind the stoic façade he was struggling to maintain.

"A bit early for that," Will Foster said.

Alex watched Dellahousaye look over at him. He didn't speak for a moment. Alex saw hard lines of age at the corners of the man's eyes and across his forehead. Finally, he said, "I need to alert the rest of our family. I've spoken with Ida's twin sister. She lives down in Charleston. I need to call Ida's mother. We're divorced."

Pepper Stokes said, "Follow us back to the Department."

Dellahousaye nodded and turned with his driver to leave, then stopped and looked back at Alex. He started to speak and then paused before proceeding on to his car.

Chapter Fourteen

Willa James sat at her desk in the newsroom of the Charleston television station where she anchored the evening news broadcast. She was in early today to follow-up on several stories she was working on before she got down to final prep for the night's show. She was dressed in worn jeans and sandals on her bare feet, a loose white blouse rolled up at the sleeves. Her long brown hair was pinned up in a bun on the top of her head. Make-up and hair would wait until four this afternoon. The clock on her computer read 11:15. She reached for another sip of coffee when her office phone rang.

"Willa James."

There was silence on the phone for a moment, then a low man's voice said, barely loud enough to hear, "Remy Dellahousaye's daughter is missing. You better check with the County Sheriff's office."

She heard the call click off.

The noon news broadcast included Willa James sitting in with a news bulletin that one of the twin daughters of business magnate, Remy Dellahousaye, had been missing since the previous night. Authorities had issued an official statement that, "... all efforts are being made to locate Ms. Dellahousaye. At this time, no sign of foul play has been uncovered."

Within an hour, the story had been picked up by the other local television stations and radio news stations and by 3 p.m. that afternoon, the cable news networks were carrying brief updates on the disappearance of Ida Dellahousaye, daughter of prominent South Carolina businessman, Remy, son of the notorious and now deceased crime boss, Asa Dellahousaye.

Willa James was thrilled to be a guest reporter on the national broadcast of her network that evening to share her local insight on the girl's disappearance.

Chapter Fifteen

It was just past four in the afternoon when Hanna pulled into her parking space behind the house in downtown Charleston that doubled as the offices for her free legal clinic, as well as the apartment she lived in on the second floor. She turned off the car and reached for her bag and phone on the seat beside her. As she got out, she thought about how disappointing it had been for Alex to have to leave the beach early. They had planned to spend a couple more days up at the old family house on Pawleys Island before he had to return to work in DC.

Her son, Jonathan, had also chosen to head back to Chapel Hill early. With all her guests gone, Hanna had decided to get back to the city and get to work on a couple of cases she had planned to deal with from the island but now felt it best to be back in her office with all resources and personnel available to her. She grabbed her travel bag from the trunk of her Honda sedan, then went up the back steps of the house and let herself in.

Occasionally, some of her staff would be in on the weekends as case work demanded, but all the lights were out, and she didn't hear anyone else about. She walked into her office and sat behind her old desk, the light from the windows behind her sufficient to work. She pulled several files from her bag and laid them on the desk. Her assistant, Molly, had left several messages for her from Friday. Anything urgent had already been texted or emailed to her over the weekend.

She took a deep breath and tried to let the events of the shortened weekend catch up with her. It was all on the edge of overwhelming and she struggled to calm herself. Thoughts of a marriage proposal, a son dropping out of school, a move to DC, was more than she could process. Her doctor had prescribed some anti-anxiety med to help her deal with the stress and effects of the past year's trauma. She found the bottle in her purse and washed the pill down with a bottle of water on her desk.

She closed her eyes and tried again to calm her breathing.

There was something about the idea of marriage, *again*, of moving away from all she had here in South Carolina, of slipping away from all that had become comfortable, that was more than she wanted to deal with. She tried to push it all aside and looked back down at the clutter on her desk.

The name on one message slip did catch her eye. *Christy Griffith.* She was the daughter of an old friend of the family, Charles. He owned four prominent restaurants in town and one out on the coast. Hanna's deceased husband, Ben, had been golf and tennis buddies with Charles, and Hanna had come to know him and his wife and family well over the past years, although the wife, Pamela, had died suddenly two years earlier in a tragic car accident.

The message just had the girl's name and call back number with no other information. It had come in late Friday afternoon. Due to her close relationship with the girl's parents, Hanna decided not to let the call wait until tomorrow morning when the clinic opened at 8am. She pressed the number into her phone. Christy Griffith answered on the second ring.

"This is Christy."

Hanna could hear the distress in the girl's voice.

"Christy, it's Hanna Walsh. I just got your message when I got back to town this afternoon." She could tell the girl had been crying and was still very upset. "What can I help you with?"

"You haven't heard?" Her voice was strained and desperate.

"Heard what?"

"About Daddy?"

"No," Hanna answered. "What's happened?" Hanna heard the girl sob, trying to compose herself.

"Daddy's gone... he's been killed."

Hanna sat stunned for a moment. She rarely had a news program on when she was up at Pawleys Island and she hadn't seen anything come across her phone. "Christy, ohmigod!"

"He's gone, Hanna!"

Hanna stood and walked to the window, looking out over the heavily shaded back yard and parking area. "What happened, dear?"

"I need to see you," the girl pleaded. "Can I come down to see you?"

Thirty minutes later, Hanna met Christy Griffith at the front door of the clinic offices. Hanna knew the girl was in her early 20's, attending college here in Charleston while she worked with her father in the family's restaurant business. She was the same height as Hanna, though rail thin and even more gaunt looking today, the grief and sorrow evident on her flushed face. She had black hair cut close with a shock of purple color along the left side of her head.

Hanna reached out to hug the girl. "I'm so sorry, Christy. Come in. Come in."

Hanna sat with the young woman in two upholstered chairs in the corner of her office. She had retrieved bottles of water from the kitchen on the way back and she watched as the girl took several short sips. Her cut-off jeans were faded and worn through in several places. Her *College of Charleston* t-shirt was also cut off at the bottom and frayed. She wore a pair of green flip flops on her pale feet.

"Tell me what's happened."

Christy gathered herself, placing the bottle of water on the table beside them. She leaned forward with her hands on her bare knees, then took another deep breath. "I found Daddy yesterday morning in his car in the garage."

Hanna reached over for one of the girl's hands, squeezing it in support.

"He was already gone, Hanna. The car was running, and the doors and windows were all closed."

"Honey, I'm so sorry."

"He didn't kill himself, Hanna! He would never do that."

"Christy..."

"No! They killed him Hanna. I know they did."

"Who?"

The girl hesitated and then wiped at her nose and eyes flushed with tears. "Daddy had investors in the restaurants. He told me they were pressuring him to sell to get their money back. He couldn't raise the money to buy them out."

"What investors?"

"A couple of years ago, after my mom died, Daddy let the business slide. He just couldn't focus after losing her. Later, he told me he nearly had to shut everything down, but he found someone to help bail out the restaurants."

"Who was it?"

"He wouldn't tell me, but I saw these men coming by his office now and then, having dinner with him occasionally. I recognized one of the men. He was in the news all the time. I asked some of the other servers at the restaurant one day. They told me the older man was Asa Dellahousaye."

Hanna couldn't hide her shock. "Your father was doing business with this man?"

The girl nodded.

"You know he died last year?" Hanna asked, choosing not to reveal the role she and Alex had played in his death.

"Yes, but someone from his organization was still involved with our business," Christy said. "The man was in Daddy's office again last week. After he left, my father was very upset, but wouldn't talk about it."

"You haven't gone to the police yet?"

She shook her head. "I'm afraid, Hanna. I know who these men are. I know they're all part of the mob. I don't know why my father took their money. I guess he had nowhere else to go."

"Who was this other man?"

"I did some digging. His name is Xander Lacroix."

Hanna had heard the name. After Asa D's death, there was a scramble for power and control of the man's extensive holdings. Lacroix was a loyal lieutenant and strongman for the Dellahousaye crime family. "You're sure about this?"

The girl nodded, then reached into her bag, pulling out a file folder. "I found this today in a locked drawer in my father's desk. It includes several documents related to the money." She handed Hanna a piece of paper from the file. "From this note he wrote, I think my father was planning to go to the police. It includes a list of several other businesses and restaurants I assume were also involved with the Dellahousaye people. They're all friends or acquaintances of my father."

Hanna read down through the note and list of businesses. "Do you think he was threatening these men about exposing their extortion ring?"

Christy took the document back and placed it in the file between them. "I don't know for sure. Just two days ago, I heard my father on the phone in his office. He was having an argument with someone. I've never seen him so mad. He was yelling at whoever was on the line about *backing off.*"

"Why would they kill your father if he owed them money?"

The girl stared back, unable to answer. She placed a hand over her eyes to stem another round of tears.

"I'm sorry," Hanna began. She tried to think through the series of events she'd just heard. "I assume your father left the business to you. Did he have a will?"

"I don't know yet."

"Who was his attorney?"

Christy reached in her bag again and found a business card, handing it to Hanna. "I found this in his office."

Hanna took the card and cringed when she saw the name, *Phillip Holloway, Attorney-at-law.*

The girl noticed the expression on Hanna's face. "What's wrong?"

Hanna shook her head and handed the card back. "Oh nothing," she responded, thinking about how much she didn't want to be anywhere near her husband's former partner again.

"Do you know him?"

"Yes, my husband used to work at the same firm. I was friends with his wife for many years."

"You *were* friends?"

"Grace Holloway is in prison now. It's a long story." Hanna stood and walked back to her desk, sitting down and pulling out a legal pad to make some notes. "I'll call Holloway and see what he knows about any of this." A troubling thought occurred to her. "If your father left the business to you, I assume these men know that and they'll be in touch soon." Hanna saw real fear in the girl's expression.

"Hanna, you need to help me with this! What should I do?"

"We need to get the authorities involved... the police, maybe even the FBI. Let me check with a couple of people," she said, thinking about bringing Alex and his office in on this.

"Whatever you think," Christy answered.

"I've got your cell number," Hanna said. "I'll call you as soon as I know more."

"I'm really afraid of these people, Hanna."

"Do you have anywhere else you can stay besides your own place?"

The girl thought for a moment. "I have a friend with a condo out on Sullivan's Island."

"I don't want you to be overly frightened, but it might be best to stay away for a few days."

"What about the business?"

"Aren't there managers for the restaurants?"

"Sure. I've already spoken to all of them after...." She paused, gathering herself again. "After my father passed."

"Stay in touch by phone for now as you need to," Hanna said, thinking about her own experience with the Dellahousaye organization. She knew how ruthless they could be and was certain they would be coming after Christy Griffith next for their money, likely thinking she would be an easier mark and could be convinced to liquidate her father's holdings. The thought of having to deal with these types again chilled her. She closed her eyes and took a deep breath. Images of the night she'd been held hostage by Asa D and his goons flashed in her mind, and then the bloody aftermath when Alex and the sheriff had killed them all.

Chapter Sixteen

Remy Dellahousaye sat in the back of his Mercedes looking out across the Low Country marshes as he was being driven back to Charleston. The afternoon sun glared hot across the water. The low ebb tide left the muddy banks exposed and black against the grasses waving in the wind. His thoughts were on his missing daughter.

An anger burned deep in his gut and he silently swore revenge for all who were involved with her disappearance. He was frustrated the authorities had found nothing to go on yet. There had still been no contact from a kidnapper. *Had she really just walked away?*

"Take me out to the beach house," he said to his driver, Vincent. "I need to see Jillian." He was referring to his second wife, Jillian Wyche Dellahousaye. He had married the woman five years ago after finally moving on from the divorce from the girls' mother, Brenda. He had called both women earlier to alert them to Ida's disappearance. Her mother was obviously frantic when he ended the call with her. She lived in Atlanta now with a second husband. She was coming out to the coast this afternoon. He had agreed to meet her at his house in Charleston.

Jillian was another matter. His much younger second wife was on her way to also becoming his ex. Their relationship had slowly faded these past years. A year earlier, he had discovered her affair with a man who belonged to their club in Charleston. More recently, another dalliance was even more troubling.

He had allowed her to stay on at his beach house as he and his lawyers prepared to throw her out completely with a small settlement to go away quietly. It wasn't so much the affair that bothered him, he thought. He had simply grown tired of her and he had his own dalliances to keep him occupied, at least for now. The woman had never grown close to his daughters who despised the woman for the affair with their father that ended their parent's marriage.

He needed to see Jillian now. Her reaction to the news about Ida's disappearance was gnawing at him. Her feigned surprise and concern were too obvious and forced. *If she had anything to do with this, I swear...*

Dellahousaye had inherited his father's massive estate on the beach on Isle of Palms. He hadn't gotten around to disposing of it yet, and he and Jillian had used it only occasionally in the past year. He had several other homes he preferred to get away to down in Naples and in Beaver Creek, Colorado, in particular. His father's second wife had returned to her home country in South America after his death with a considerable nest egg to live out the rest of her life.

Vincent pressed the code at the gate to the house and the car made its way slowly up through the shaded road lined with ancient live oak and palms. The house came into view with a sweeping circle drive across the back around a large ornate fountain that sent water shooting out in multiple directions. The grounds were still immaculately kept, though the house sat mostly vacant since the passing of Asa Dellahousaye.

Remy thought about his father as the car came to a stop. He had attended many of the lavish parties the man had thrown here at the beach and had occasionally come out for family holiday gatherings. The gregarious Asa Dellahousaye had thrived on his highly public lifestyle. Remy had preferred to stay in the shadows, though his business success had certainly garnered considerable attention by the media.

He saw his wife's green Jaguar parked in front. He thought about her recent attempts to rekindle the marriage. He had rejected all her advances and could barely stand to be in the presence of the woman.

He walked through the glass double doors at the back of the sprawling contemporary house, opening into a large open view with windows to the beach across the front. Jillian was sitting on a couch looking out at the beach, a glass of wine in her hand. Remy looked at his watch... a little after four. *Typical*, he thought.

He watched as she jumped up, placing her glass on a table and coming across the room toward him. Her fitness instructor body had lost little of its tone during the short years of their marriage. She still worked out religiously almost every day. Her skin was deeply tanned and freckled from her devotion to "pool time" on most afternoons. She was barefoot in faded jeans with a lime green bikini top above showing off her surgically enhanced curves.

"Oh, honey," she said, "I'm so sorry. Do we know anything yet?" She wrapped her arms around him and kissed his cheek, but he didn't return her greeting.

Brushing past, he walked to the front of the house and through one of the many sliders out onto the long deck across the front. Over the vast lawns and dunes beyond, he could see the afternoon sun sparkling on the calm blue surface of the Atlantic. He heard Jillian come out behind him. He turned and stared at her without speaking. He pushed away thoughts of his past attraction and lust for this woman. Instead, his anger continued to build, not just at her indiscretions, but...

"What's happening?" Jillian asked, the wine glass in her hand again.

"Why don't you tell me," Remy hissed.

The look of surprise on her face was expected. "What are you talking about?"

"I swear, Jillian, if you had anything to do with this!"

He watched as her mouth fell open. "Remy, how could you think..."

"Shut-up!" he snarled.

She recoiled, a look of fear replacing her earlier surprise.

"What were you doing with Xander last week? One of my guys saw you at lunch with him in town." When he had learned of his wife's liaison with the man who was still struggling to take over much of his father's network of businesses and affairs, he had immediately gone on the defensive.

Jillian stood stunned, unable to respond.

"I asked you a question... and don't lie to me!"

The woman took a long drink of the wine and then walked up to her husband. "It's not what you think."

"What should I think?"

"I've known Xander Lacroix for years. His wife's a friend...."

"I'm well aware of that, but what were you doing with him now?"

She hesitated a moment, collecting her thoughts. "He called me. He wanted to catch up."

"Bullshit!"

"Okay," she said. "He's worried about you... about how you feel about his moves to take over your father's businesses."

"How do you think I feel!" he shouted. "He should come to me."

"Honey..."

"Don't call me that," he snapped, grabbing the wine from her hand and throwing it against the house, the glass shattering. He saw real fear in her eyes now. "Jillian, I swear if you and Lacroix had anything to do with Ida..."

"Remy, no!" she pleaded. "I would never do anything like that. Why would you think that?"

"You know I'm about to throw your sweet little ass out the door!"

He watched anger come across her face now. "What do I have to do to make all this up to you?"

"We're way past that now."

Her expression softened and she came up to him, hugging him again. "We can make this right again, honey. Let me make this right." She reached a hand up and caressed his cheek.

He pushed her away in disgust. "What do you know about Ida?"

"Nothing! I swear to you."

Chapter Seventeen

Ophelia Dellahousaye drove along the Battery in Charleston, approaching her father's house. The street was deeply shaded in the early evening light. Traffic was heavy as usual along the scenic route on the confluence of the Ashley and Cooper rivers.

On the drive over, she had struggled to stay awake. The previous night's partying was still taking its toll. Her head pounded and her body ached no matter what position she tried in the comfortable seats of her sports car. She wasn't looking forward to seeing her father. She anticipated another round of bitching about her life, her friends, everything she was currently doing. She had never been able to please him. The perfect Ida was another story.

She had spoken on the phone with her mother an hour earlier. She was on her way into town from Atlanta and would probably be at the house by now, she thought. *Mom will be hysterical, as always.*

Her mother, the former Brenda Dellahousaye, her father's first wife, was now living in Atlanta with husband #2, an investment banker named Walters who had amassed a sizable fortune and a big house on West Paces Ferry Road in Buckhead. On the few visits Ophelia had made to Atlanta to visit her mother, she had found her to be comfortably established in the social pecking order, a member of all the right clubs and women's groups and charities. She seemed to have successfully moved past her chaotic life with her father and her mercurial twin daughters.

Ophelia turned into the drive at her father's house and drove around back to a parking area next to the large detached garage. The grounds of the house were lavishly landscaped with flowers and flowering shrubs creating a striking colorful contrast to the deep greens of the surrounding foliage. A large wooden pergola hung with clematis and bougainvillea shaded a brick patio filled with comfortable furniture and a kitchen built into a brick wall across the back, all overlooking a small pool.

Her father's man, Vincent, met her at the back door and let her in. "Hello, O, he said. "Welcome home."

She tried to brush past, but he held her arm and pulled her close, trying to kiss her neck. "Are you crazy!" she said, looking down the hall to make sure her father hadn't seen them.

"What're you doing later?" he asked, quietly.

"Nothing with you," she said, trying to pull away.

Vincent smiled back. "Yeah, right."

"Let me go!"

"I'll see you later..."

"Don't count on it." She was able to free her arm and walked away through the back hall and into the kitchen. The thought of another roll with her father's amorous bodyguard sent a guilty thrill through her. *Wouldn't it be fun to get him over with Josh and Susanna*, she thought?

Her parents were standing on opposite sides of the big marble-covered island, obviously in the middle of a serious argument. They both looked up when Ophelia came in. Her mother moved quickly to give her a hug. Ophelia could see tears streaked down her cheeks. Her eye make-up was flushed, marring her pretty face, still stunning in her late forties.

"Oh, honey," her mother gushed.

Ophelia felt her mother's body pressed against her in a tight hug. She returned the embrace and patted her back gently. "We'll find her, Momma."

She heard her father say, "It's about time you got here, where....?"

Her mother interrupted. "Remy, don't start. We need to be thinking about Ida. If you had provided the security for the girls, I've talked to you about, none of this would have happened."

"Dammit, Brenda, we've been through all this how many times? The girls don't want anyone hovering over them night and day."

"This is your fault!"

"Stop it, Momma!" Ophelia shouted, pulling away. "Can the two of you take a break? We need to find Ida."

Remy said, "You obviously haven't heard anything from her?"

Ophelia shook her head, going to a cabinet next to the sink, pulling down a glass and filling it with water. The cool chill was a welcome relief. "Have the police found anything yet?"

"Nothing," her father responded.

"Did Ida give you any reason to believe she might be thinking about running away?" her mother asked.

"Absolutely not. She was excited to get back to school and finish up this last term. God knows why!"

A small television was set in the corner on the counter tuned to CNN, the sound turned down. Ophelia saw the talking head, then the crawl of copy across the bottom caught her attention. She rushed over and turned-up the volume.

"... the daughter of prominent businessman, Remy Dellahousaye of Charleston, South Carolina has been reported missing for nearly 24 hours now. Representatives from the Sheriff's Department, the State Police and the FBI have all acknowledged a search is underway for the missing Ida Dellahousaye."

A picture of her sister flashed across the screen, her smiling face a mirror image of her own. *They must have taken it off her Instagram feed*, Ophelia thought. The news anchor came back on.

"Remy Dellahousaye, a high profile and legitimate business leader with interests around the world, is the son of deceased crime boss, Asa Dellahousaye, who was killed in a shoot-out with authorities a year ago after abducting two South Carolina women.

Ophelia saw her father's pained expression as he watched the broadcast. He walked over and turned the sound back down. As she stared at her sister's face on the screen, her mind flashed to an image of a dirty window, heavy trees and brush beyond. She looked over when her father spoke, and the image faded.

"It's not like Ida to just run away like this," he said. "And wouldn't she have called at least one of us to let us know she's okay?"

Brenda started crying again and turned her wrath back to her ex-husband. "If anything happens to her, I'll never forgive you!"

Ophelia was not in the mood to witness another of her parent's typical skirmishes. "Can the two of you please stop!"

"Do you have any idea where she might have gone if she did run away?" her father asked.

Ophelia took a moment to respond. "I'm sure the cops have checked her house back at school." She thought again about the old window. *Where have I seen that before?*

"No sign she's been back to school," her father said.

"Can't they trace her credit card if she tried to buy a plane or bus ticket?" Brenda asked.

Remy's tone hardened again. "She would have had to walk miles from the beach to get any transportation. All the cars were still out there."

"So, you think she's been taken?" Ophelia asked.

"We have to assume that's the case," her father said. "I still don't know why we haven't heard any ransom demands though."

Ophelia walked to the window of her father's office and stared out at the familiar street and park beyond. She closed her eyes and tried to bring back the view through the old dirty window. *Where are you?*

Chapter Eighteen

Ida dozed uncomfortably off and on through the afternoon and into early evening. Her masked captor had brought in a sandwich earlier which still lay on a plate on the floor uneaten. He hadn't spoken and didn't respond to any of her pleas to let her go. About an hour earlier she had heard the door in the other room close and then the sounds of a car driving away from the old shack. There had been silence ever since.

She felt her heart pounding heavily as she listened for any sound. *Had they left her here?*

She sat up as quietly as she could and stretched to get some circulation back. Her right wrist was still held fast to the metal bed frame. She got closer to look at the cuff that held her to the bed. The other end was secured to a cross piece that was bolted to the legs against the wall. She tried to turn the heavy black bolt, but it wouldn't budge.

Shifting her position for leverage, she tried to free her wrist from the cuff. The hard steel cut into her skin as she pulled hard. She winced in pain and then tried again, the cuff painfully digging into bone now. Blood began flowing down her arm. She gritted her teeth and desperately pulled hard again to slip her wrist through. The pain was excruciating, but she pulled hard again and felt nerve endings flare as the cuff ripped through skin and tissue. She felt a bone in her hand flare with pain, probably breaking. She deadened her mind to the pain and pulled hard again once more. She fell back on the bed as her hand slipped free. Her wrist and hand were on fire with pain and blood dripped from the wound along her wrist.

Standing unsteadily, she stood, looking around the room, then walked over to the window against the side wall. The glass was dirty and cracked along the bottom. The sill was held with a single lock that she opened easily. With her good hand and arm, she tried to lift the window. It came up only an inch and squeaked loudly. She turned in alarm to the door, terrified she would alert anyone still in the house. There was no sound. She crouched and placed her hand under the sill of the window and then pressed up with all her strength. The window gave another inch. After several more attempts, she was able to get it fully open. There was no screen.

Ignoring the pain in her hand and her shoulder from her fall the previous night, she pushed her upper body through the window. There was a weathered wood deck four feet below and she tried to catch her fall with her good arm. She crashed down hard and paused for a moment waiting for the expected pain of another injury, but there seemed no new damage.

Ida quickly looked around for signs of her captors. She crawled along the deck as quietly as she could, holding her injured hand up, blood still dripping on the wood deck. The front door to the place was now just a few feet ahead. Steps down to the drive were to her left. A black Ford sedan sat parked in the trees and her heart sank. *Someone is still here!*

She got to her feet slowly and as quietly as she could, crouched now to keep a low profile. She inched her way toward the steps. *I need to run! I need to get to the woods!*

Thoughts of snakes and alligators flashed in her brain, but she pushed them aside. *I have to get away. These people are going to kill me!*

Each step on the stairs moaned and creaked as she stepped slowly and as carefully as she could. She looked back at the old screen door, the inner door open to inside. There was still no motion or sound.

Her bare feet touched the warm sand at the bottom of the steps. She moved quickly now to her left and then around the back of the house. Deep woods surrounded the place in all directions. She paused once more to gauge the possible danger inside the house. All she could hear was the wind blowing through the trees and birds squawking and whistling in the distance.

She started running and crashed into the heavy brush of the woods, tripping almost immediately on a fallen branch. The pain in her shoulder and hand was as hot and searing as a lightning bolt. She lay on the ground, trying to catch her breath, trying to push aside the pain. She suddenly felt like she might pass out and she steeled herself to stay conscious. *I need to get away!*

Managing to get back to her feet, she started off again, slowly now, making her way through the heavy brush of palmetto and fallen limbs. She cringed as the sharp roots and knife-edged palmetto leaves cut at her feet, but she kept on, only darkness ahead.

She tripped again on something and fell hard, then lay there panting in near exhaustion, fighting the urge to just give into the night and close her eyes to the danger all around.

Raising herself up on all fours, she struggled to get some breath, to calm herself. Something crashed through the brush to her right and she felt a rush of cold fear again. She stayed there motionless, listening for the sound again. *What in hell is it now? An alligator? A wild pig?*

She almost cried out when the bushes nearby rustled again even closer. Her only instinct was to *get away*. She struggled to her feet and began running, stumbling again, then continuing on, trying as best as she could to thread her way through the dense forest.

Coming up against the trunk of a large live oak, she stopped, leaning into the tree, hugging it as if there might be some comfort and safety there. She listened again and only the screech of the chorus of tree frogs broke the stillness of the night.

Chapter Nineteen

Hanna met Alex for dinner at one of their favorite restaurants in downtown Charleston. It was a small family-owned place known for its great Italian food. The lighting was low and the smells coming out of the kitchen were mouth-watering. They had already ordered a bottle of wine and the two glasses of Cabernet rested between them on the table.

"Still no leads yet on the missing girl?" Hanna asked. She noticed how tired Alex looked and he seemed distracted. "Are you okay?"

He nodded, then replied, "Long day. Nothing yet on Ida Dellahousaye. I met her father today, Remy. It was not a comfortable encounter. He knows I killed his father."

"I had my own Dellahousaye moment today," Hanna said.

Alex looked up but didn't respond.

"I don't think you know the Griffith family," Hanna continued. "Old friends of ours. Charles owns several restaurants in town and out on the coast. His daughter came to see me today down at the clinic."

"You're doing office hours on Sundays?" Alex asked.

"I saw her call message from Friday when I was out and didn't want her to wait any longer. She found her father dead in his car in his garage, apparently a suicide by asphyxiation."

"I'm sorry."

"The girl doesn't think her father killed himself." Hanna went on to tell Alex about Christy Griffith's suspicions of the Dellahousaye organization in her father's death."

"Xander Lacroix," Alex repeated when she finished. "Everything we hear, this guy has quickly stepped in to take over the Asa D crime network."

"Including extortion?" Hanna asked.

Alex nodded, taking a drink from his wine. "So, this girl thinks her father was threatening to expose Lacroix to get him to back off?"

"That's what she thinks."

Alex sat staring back at her for a moment, then said, "Obviously not a smart move."

"I'm afraid they'll be coming after her next... an easier play to get their money back with her father out of the way."

"Very possible."

The waiter came up with two plates of pasta and set them down. "Can I get you anything else?" he said, reaching for the wine bottle and refilling their glasses.

Alex said, "No, we're good, thanks." The man walked away. Alex looked around the room. There was one other couple two tables away. He leaned in and spoke softly. "The Bureau has been all over the Dellahousaye organization since Asa died last year. They've had me helping with the case while I was up in DC. This Lacroix guy makes Asa D look like a saint. Apparently, he's got backing from one of the major New York crime families. He's moving fast to secure his position and ratchet up the business to please his new friends up North."

"So, we should be worried about Christy Griffith's safety if she doesn't go along with this guy?"

"No question."

Hanna pushed the food around her plate without eating. She realized she had no appetite for the food. "Guess who her father's lawyer is?"

Alex rolled a long piece of pasta on his fork, took a bite and shook his head.

"Our old friend, Phillip Holloway."

He looked away in disgust, then swallowed and said. "Don't tell me you need to work with him on this?"

"As little as possible. I need to help Christy with her father's estate. We're assuming he's left everything, including the restaurants, to her. The mother died a couple of years ago in a car accident."

"So, Lacroix will definitely be coming after the girl next."

"She really believes they killed her father."

Alex shook his head. "I wouldn't be at all surprised." He thought about the death of his partner and best friend, Lonnie Smith, in a shootout with one of Dellahousaye's hired guns a year ago. The assassin had almost taken him out with a bullet wound that creased his neck. He wondered who else in the Dellahousaye organization had their hand in on his partner's death. *There is nowhere on this green earth they can hide,* he thought.

Hanna watched him look away in thought. Finally, he said, "Can you get us a meeting with the girl?"

"Sure."

"She could be very helpful getting to Lacroix."

Alarm bells went off in Hanna's mind. "I don't want her put in more danger than she already is."

"I know, but if she's right about her father being murdered, this may be the best way to get some justice."

Alex held Hanna's arm as they walked along the dark streets back to her office and apartment. He said, "I have to check in with the office when we get back, see if there are any new developments."

"I hear she has a twin sister," Hanna said.

"Quite a piece of work... wild child from all we hear. We got her statement earlier over at her father's house. The first wife was there, too. Their daughter lives here in Charleston. Daddy's got her set up with a nice condo downtown and an art gallery to run."

"What do you think about the girl's disappearance?" Hanna asked.

"Doesn't seem likely she just ran away. The kid's a serious student, one term to go, then medical school. Everything we're seeing, she's the sane one of the two."

"If she's been abducted, why hasn't there been a ransom demand?"

"I know, it doesn't make sense."

Hanna thought for a moment, then said, "So it's possible she's been taken and killed?"

"It's possible."

They walked in silence for a while, holding hands, both thinking about the cloud of the Dellahousaye family hovering over them again.

Hanna stopped and pulled Alex's arm to turn him to her. "I'm not sure I can do this again."

"What is that?"

"These people killed my husband. They kidnapped my son and nearly killed both of us."

Alex didn't answer at first, instead pulling her into his arms and holding her close. With his mouth close to her ear, he said, "We'll take care of this Dellahousaye situation. Asa D is gone, and his son only wants his daughter back."

"Yes, but..."

"But," Alex continued, stepping back and looking into her eyes, "you need to stay away from Xander Lacroix. This guy is more than trouble."

"I can't leave my client..."

"She needs to be working with the police and we're already investigating this guy."

Hanna thought about his advice for a moment, then knew she couldn't walk away from Christy Griffith. "She also needs legal help... her father's will, and..."

"Hanna, please listen to me," Alex said, reaching out to hold both of her arms in a firm grip. "You know these people don't fool around."

She knew he was right and the thought of getting on the wrong side of Lacroix and what was left of the Dellahousaye crime syndicate made her stomach feel like she might be sick. She also couldn't push away the thought she would never be able to live with herself if she walked away from this woman. "Are you sure she can be protected if she agrees to cooperate and go after Lacroix?"

Hanna wasn't reassured when Alex didn't answer immediately. Finally, he said, "Look, there is always a risk."

He wasn't telling her anything she didn't know and deep in her gut she was sure there was an incredible risk, not only for Christy Griffith, but for anyone else involved. She closed her eyes and took a deep breath, then looked back. "I at least need to help her through the estate issues with Holloway tomorrow."

"Of course, although I trust that bastard about as far as..."

"Oh, believe me, I know," Hanna said.

Chapter Twenty

Ida Dellahousaye sat shivering against the trunk of the big live oak tree, her arms wrapped around her bare legs. She was dressed in only her two-piece swimsuit with a sweatshirt over it. The woods around her were still in almost total darkness. She'd been struggling through the heavy underbrush for what seemed hours. She had no idea where she was or what direction she was heading. Her legs were scraped and bleeding from numerous falls and cuts from the heavy brush. Her shoulder and wrist ached unbearably.

She closed her eyes, willing herself not to panic any more than she already was. *Who are these people? What do they want from me?*

She thought again about the man who had taken her, the frightful mask he wore when he came in to check on her. *And who was the woman?* She continued to think she knew her. *But where?*

The echoes of the night, tree frogs and a few birds, were suddenly interrupted by the faint sound of a car engine passing nearby. Ida stood, every muscle in her body screaming in pain, her bare feet cut and bleeding. The noise had come from off to her left and she started in that direction, making her way slowly, her hands out ahead to protect her face from low branches and brush.

She walked for several minutes, then heard another car pass. Her hopes soared as she thought of waving down a passing car, getting to safety, seeing her family again, surviving.

The night continued to close in around her like a dark blanket. She tripped again but caught herself on the bark of a large tree trunk. She paused to catch her breath, to try to push aside the agony wracking her body.

Then, she saw the lights of a car passing ahead. She continued forward, quickening her pace as best she could. Her next step was down a steep bank and she fell, tumbling in pain and landing in a pool of warm water, a ditch along the road above her. She cried out from the pain and lay there shuddering for a minute before willing herself to crawl up to the road. The sky above, clear of trees, now looked brighter and she could see a few stars. Her hands felt gravel, then the hard surface of the road. She rose up on her knees looking in both directions, no lights coming from either way. Only the sounds of the screeching frogs in the trees split the night.

To her left, she saw the glow of approaching headlights around a turn, then the bright lights of the car. She forced herself to her feet and walked two steps out into the road. As the car approached, she began waving her arms above her head, willing herself to ignore the pain. The car didn't appear to be slowing and she was about to jump out of the way when she saw the lights swerve, then begin pulling over to the roadside.

Her spirits soared as she ran to the car. The passenger door opened, and a man got out. The interior lights came on and she saw another man driving. Before she could react, the first man grabbed her hair and pulled her along the side of the car. The trunk opened and she felt herself lifted and then tossed like a sack of potatoes inside.

"No!" she yelled out into the night, but the trunk lid came down and she was in total darkness again.

Chapter Twenty-one

Ophelia Dellahousaye settled into the plush couch in the living room of her apartment in downtown Charleston. The windows looked out over the lights of the city skyline and out to the lights of boats passing through Charleston harbor. A glass of vodka over ice rattled in her hand. The television was tuned to another news network, but she had the volume turned down. She saw her sister's face looking back at her on the screen. *Still, nothing new.*

Suddenly, she felt cold and reached for a blanket she kept on the back of the couch. Wrapping it around her shoulders, she shuddered, thinking the A/C must be turned up too high.

The buzzer from the lobby went off and she walked over to the speaker on the wall by the door. She pressed the button, "Who is it?"

"It's us, baby." She recognized the voice of her friend, Josh.

"Let us in, honey," Susanna echoed.

Ophelia buzzed them in and left the door open. She started back to the couch and stumbled as a searing pain shot through the bottom of both feet. She sat and sipped at her drink, the pain slowly fading.

The return of her friends, who had gone out for food, did little to lift her mood. When they walked through the door, she didn't get up. They both came over and sat on either side of her, kissing her neck and nuzzling close. She pushed them away and stood to go into the kitchen to refill her drink.

"We thought you needed some distraction," Josh said, his voice tinged in disappointment.

"How are you doing?" Susanna asked.

Ophelia came back in and sat across from them on a deeply cushioned chair with two stuffed pillows. She took a deep breath, staring at her friends. The vodka was having its desired effect. She was calmer now, thinking about her sister and her earlier confrontation with her father and mother.

"How do you think I'm doing?" she finally said.

"We were watching the news down at the bar," Susanna said. "It's just awful. There's no sign of her yet?"

Ophelia shook her head *no*.

Josh said, "We're here for you, baby."

Ophelia could tell he was high. The smell of weed lingered on his clothes.

"The feds came by this afternoon," Susanna said, "looking for you."

"I already talked to them at my father's house."

"The bastards grilled us for an hour," Josh said, his voice unsteady and slurred.

Ophelia looked at the two of them. They'd become close friends and now lovers these past months. She really could lean on them for support. *Who else do I have?*

Remy Dellahousaye sat at his office desk at his house in Charleston. He'd had his ex-wife, Brenda, driven to a nearby downtown hotel. A single lamp with a green shade on the corner of the desk lit the room in soft shadows. CNN was on the television on the wall. He'd been watching for over an hour as periodic reports of his daughter's disappearance came on. Still no news or demands from her captors, if she had indeed been taken. He had forced away thoughts of the possibility his daughter had been murdered on numerous occasions through the night.

There was a knock at the door and Vincent stuck his head in. "Anything else tonight, boss?"

"No, get some sleep. Long day ahead tomorrow."

Vincent nodded and backed out of the room.

Dellahousaye's thoughts returned to his current wife, Jillian, and her recent contacts with Xander Lacroix. He shook his head in anger, wishing she was here with him now so he could strangle the truth out of her.

His recent *negotiations* with Lacroix had proved troubling. While he wanted to stay above the fray of his father's illicit dealings, he also needed to keep control behind the scenes. He had his own people working on it, but Lacroix had surprised him with the speed of his takeover and the support he had garnered from New York. That was the point that troubled him the most.

Rico Terrelli ran the strongest of the crime syndicates in the North. His father had always been a partner with Terrelli, though their relationship was often shaky. Remy had met him on only two occasions, again trying to stay out of direct contact with his father's business as much as possible. With Terrelli's support, it was just a matter of time until Lacroix had full control of everything, even back in New Orleans, he thought.

He reached for his cell phone and looked up a number in his directory. The call was answered on the third ring.

"Yessir."

Remy heard the voice of the person he had placed inside the Lacroix organization.

"We need to talk."

"What?" he heard the man ask.

"Get your ass over here as soon as you can."

"It's past midnight..."

"Now!"

Josh and Susanna tried to convince Ophelia to come to bed, but she had filled her glass with vodka again and returned to her couch, turning up the volume of the television just loud enough to be heard above the moans and giggles coming from the bedroom.

The late-night anchor on CNN said, "Missing for nearly 24 hours now, the whereabouts of Ida Dellahousaye, daughter of prominent businessman, Remy Dellahousaye, remains a mystery. Local, state and federal authorities working on the case continue to report no progress in locating the girl..."

Ophelia looked away out the window. Living in near constant contact with her twin sister through the years, the two of them seemed to have an almost telepathic connection, often completing the other's thoughts before they could finish a sentence. Though her mind was dull and clouded by the alcohol,

Ophelia could sense her sister's fear as keenly as if she was there in her place.

Remy's plant inside Xander Lacroix's inner circle sat across the desk from him. The clock on the wall showed it was just past 1am.

Danny Wells was in his late forties, not aging well, and trying his best to cover the bald spot creeping forward by combing over his thinning gray hair. His eyes were swollen and bloodshot from a late night drinking with some of Lacroix's guys at a bar downtown.

"You look like shit," Remy said.

"Thanks, I really needed that reminder," Wells said. "Sorry to hear about your daughter. Any news?"

"You tell me."

"What?"

"This has Lacroix written all over it. What are you hearing?"

The man sat for a moment considering the question, then shook his head. "Sorry man, but I haven't heard a word other than a couple of the guys tonight seeing the news coverage down at the bar and laughing about it."

"Laughing?"

"They were drunk..."

"Who was laughing?"

"A couple of the new guys. You don't know them," Wells said. "You got to understand, since Asa's been gone and Lacroix has moved in, the Dellahousaye name ain't exactly popular."

"I need you to dig deeper on this," Remy demanded. "If Lacroix had anything to do with Ida, I swear..."

"I'll check it out."

Chapter Twenty-two

Jordan Hayes sat with three friends in *Gilly's Bar* in Dugganville, South Carolina. They had checked out of their rented beach house earlier in the day and had planned to drive back to school. Ida Dellahousaye's disappearance had changed all their plans.

He had spent over an hour being questioned first by the local Sheriff's Department and then by two very serious people from the FBI. Everyone attending the beach party bonfire the night before had gone through the same drill at the house before they were allowed to leave.

They had stopped at *Gilly's* to get a burger and beer before starting back to school, but one beer led to several and they were still glued to the news broadcast on the TV above the bar. Coverage of Ida's disappearance had been coming on every fifteen minutes or so, even though there was little new to report.

Jennifer Wallace startled him by placing her hand on his thigh under the bar. He looked over at the tanned face of Ida's sorority sister, her blonde hair rolled up in a bun on top of her head. Her eyes were glazed and vacant from the drinking.

"Hey babe," she said with a groggy slur in her voice. "We need to get home. I'm exhausted and I've got classes in the morning."

Jordan saw his other friends nod in agreement. He took another drink from his beer glass and looked up at the picture of Ida Dellahousaye on the news broadcast. Her father had put out a $50,000 reward for information earlier in the evening and the news headline along the bottom of the screen repeated the offer. He thought about the conversation he'd had with his father, the son of the once powerful, now disgraced Senator from South Carolina. His father was an attorney in DC but had been jockeying for a Senate run in the next election. Jordan's grandfather, still a powerful force with all the right connections in Washington, was pulling strings behind the scenes to make it happen.

Jordan's family had never been happy about his relationship with Ida Dellahousaye. Even though her father was seen as a legitimate businessman, any connection to the crime family was considered a liability, particularly after his grandfather's role in Asa Dellahousaye's bid to control expanded gambling in South Carolina had been uncovered. Jordan had been listening to his father and grandfather complain about this for over a year, but he continued to reassure them it was just a fling.

Jennifer pulled at his arm. "Really, Jordan, let's get out of here."

He remembered his night in bed with her after they'd all finally got back to the beach house last night. It was all a bit blurry in his mind. It was late and they'd been drinking all day, then staying up half the night with the police after Ida went missing. Jennifer had been coming on to him for days. She didn't seem to have much guilt moving in on her sorority sister's boyfriend. She certainly wasn't too concerned about Ida's disappearance as she pulled him into her room last night.

Thoughts returned of Ida in those last few minutes at the beach bonfire. She was obviously getting upset about his interest in Jennifer. *Good!* he thought.

Then, there were the events of the past night I didn't tell the police about.

Chapter Twenty-three

Hanna poured another cup of coffee in her kitchen. Alex was in the shower in the small bathroom at the back of her apartment. They had both set alarms early. Hanna had a full day ahead catching up at the legal clinic downstairs. Alex had to be downtown for a meeting with the team assembled to investigate the disappearance of Ida Dellahousaye.

Alex came into the kitchen, buttoning his shirt. His dark hair was combed back wet. He came over and hugged Hanna from behind as she sipped at her coffee and watched the morning news. News crews were now assembled outside the house of Remy Dellahousaye down on the Battery. All the national and local news shows were reporting frequently on the ongoing disappearance of the daughter of the prominent business icon and son of the late mob boss, Asa.

"Anything new?" he asked.

She felt his warm hands inside her robe and turned to kiss his cheek. "You heard about the reward the father put up?"

"Yeah, he talked to us about it yesterday. I just checked in with the office. The hotline is getting a lot of calls but nothing real yet."

She stepped away to pour coffee for Alex. "With no word after all this time, are you getting worried she's been hurt?"

"It's certainly a possibility."

"Poor girl," Hanna said, thinking back on the frightening time her own son had been held hostage by her deceased husband's partners trying to recover lost money they thought she was holding.

"What have you got this morning?" he asked.

"I'm taking Christy Griffith to the police this morning to tell them about her suspicions that her father's death wasn't a suicide."

"So, you're going to go ahead with this?"

"I have to..."

Alex shook his head with concern, then said, "You're sure?"

Hanna nodded back.

"Let me check with the locals here on Lacroix and what they know about any other extortion activity."

"Thank you. If she's right, it's just a matter of time before they come after her for the money or to liquidate her father's holdings."

"I don't need to tell you again to be careful with this," Alex warned. "We know all too well these guys don't play around."

Hanna winced and said, "Someone needs to help this girl."

"Just be careful." He came over and kissed her. "I need to get going."

Hanna spent two hours in her office going through email and messages, updating files for the week's work ahead, then left to meet Christy Griffith at the downtown precinct of the Charleston Police Department.

They both sat in a small windowless conference room, cups of coffee steaming in front of them.

Hanna said, "I called your father's attorney this morning." She remembered her brief conversation with Phillip Holloway. He had been delighted to hear from her and started in immediately about how they needed to get together to *catch-up*. He had been coming on to her for years, even before his wife and her ex-friend, Grace, had been sent off to prison for her role in the failed land deal that cost her husband, Ben Walsh, his life. Hanna had kept the conversation strictly to business, quickly as always, rebuking his advances. She learned that Christy's father indeed had a will. Phillip would be able to meet with them later this morning to review the document. She was not looking forward to seeing the man again.

"He has a copy of your father's will and can review it with us later today," she told Christy. "We have an appointment at 11:30."

Christy nodded back, sitting sullen, her face drawn and pale.

The door opened and a familiar face walked in. Nathan Beatty had worked with Alex in Homicide at the Charleston PD. Hanna had met him on several occasions while Alex was still working with the Department.

"Hello, Hanna," Beatty said, "Nice to see you. How's Alex doing with the Feds?"

Hanna rose and shook his hand. "He's fine, Nate. Caught up now in the disappearance of the Dellahousaye girl."

"Give him my best."

Hanna nodded and introduced her client.

When they were all seated around the small table, Beatty said, "I understand you think your father's death wasn't a suicide."

Christy proceeded to walk through her suspicions of the Asa Dellahousaye organization, now under the growing control of Xander Lacroix."

When she finished, Beatty said, "Those are pretty serious allegations, Miss Griffith."

"They killed my father, Detective! I'm sure of it."

Beatty looked over at Hanna for a moment, then back to Christy. "And no one's contacted you yet?"

She shook her head *no*.

Beatty thought for a while, then said, "Would you be willing to help us build a case against these people, if indeed they do reach out to you?"

Hanna sensed warning alarms going off in her brain. "Nate, these are dangerous people..."

He cut in, "Hanna, I'm well aware of that. We can provide the necessary protection."

Hanna still had her doubts.

Christy said, "What do I have to do?"

"First, we would set up surveillance on your phones."

"Okay," she said, tentatively.

"If they do want to meet with you, we might have you wear a wire."

"Nate, really..." Hanna began.

"Let's not get ahead of ourselves," he said. "They haven't even made contact yet."

Hanna looked over at her young client who stared back, then said, "Whatever it takes."

Hanna shook hands with Christy on the sidewalk outside the precinct. "I'll see you at 11:30 down at Holloway's office," she said. "I'll text you the address. Are you going to be okay?"

Hanna saw an expression that was both fearful and yet determined. "We need to stop these guys," Christy said.

She watched the girl walk away down the street, then turned to go to her car and back to the office.

She didn't notice the dark brown SUV across the street pull out and then proceed slowly in the far lane following Christy Griffith.

Hanna arrived at Holloway's office first and was shown to one of the elegantly appointed conference rooms. Phillip came in almost immediately with a broad smile, a single file folder in his right hand. He came across the room and before she could back away, gave Hanna a tight embrace, his other hand patting her on the back.

"Hello, dear," he said, stepping back. "You look incredible, as always."

Hanna pressed back her revulsion for the man.

He noticed the ring on her finger. "Looks like congratulations are in order."

She nodded.

"Lucky man. Alex Frank, I assume?"

Again, she just nodded.

"Or should I say, *Special Agent* Alex Frank?"

"That's correct."

"Well, I'm happy for you."

I doubt that. "Thank you, Phillip. Christy should be here any minute."

"Really sorry about her father. Nice man."

"Is my client the only person named in the will?"

"That's correct."

"So, she will have ownership and control of the restaurants now?"

"You'll see in a moment, he left everything to his daughter. Pretty straightforward, except..."

"Except what?"

"He had some investors in the business."

"You know about that?" Hanna said, surprised.

"Sure, it's no secret. The girl's father had me keep a copy of the agreement."

"Who's named in the documents?" Hanna asked.

"Some holding company out of Florida. Can't recall the name. Griffith told me they were investing in restaurants all around the country."

Hanna's spirits flailed. *Probably a dummy company to hide their tracks.* Can we see those papers this morning?"

"Of course." He picked up a phone off the table and pressed a single button. "Bring me all the files on Charles Griffith."

The door opened and Christy peaked in, then entered. One of the office assistants closed the door behind her.

Hanna introduced the girl to Holloway.

"Very sorry for your loss, Christy," Holloway said. "I was always impressed with your father. He ran a good business."

"Thank you, sir."

Holloway opened the file in front of him and walked through the details of the will. It was all as he had described earlier. He got her signature on a couple of documents and then had someone come in to make copies. The woman left two other files on the table. "I believe you're aware of your father's partners in the business."

Christy said, "Yes," leaning over to look at the document on the top of the file folder.

Phillip read for a moment, then said, "Horizon Properties holds a $500,000 interest in the restaurants. Your father has been paying them an annual dividend of about..." He read further down in the document. "The dividend is 9%, paid monthly."

"That's pretty steep," Hanna said. Holloway just nodded. "Can I see that?" She took the contract and quickly read through the two pages in the agreement. It was signed by a *William Rodriguez* on behalf of *Horizon Properties.* "Do you know this man?" she asked.

Holloway said, "No, never met anyone other than Christy's father."

Hanna noticed Christy sitting silently by, taking in the news of her father's investors. "We'll need copies of all this," she said.

Holloway called for his assistant again. He turned back. "Anything else I can help with today?"

"No, thank you, Phillip," Hanna said.

"You'll have to stop by the house... with Alex, of course. See what I've had done to Grace's kitchen. I think she'd love it."

Hanna just shook her head, forcing a thin smile. *Not going to happen!*

On the way down the elevator with Christy, Hanna said, "Let me know if you hear from anyone on this."

"I will," Christy replied. "A $45,000 dividend is a lot of money."

Hanna nodded.

"From what my father let on, they want all their investment back. I didn't realize it was half a million. I'm sure I'd have to sell everything and there still probably wouldn't be enough. He didn't have a lot of equity in the business, I'm finding. I suppose it's why he went to Lacroix in the first place. I'm meeting with my dad's accountant later this afternoon."

"Fill me in after you speak with him."

They said their goodbyes out on the street in front of the law offices. Neither woman noticed the man sitting in a window of a coffee shop watching them across the plaza.

As Hanna walked the few blocks back to her office, she sorted through the events of the morning in her mind. She kept coming back to the police suggestion her client wear a wire and agree to the surveillance efforts to try to take down Xander Lacroix. *If he ever discovers what's going on...* she grimaced as she walked on, thinking about how badly this could go.

When her son was kidnapped, she was sure now they had been connected to the Asa D crime family. She had also agreed to help. Her son had ultimately been returned safely, but it was one of the most harrowing experiences of her life. *Is it really best for Christy to go forward with this?*

She stepped off the next curb, her thoughts distracted. A loud car horn blared, and she jumped back, narrowly missing the front of the car speeding by. Her pulse jumped immediately to redline, and she nearly stumbled as she moved back from the street.

The car continued on without slowing and then turned right at the next street. She stood for a moment to catch her breath. She felt a hand on her shoulder.

"Are you okay, miss?"

It was an older woman, pushing a small cart of groceries.

Hanna looked back at her, still stunned by her near accident. "Yes... yes, I'm fine, thank you."

"You need to be more careful," the woman scolded. "Everyone's in a hurry in this town."

Yes, I do need to be more careful!

Chapter Twenty-four

Ida felt a humming rhythm. She opened her eyes and squinted at the bright sunlight coming through a small round window. She lay in her same clothes, the bathing suit and sweatshirt, on a small bed in what she now realized was a boat. Her body was drenched in sweat.

She had no idea how long she had been out or sleeping. She remembered her flight through the woods, then her capture again. *Did they drug me?* She couldn't remember anything after just a few minutes locked in the car's trunk the previous night. Her wrist was bruised and swollen from her efforts to get free from the old shack. She couldn't move her hand or fingers without intense pain.

She looked down at her bare legs and hands and saw the cuts and bruises she had received trying to make her way through the heavy brush. She looked out the window and saw only the distant horizon across endless water, steel blue and pushing up against a far bank of white clouds. There were no other boats in sight.

She stood and tried the latch on the door, but it wouldn't open. Sitting back down on the bed, she tried to keep the panic from rising again. *If they were going to kill me, I'd be gone by now, right?* she thought.

Food and water were placed on a tray on the floor beneath her. She took the water bottle and quenched her dry and stale mouth. Her body smelled foul and rank. She pulled the dirty sweatshirt over her head for some relief from the warm and close air in the cabin.

Have I been kidnapped? Are they trying to get money from my father? she thought. *I'm certain he'll pay. What's taking so long?*

Ophelia woke to the sound of the shower running. She willed herself out of a deep sleep. The familiar dull ache in her brain from another hangover greeted her. Susanna was still asleep beside her. Josh was singing in the shower. They both had been passed out when she finally came to bed last night.

The ringtone from her phone startled her. She picked up the cell and saw the number for her father on the screen. "Hi, Daddy."

"Where are you?"

"At my apartment here in Charleston."

"I assume you haven't heard anything from Ida."

"No, nothing. I would have called."

Josh came out of the bathroom, dripping on the carpet with a towel around his waist. "Morning, babe!"

Ophelia put her finger to her mouth to shush him.

"Don't tell me they're still there with you?" her father said.

"They're just trying to help," she said, impatient now with his constant irritation about the friends in her life. "There's been no word then?" she asked.

"No, but if she's been abducted, the cops think we'll likely hear from someone today."

Ophelia hesitated, then said, "And what if she wasn't abducted?"

"Let's not think about that," she heard him reply.

A wave of nausea came over her and she felt like the bed was shifting beneath her. She reached for the nightstand to steady herself.

Chapter Twenty-five

Alex walked into the field office of the Federal Bureau of Investigation at 177 Meeting Street in downtown Charleston at 8:01. He was cleared through to the offices in the back where he had been assigned a cubicle for his temporary assignment to work on the missing Dellahousaye girl case. Fellow agent, Sharron Fairfield, was coming back from the kitchen with a cup of coffee. She stopped as he was pulling some files from his bag and sitting at his small desk. As usual, she was dressed smartly in pressed blue slacks and a white button-down dress shirt. Her FBI credentials hung from a lanyard around her neck. A 9mm semi-automatic pistol was secured in a black holster on her belt. Her blonde hair was pulled up tight in a ball at the crown of her head. Alex had always thought she looked like a television actress whose name he could never remember, though he hadn't mentioned it.

"Morning, Alex."

"Any news?"

"Lot of calls to the hotline for the ransom as you would expect. Nothing of value."

"What's the plan for today?"

Fairfield sat in the metal chair next to his desk. "There's a meeting and conference call with the full team at 8:30." She looked at her watch. "What's your take on this?"

Alex pushed back his chair and gathered his thoughts for a moment. "I keep thinking about who can be squeezed the most, if this is truly an abduction. Obviously, the father, Remy Dellahousaye, is the logical target. His reported net worth is huge, making him a very likely target."

"Yet still no ransom demand," Fairfield said.

"I know. All I can think is they're trying to build the panic factor with the family."

"The media is making this into a circus, as usual."

"Only adds to the stress the family must be feeling."

Fairfield asked, "What do you think about Remy? Hard to believe he's clean with a father like Asa D."

Alex shook his head. "I agree, but you know all the scrutiny he's been under, particularly these last couple of years when his father was directly in the cross-hairs of all the law enforcement agencies. Remy D always comes up clean."

Sharron stood and looked out over the tops of office cubicles, then back to Alex. "Have you talked to Hanna about being assigned back in DC?"

Her question caught him off guard for a second. He hesitated, then said, "We've talked about it."

"Shame you two will have to be apart so much." A strange smile came across her face. She looked down at her watch. "See you in a few minutes at the meeting," she said, turning to walk away.

Alex was back at his desk at ten. The Dellahousaye meeting had turned up little in terms of new information or leads. *At least all the agencies involved seem on the same page*, he thought as his office phone buzzed. A man at the front desk said, "A Mr. Dellahousaye is here to see you."

Alex took a deep breath as his pulse quickened. "I'll be out in a minute."

Agents Fairfield and Foster joined Alex in the small conference room, sitting across the table from Remy Dellahousaye. The man's handsome face was understandably drawn and tired, his eyes bloodshot and cloudy.

Dellahousaye said, "Are any of the leads coming in on the reward hotline proving helpful?"

Alex responded first, "I'm afraid not." He watched as Remy looked across at them. His tired expression suddenly turned hard, "What in hell do I have to do to light a fire under all your asses?"

Will Foster jumped in. "I can assure you, sir, every agency and department involved is doing..."

"Enough with the bureaucratic bullshit!"

Foster didn't back down. "Your anger is understandable, but frankly, you're wasting our time here. We need to get back to work."

Dellahousaye seemed to soften. "What can I do to help? Should we raise the reward?"

Sharron Fairfield said, "I don't think that will make much difference. Our best hope today, if your daughter is indeed being held, is her captors will finally reach out with their demands. Now, if you'll excuse us."

Alex rose with both his colleagues.

Dellahousaye said, "Agent Frank, can I have a moment, please?"

Alex looked over at the puzzled expressions on his colleague's faces, but then they stepped away from the table and closed the door as they left. Alex sat back down.

"I want to be honest with you, Alex. Can I call you Alex?"

"Of course."

"I'm concerned about your history with our family."

Alex wasn't surprised by the comment.

"I'm afraid your judgment and commitment will be clouded by your past encounters with my father and..."

Alex cut him off. "Sir, I can assure you..."

"Frankly, I'm surprised the Bureau would even assign you to this case, knowing you killed my father."

The comment hung in the air between them for a moment. Alex felt his pulse surge and he struggled to maintain his temper. He locked eyes with Dellahousaye and refused to blink. Finally, he said, "I'm sure you remember what really went down that night."

"Oh, I know exactly what went down." The edge and anger in his voice was clear and his faced flushed as the tension between the two of them continued to rise. "I don't dispute my father ran a tough business..."

"Tough business!" Alex said, his eyes wide in disbelief. "Drugs, prostitution, illegal gambling, bribery, extortion... murder! Did I miss anything?"

Dellahousaye stood defiantly. "You and your sheriff friend came in with guns blazing that night. Is that how you do business?"

Alex struggled to maintain control. All he could see was the enraged face of Asa Dellahousaye the night he held Hanna hostage, a gun to her head, moments before he would have killed her. A younger version of that face stared back at him now, the man's fists clenched as if he was about to attack.

Suddenly, Alex remembered the discussion with Hanna about the Griffith family and the suspicious death of the father, Charles. "Tell me what you know about the restaurant business," he asked, standing and moving to the end of the conference table.

Dellahousaye's eyes followed him and he looked back with a puzzled stare. "What?"

"Do you know Charles Griffith, local restaurant owner?"

"I have no idea what you're talking about," Dellahousaye said.

Alex tried to read the man's face but detected nothing but confusion.

Dellahousaye stepped back and turned to leave. "I've made some calls to DC, to express my doubts about your assignment on this team. Surely the Bureau has personnel who will be more objective and devoted to actually finding my daughter."

It took all his will for Alex not to lose it with this pompous asshole. He stared back for a moment, gripping hard on the table between them. At last, he said, "You do what you have to, but if I were you, I wouldn't be trying to disrupt our efforts to find your daughter. I think we're through here. I need to get back to work!"

Chapter Twenty-six

Hanna worked through lunch at her desk, one bite out of a sandwich sitting on a plate to the side of the papers she was going through. She was trying to concentrate on the case in front of her, but her thoughts kept wandering back to Alex and the news he would be assigned to Washington for the foreseeable future. He wanted her to come with him. He had asked her to marry him. *Why is the prospect of moving so upsetting?* she thought. *Is this all so important here in South Carolina? Why not a new start?*

The idea of a second marriage still gave her pause. She knew she loved and cared deeply for Alex, but trust issues from previous relationships continued to keep her up at night. She was having trouble thinking clearly about any of this and even her work now seemed a distraction when once it had meant everything to her. Sleep deprivation and stress had magnified soon after her terrifying and near deadly encounters a year earlier with the mob boss, Asa Dellahousaye, and his hit man she came to know as Caine.

Her therapist had helped her deal with this to some extent, but she knew she was still far from healthy psychologically and now physically. The symptoms continued to take their toll on her body. She had tried to spare Alex all the drama around her condition. He had enough to deal with getting through the training program at the Bureau.

She noticed the ring on her left hand and her face stretched into a thin smile. She thought about calling Alex to get an update on the missing girl case but decided not to bother him. They had plans to meet for dinner.

The ring tone for a call on Hanna's cell broke the stillness and she saw her father's name on the screen.

She realized it had been several weeks since she'd spoken with him and the thought of catching up and sharing the news of her engagement brightened her mood. She had been waiting to call him about the engagement until she had sorted out all the related issues with Alex in her mind. *What the hell!*

"Daddy, how are you?"

"Fine, fine. How's my favorite daughter?"

"Your *only* daughter is just fine, thank you." She heard him laugh in his deep throaty way. "What's happening in Atlanta and the firm?" Her father was senior partner at one of the city's leading law firms.

"Well," he began. "I do have some news."

Hanna waited expectantly.

"I've decided to step aside and let the young guns run this place."

Her eyes opened wide in astonishment. "You're really going to retire?"

"I submitted my terms of retirement to the management committee this morning."

"Daddy, that's wonderful!" She had been after him for years to cut back on his work. He had been through several near fatal cardiac events. She also knew he had been concerned about leaving the firm without her taking a leadership role to replace him. She waited for this next.

"Martha is just tickled," he said. "She's got a dozen trips mapped out for us to start getting away."

"I'm so happy for you," she said, but couldn't bring herself to believe that her father's second wife truly had the best intentions. Hanna's relationship with the woman had been strained at best since her father had remarried two years after Hanna's mother and brother were killed in a plane accident piloted by her father.

"Of course, you know I want you to come back to Atlanta…"

"Allen!" she jumped in, calling him by his first name which he preferred over *Daddy*. "We've been over this how many times? You know how I feel."

"I know, I know, but I have a solution. The committee has agreed to my terms and will hold a seat on the board for you to rejoin the firm at any time. If I pass before that eventuality, my stake in the firm will obviously pass to you and you can decide from there."

"And how does Martha feel about that?"

"About the money? She has nothing to worry about."

Allen Moss had already informed Hanna over a year ago he planned to leave the large family home in Buckhead, north of Atlanta, to his second wife. Hanna was sure he also had a sizable investment portfolio of which some significant portion would find its way to Martha Wellman Moss. Hanna had never cared about her father's money or the big house she had grown up in and had told him that on numerous occasions."

"I really am so happy for you, Allen!" she continued. "There's so much more of the world to see than your grand office at the law firm."

He laughed again. "I'm sticking around for a couple months to hand off my case load but then, Bon Voyage!"

"Well, I have some news for you, too, Allen."

"And what is that?"

"Alex finished his training at Quantico. He is officially Special Agent Alex Frank now."

"A damn G-man!" her father said. She heard his deep chuckle follow.

"He's assigned to a case here in Charleston at the moment."

"The missing Dellahousaye girl?" he asked. "Can't get any other news lately."

"Yes, he's on the joint team."

"Hope they find her soon. You stay away from those Dellahousayes," he warned.

"I'll be fine," she replied, pushing away dark images. "Alex will be heading back to DC after that's wrapped-up."

"I'm sorry to hear that, dear."

"He's also asked me to marry him, Daddy."

There was silence on the other end of the phone for just a moment, then, "What took him so long?"

"Well..."

"No, I think it's just great," she heard her father say. "Have you set a date?"

"Not yet. With Alex going back to DC, we have to sort all that out." She dropped the final bit of news. "He wants me to move up there with him."

Again, silence. This time with no response coming.

"We'll work it out, Allen."

"You've built a fine life there in South Carolina, honey. After Ben's passing..."

"I know, Allen. Like I said, we'll work it out."

"Of course, you will. Hey, they're planning some big retirement shindig for me soon. I'll let you know the details. You and Alex and Jonathan will have to come over to Atlanta."

"Wouldn't miss it." She decided not to tell him about his grandson's decision to take a break from school. Her discussion with Jonathan had been far from satisfying and she had been stewing about his plans ever since.

"Give my best to Alex," she heard her father say, still thinking about how a move to Washington was the last thing she needed in her life.

Chapter Twenty-seven

Remy Dellahousaye was in the back of his car on the way to a lunch meeting. He was still fuming about his discussion with Alex Frank. He had convinced himself the cop still held a grudge against the family for his father's role in the girlfriend's incident a year earlier. Then, there was the death of Frank's partner at the hands of one of his father's *enforcers*.

He knew the FBI and other law enforcement agencies were putting considerable resources into finding his daughter but couldn't get over the notion that Frank would undermine the investigation. *Hopefully, my contacts in Washington will get the bastard pulled*, he thought as the car pulled up to the curb in front of the restaurant.

He remembered Frank's questions about Charles Griffith. He did indeed know about the shakedowns Lacroix was engaged in with many businesses across the south. Lacroix was continuing his father's practice of "investing" in struggling businesses at extravagant interest rates, then using whatever means necessary to recoup those investments when businesses continued to falter.

Vincent said, "We're a few minutes early, boss."

He didn't answer, still thinking about Special Agent Alex Frank.

Brenda Dellahousaye Walters ended her call back to her husband in Atlanta and put the cell phone down on the nightstand next to her bed in the well-appointed hotel suite in downtown Charleston. She shook her head in disgust at his response as they'd talked about her daughter's disappearance. He seemed barely interested, more concerned he had to get down to his office for some meeting. She had tried her best not to lose her patience with him. It had been getting harder these past months as his infatuation with her was clearly faltering.

She got out of bed and went into the bathroom, cringing when she saw the disheveled face staring back at her. She splashed cold water on her face and then ran her wet hands through her hair, pushing the random strands away from her face. Her silk nightgown hung over her body loosely and she assessed the toll her upcoming fiftieth birthday was taking. She pushed her shoulders back and sucked in her stomach, turning to see her profile. She looked away with a frown.

She had slept little through the night, imagining the horror her daughter, Ida, must be facing. Her anger with the girl's father burned fresh and she thought about the new Mrs. Dellahousaye and her tight body and stunning looks, living comfortably out at the palatial beach house on the ocean. *Hopefully, I won't have to be in the same room with her*, she thought.

Jillian Dellahousaye had slept far better. She always slept well after sex. She propped herself up on pillows against the headboard, not bothering to cover herself, and looked out across the beach and ocean beyond the big master suite of her husband's house. The bare back and wide ass of Xander Lacroix lay beside her. He was still snoring loudly. He had come out to the beach house just past midnight. She smiled as she thought about their night together. He certainly enjoyed screwing his rival's wife.

She also knew it was dangerous for them to be this reckless, but frankly, she didn't care. Remy had made it clear he was through with her. She had to look out for herself. She had no trepidation with Xander being *Plan B*.

The Starbucks around the corner from her apartment was typically full, but Ophelia had found a small table and chair at the back. She sat nursing her latte with skim milk, a laptop open in front of her on the table. She had been scanning news sites, reading all the latest conjecture on the whereabouts of her sister.

Her cell phone chimed. On the screen she saw a text from Vincent. *"I'm free at lunch. Your place?"*

Her first reaction was anger at his incessant attempts to get into her pants. If her father ever found out his right-hand man was banging his daughter, he would pay a heavy price. It didn't seem to deter him. Then, the thought of Vincent meeting the *love couple* and the four of them together seemed intriguing. She texted back, *"Noon."*

Her next text was to Josh and Susanna back at the apartment. *"Don't go away. I'm bringing a friend home to play."*

Guilt rushed through her mind as she thought again about her sister. *We're not forgetting you.*

Chapter Twenty-eight

Jordan Hayes woke late when he heard a knock on the door to his room at the fraternity house. "What?" he yelled out, pushing back covers and rubbing his eyes to gain focus on the morning.

A head peered around the door. "You better come down here, man."

A few minutes later, Hayes walked down the stairs to the landing at the front door of the house. Several of his fraternity brothers were standing at the open door looking out at the street. He walked over to a window. Three television satellite broadcast trucks were parked at the curb. Another pulled up as he watched. *What the hell?*

"They want to talk to you," he heard one of his brothers say. "They want to talk to you about Ida."

He felt the empty pit in his stomach churn. He had pulled on a pair of shorts and was wearing the Clemson t-shirt he'd slept in. He reached for his cell phone in his pocket and walked away into another room. His father came on the line after a few rings.

"What is it?" His father, Jordan Hayes, Jr., was all business, all the time. As a high-profile lobbyist in DC and now potential Senate candidate to fill his own father's seat, he had little time for niceties.

He quickly told his father about the news trucks on his front lawn.

His father didn't hesitate. "You need to show full cooperation with the investigation. Tell them everything you told the police. Don't appear evasive on anything."

After a few more coaching suggestions, his father rang off. He took a deep breath and walked back to the front door and then out onto the sprawling porch across the front of the house. He heard one of his fraternity brothers say, "Holy shit!" as four reporters with camera people following came quickly up onto the porch to confront him.

A female reporter with CNN on her microphone stepped in first. "You are Jordan Hayes?" she asked.

"Yes ma'am."

"The grandson of former Senator Hayes?"

"That's correct." He forced himself to remain calm, though he could feel his knees quivering.

An MSNBC reporter pushed in. "Can you confirm you are dating the missing girl, Ida Dellahousaye, and that you were there at the beach when she went missing?"

He looked for a moment at all the cameras trained on his face and could imagine television screens across the country carrying the interview. He put his hands in the pockets of his shorts so no one could see them trembling. "Yes, Ida and I have been dating and we were with friends down at the beach for our break from school. I just got back last night."

A man with a *Fox News* microphone pressed in. "We're told by another attendee at the party that Ida just walked away and never came back."

"That's correct," he responded quickly.

The reporter continued, "We are also told you followed her shortly after, though that wasn't mentioned in the police report that's been released."

He felt his heart start thumping in his chest and a cold chill swept over his skin. He gathered himself and tried to regain some sense of composure. He knew what they were implying, and he could see his father and grandfather cringing as they watched the coverage. "We all eventually started looking for Ida when she didn't come back."

"Our source said you followed her soon after she left and were gone for ten to fifteen minutes."

He heard other reporters start yelling questions at him. He couldn't respond. The panic was paralyzing. *They think I had something to do with this! They think I hurt Ida!*

He heard one of the reporters yell, "The authorities say you are a person-of-interest in Ms. Dellahousaye's disappearance."

"What?" he stammered, totally overwhelmed and confused.

"Do you know where the girl is?" someone yelled out from the crowd. "Is she still alive?"

Hayes started backing away. He bumped into some of his fraternity brothers standing behind him. He pressed through and back into the house. His cell phone was ringing as he ran up the stairs to his room. He knew it was his father before even looking at the screen.

Chapter Twenty-nine

Christy Griffith was in the kitchen of her father's restaurant in downtown Charleston talking to the head chef about the food orders for the coming week. The place was bustling with activity in preparation for another busy lunch. A server walked up and said, "There's a man out front who wants to speak with you."

She excused herself and pushed through the doors into the dining room. In the dim light before opening, she saw a tall and thick figure of a man standing by the host station. She felt her nerves flare in fear as she got closer. She'd seen him before, speaking with her father. *He was one of them*, she thought. She willed herself to keep on toward the door and when she walked up, managed to say, "What can I help you with?"

The man reached out his hand. "Miss Griffith, my name is Joseph. I represent a group of investors who were partners with your father in his business. We wanted to express our sympathies at his passing."

She shook his hand quickly and looked at the wide chiseled face beneath a shaved head staring back at her. *Joseph*, she repeated in her mind. "Thank you, sir," she finally said.

"In the next day or so, we would like to speak with you about our investment."

She remembered the detective's request to enlist her help in getting evidence of extortion on these people, even wearing a wire to record their conversations. The thought of it terrified her. She willed herself to remain calm. *These people need to pay for what they've done.*

"I just buried my father."

"Of course," he quickly responded. "We don't want to rush you on any of this."

"I'm very busy right now. Trying to pick-up my father's duties..."

"We totally understand." His voice had the slightest hint of an accent she couldn't place. *Cajun?*

"Let me call you later today," Christy said, more assured now. "We'll get something scheduled."

The man wrote a phone number on a piece of paper on the host stand, then left.

Christy sat in a small interrogation room with her attorney, Hanna Walsh, Charleston Police Detective, Nathan Beatty and a man who had been intro-duced as the new Captain of the precinct, Harold Zeils. The clock on the wall read just past four in the afternoon. She had called Hanna immediately after her visit from the man at the restaurant. Hanna had arranged for the meeting down at the police station. Neither of the police officers had spoken as Christy shared the details of her discussion with Joseph.

"He wants me to meet this group of *investors*," she said in conclusion.

Beatty looked at his Captain, who nodded back, and then turned to Christy. "We'd like you to set this up for tomorrow morning at your downtown location where you were today."

"Okay," she answered, her skin crawling with the pinpricks of nervous-ness.

"We'll be there early," Zeils said. "We'll get the recording wire set-up on you as well as surveillance video if possible. We'll also have people outside at a discreet distance to get whatever they can on audio and video. We'll have to get a warrant, but that shouldn't be a problem."

"Are you sure you're okay with this?" Hanna asked, looking carefully at her.

She felt a rush of resolve to bring these men to justice. "Whatever it takes."

Chapter Thirty

The call came across his office phone in Charleston just before 5 p.m. Remy Dellahousaye saw the caller ID was blocked. He considered dropping the anonymous call for just a moment, then realized he had to make sure it wasn't related to his daughter.

"This is Dellahousaye." He listened, waiting for a response. Finally, a deep and muffled voice began to speak. Remy sat up as he listened to the man carefully lay out his demands for the safe return of his daughter.

His first reaction was relief that Ida appeared to still be alive. Almost immediately his anger flared hot as he listened to the very specific instructions. He let it all sink in without responding.

"Am I clear?" he heard the voice ask.

He didn't respond, thinking about all he had just heard. Finally, he began in a low and steady voice. "If one hair is out of place on my daughter's head... if you've hurt her in any way, I will personally gut you and everyone involved and feed all your bowels to the fish. Am I perfectly clear?"

There was no response.

"I need proof she's okay," he demanded. Again, no response and then his cell phone chimed. He saw the notification for a text message. He clicked into the phone. There was no message, just a close-up picture of his daughter's face, holding today's issue of the Charleston newspaper, the date across the masthead clear. Ida looked tired, dirty... and petrified.

"You sonofabitch!"

He heard the call click off.

It isn't the money, he thought, driving himself across the bridge in his Land Rover. His driver and bodyguard, Vincent, had called with some excuse about *personal business* and that he'd be back to the house by dinner. Five million dollars was a significant sum but wouldn't put a dent in his holdings. Getting the cash freed-up would be problematic and the Feds would want to be involved in the exchange. He wasn't about to let that happen. The man had been very clear. *Ida is still just missing as far as the cops are concerned.*

No, it isn't the money. The fact that whoever these people were, they thought they could get away with this and may have done anything to hurt Ida, was eating into his gut. He had been serious about slow and painful retribution if he ever found out who was involved.

Their deadline was midnight tomorrow. The money would be wired to a Cayman bank in an untraceable transaction. They would be back in touch with him in the morning with instructions.

Jillian Dellahousaye met her husband at the door of the beach house on Isle of Palms. She had seen him press in the code at the gate on the security system camera. She was dressed in a short silk robe over a thin red bikini she'd been sunning in by the pool.

Before she could speak, he rushed in, grabbed her by the throat and slammed the door shut with his foot. His face was a mask of fury and rage. Her first thought was, *he's going to kill me!*

She tried to speak but her windpipe was nearly crushed in his grip. She struggled to pull away, but he dragged her by the throat down the two marble steps to the vast room across the front of the house. Throwing her down on the cold stone floor, she slid and hit her head on the sharp metal edge of a lamp table next to a couch.

"Remy!" she cried out in a garbled moan, trying to catch her breath. "What the hell!"

He moved quickly to kneel beside her and reached for a glass on the table. She cringed when he smashed it on the floor beside her and then grabbed a jagged piece of the glass and held it just beneath her left eye. She tried to crawl away, but he had her pinned up against the couch.

"Remy, please..." She felt the sharp point of the glass pressing into the soft skin below her eye. "No... please!"

"Tell me now who's involved," he spat. "I won't hurt you anymore if you tell me who's behind this."

Her body was trembling, and she felt an icy chill through her body. "I don't know..."

He grabbed her by the throat again, the glass pressing painfully now into her face. She was sure she was bleeding. She couldn't breathe and clawed at his hand to let go.

"I know Lacroix was here last night," he yelled. "Do you think I'm an idiot?"

She tried to shake her head, but he held her fast. Tears filled her eyes and streaked down her cheeks. She felt a wave of nausea and suddenly realized she was passing out. She looked into the enraged eyes of her husband... *a man she had loved... the man who was going to kill her.*

Xander Lacroix hung up the phone and smiled at the man sitting across the expansive desk from him. "Well done," he said, taking out a cigar from one of the desk drawers and slowly going through the ritual of lighting it. Not offering one to the other man, he blew the cloud of blue-gray smoke up into the air above him. *We need to get all of this cleared up, soon,* he thought.

Remy Dellahousaye backed away from the prone figure of his wife, lying on the floor, apparently unconscious. He tried to control his fury and calm himself. He could see Jillian was still breathing, just passed out. She hadn't admitted anything to him, but he was convinced she was working with Lacroix and kidnapped his daughter to scam this money from him. The thought of Ida held captive, frantic and alone continued to infuriate him. He was tempted to kick the woman to let off more of his anger, but he stepped back.

His cell phone buzzed. He pulled it out and looked at the screen. It was his CFO, the man who ran the finances on all his businesses. "What!" he shouted, his pulse still racing.

"We got trouble, Remy."

He took a deep breath. "Talk to me."

"It's on the street and all over the news."

"What the hell are you talking about?"

"An informant has come forward, anonymously. He's gone to the press, telling everyone you're secretly connected with the mob in New York, just like your old man... that your daughter's disappearance is a mob vendetta."

"Shit. Who is it?"

"Don't know, but all your publicly traded companies, the stocks are going to fall like a rock in the morning. He's been all over the TV this afternoon. His identity is shielded."

"How can they run this bullshit?" he said, tempted to throw the phone through the front window. "No one has called me for confirmation or a comment."

"You're not answering your phone, boss."

Chapter Thirty-one

Hanna and her client, Christy Griffith, walked back into the Charleston Police Department precinct office downtown. Neither noticed the SUV pull up across the street and park, two men inside watching them enter the building.

They were cleared through security and escorted to a large conference room. FBI agent, Sharron Fairfield, was sitting on one side of the table. Detective Nathan Beatty and another police officer they hadn't met sat across from them, deep in conversation. Everyone rose to greet them. Introductions were made. The second police officer was an audio technician who would work with them on the recording equipment for her meeting the next day with Xander Lacroix's men. Hanna made eye contact with Sharron and she smiled back at her.

Beatty began, "Christy, we've secured the warrant authorizing us to record your meetings and phone conversations. We want to walk through how this will all work tomorrow and what you can expect. Thank you for your cooperation."

Christy looked over at Hanna who nodded, hesitantly.

Hanna listened as the police technician walked them through the process of both the personal wire her client would wear as well as the business and cell phones that would be tapped. He also explained that the FBI was in attendance because of their ongoing investigation in Xander Lacroix's operation. When the tech finished, he asked if anyone had any questions.

Christy shook her head *no*, then paused and said, "What if they find out about all this?"

Hanna watched as all the law enforcement officials around the table exchanged glances. Detective Beatty jumped in. "That's very unlikely, but we will have back-up for your protection in your restaurant as well as around the building."

"These people killed my father," Christy said, her voice faltering. "Why should I believe they won't come after me?"

Agent Fairfield said, "We understand why you would be nervous about this. No question, these are dangerous people. Your assistance will help us take them off the street, Christy."

Hanna watched the face of her client and could tell she was having second thoughts. "If you have any concerns about this, we can pull the plug." She noticed the disapproving stares coming back at her from the police and FBI attendees.

Beatty said, "We will be right there with you, Christy."

The girl nodded and looked back at Hanna for reassurance. Hanna reached for her arm on the table and squeezed it.

They all agreed that Beatty and his team would be at the restaurant early the next morning to get Christy ready for the meeting. Beatty told them all the phone taps would be operational within the hour.

Hanna said goodbye to her client out on the sidewalk in front of the police precinct. "Call me at any time tonight or in the morning if you have more questions or concerns, or if you just want to talk."

"Thank you, Hanna. We're doing the right thing, aren't we?"

"You can help to put these people away where they won't be able to hurt anyone else."

"I know," the girl said and then leaned in and hugged Hanna. "Thank you for helping me with this."

"Of course." Hanna watched her walk away down the street and turned to go back to her offices. Again, she didn't notice the vehicle across the street pull out and proceed in the direction of her client. She heard her name called from behind.

"Hanna!"

She turned and saw Sharron Fairfield walking toward her. When they were face-to-face, Hanna said, "Please tell me you all will be able to protect her."

"We'll be working closely with the Charleston PD to provide adequate measures for her safety tomorrow and going forward."

Hanna wanted to feel reassured, but a nagging doubt stuck with her. From personal experience, she knew these organized crime people would not hesitate to take drastic action to protect their interests. "I hope you're right."

Fairfield nodded back.

Hanna said, "How are you all coming on the missing girl search?"

"Nothing really, yet. Seems she's simply vanished."

"As you know, Alex and I both have a history with the Dellahousaye family. It's hard to imagine there isn't foul play at work here."

Fairfield said, "Alex is doing a great job." She hesitated a moment, then said, "You know, back when we were dating, he always talked about joining the Bureau. I'm glad it's worked out for him."

Hanna tried her best to hide her surprise, but obviously failed miserably.

"You didn't know... about Alex and me?" Fairfield asked, looking away down the street then back into Hanna's gaze. "It was before the two of you were together. We met when we were working on your husband's case. It wasn't meant to be for the two of us."

Hanna's thoughts were swirling, and she struggled to respond.

"I'm really happy for both of you," Fairfield said.

Hanna finally managed a confused reply. "Thank you."

Hanna sat in the restaurant, waiting for Alex to join her for dinner. She looked at her watch and saw he was already fifteen minutes late. A glass of white wine sat empty in front of her, and she nodded when the server came up and asked if she'd like another.

Since leaving Special Agent Sharron Fairfield downtown at the police precinct, she had been trying to calm her emotions and not overreact to the news that her new fiancé had once dated the woman he would now be working closely with in the FBI. She had asked herself repeatedly, *why in hell didn't he tell me about this?*

As hard as she tried, all her trust issues with the men in her life kept screaming back in her mind. Again, she tried to be objective. *It's not like he lied to me about this.*

Her cell vibrated on the table next to the silverware on a blue cloth napkin. She saw Alex's name on the caller ID. Harder than intended, she pressed down on the call button and placed the phone to her ear. "Hello." She knew her tone would surprise him.

"*What's wrong?*" she heard him ask.

She didn't answer, trying with all her will to calm down.

"*Hanna?*"

"Where are you?" she finally asked.

He hesitated, then said, "*I'm sorry. I should have called earlier. I'm hung up here at the office.*"

Hanna couldn't help picturing him sitting in his office with Special Agent Sharron Fairfield.

Alex continued. "*I'm not going to be able to make it for dinner. I'm really sorry. I should have called, but...*"

"No, I understand," she said, not believing her own words.

"*Can I stop by the apartment later?*" he asked. "*Not sure when.*"

She couldn't hide the irritation in her voice. "You know, it's already late and I have a ton of paperwork to get through before work tomorrow."

"*Is everything okay?*" she heard him ask.

"Oh fine, just fine."

Chapter Thirty-two

Ida Dellahousaye watched the sky slowly darken through the small window in the boat cabin she was locked in. She lay on the small bunk and willed herself not to be sick. The boat had been rocking slowly in the offshore swells of the ocean for hours now. She had already thrown-up several times in the small toilet in the room. The air was close and smelled of vomit and dead fish. Her eyes were crusted with dried tears and she struggled to keep from shivering under the rough blanket she'd found. Her wounds throbbed and ached.

Her captors had pushed food and water through the door, but she had not seen anyone in hours. She thought again of her family and what they must be feeling, their panic about her disappearance... what they were all doing to find her. She had been trying to press down a sense of desperate hopelessness. *Will anyone ever find me? When are they going to just throw me overboard and leave me to die out here?*

Ophelia Dellahousaye stood on the small balcony off the living room of her apartment in Charleston, four floors up above the traffic crawling by below. The sun was setting to the west and cast a purple and pink glow on the wispy clouds moving over the town. Inside, she could hear her two friends laughing in the kitchen. Their afternoon in bed with her father's bodyguard, Vincent, had been as crazy as she had imagined. The man had left over an hour ago. She shook her head as she thought about her father and what he might do if he ever found out. She knew how close he was to cutting off all support. This would surely seal the deal, but, *what the hell.*

She thought of her sister and her already gloomy mood darkened. *Where are you?*

A sense of complete desperation and panic came over her. She gripped the balcony rail to steady herself.

Their father was back at his house in Charleston, sitting in his office, staring at the phone on his desk. He was waiting for a callback from his CFO on arrangements for the ransom payment the next day.

He had left his wife over an hour ago at the beach house. When she had regained consciousness from his attack, he had gone after her again about her duplicity with Lacroix. She continued to deny they had anything to do with his daughter's disappearance. She didn't deny the affair with his rival. *She'll be out on her ass in a matter of days.*

There was a knock at the door to his office. Vincent leaned in. "Get you anything for dinner, boss?"

"No," he replied abruptly. Food was the last thing on his mind. "Where in hell were you this afternoon?"

"Doctor and dentist," Victor said quickly. "Finally got appointments scheduled."

Remy looked back at his phone, his nerves a raw edge of anger and anticipation... *the money transfer tomorrow. Getting Ida home safely.*

"Any news on Ida?" he heard Vincent ask.

He looked up, thinking about how this would all come down tomorrow. "The bastards finally came forward with a ransom demand. I'm transferring the money tomorrow. We're not telling the Feds. You hear me?"

"Sure," Vincent said, walking over and sitting across from Dellahousaye. "She's okay, then?"

"Yes, they sent a picture." He pulled it up on his phone and handed it to Vincent.

"Damn, she looks terrible... sorry, boss."

Remy took his phone back. "I need you to stay close. This is going to come down quickly. Again, not a word of this to anyone. The cops get involved and God only knows how they'll screw it up."

"Right."

"You see the news?"

"What?" Vincent asked.

"Some asshole's come forward, telling the press and the cops we've been linked to the Old Man's syndicate the whole time."

"Who the hell?"

"I don't know, but when I find out, the prick is a dead man." He turned up the sound on the television on the wall when the news feed came back on about him, his daughter's mysterious disappearance and his long-time ties to his father's crime network. He grabbed a glass of water and took a long drink, not able to keep his hands from shaking. He sat staring at the television, watching his life unravel before his eyes. He reached for a brass letter opener laying by his office phone. With a sudden motion, he slammed it down into the rich walnut desktop. It stuck there, embedded, as he stood and walked to the bar on the far wall to make another drink.

Vincent jumped up in surprise. "Boss, it's okay. We'll find out who's behind this."

Chapter Thirty-three

Alex got back to his own apartment just before 10 p.m. He walked into the kitchen and threw his mail on the counter, then pulled a bottle of lime soda water out, taking a long drink. He sat on a stool and let the exhaustion of the day finally catch-up with him. They had made virtually no progress in their search for Ida Dellahousaye. None of the calls coming into the hotline had proved helpful, but each tip had to be tracked down. The head of the Charleston FBI office had sent him home to get a few hours of sleep.

The dark apartment was silent, and the air was stale from being closed up for so many months while he'd been away. He looked out a small window in the kitchen and saw the lights of the skyline of downtown Charleston on the horizon. He thought about Hanna and their abrupt phone conversation earlier. *What was that all about?*

He could imagine she was frustrated with the long hours he was spending on this case. They had planned to share a few days together before he had to report back to Washington. He had no idea how long he would be assigned to the Dellahousaye search here in Charleston, but eventually, he would have to go back, and he knew Hanna was still upset about his invitation to have her join him. *Am I being selfish about this? Everything in Hanna's life that's important is here in South Carolina.*

He knew she was also upset about her son deciding to take a break from school, and he could certainly understand her feelings. Jonathan had been doing so well and then suddenly, to just walk away? He had told them it was just for a term to take a break, but Hanna was right to be concerned that one term might turn to many.

His thoughts shifted to his last encounter with Remy Dellahousaye earlier in the day. Of course, he was upset about the disappearance of his daughter but trying to get him pulled from the case wasn't going to help. He had also seen the news on the television monitors down at the FBI offices about Dellahousaye's ties to the mob. Alex had not been surprised in the least and was pleased the man's true nature and business interests had finally been revealed. The timing of the anonymous informant coming forward was puzzling, though.

He couldn't help thinking about the Dellahousaye family's role in his partner's murder. Lonnie Smith had been gunned down in front of his eyes and the assassin had come within a hair of taking Alex out, too.

There had been some sense of revenge and justice the night he and Sheriff Pepper Stokes had burst in on Asa Dellahousaye and his men who were holding Hanna hostage. Seeing Dellahousaye lying on the floor, his guts splattered against the wall as his life ebbed away had given him some sense of peace in the matter, though the image still haunted him in his sleep. He wondered if the son, Remy, had also been involved in his partner's death, and his anger burned hot.

We'll find your daughter, he thought as he considered what to do about Remy Dellahousaye. *But, the two of us may still have some business to take care of.*

Alex crawled into bed and was about to turn out the light on the nightstand when he decided to call Hanna. It was only 10:30 and he assumed she would still be up. His cell phone rang four times and he was about to hang-up, fearing she might have gone off to sleep and he didn't want to wake her.

She answered, "Hi."

Again, the distant tone in her voice, he thought. "I just wanted to check in on you."

"I was almost asleep."

"I'm sorry." He waited a moment for her reply, but none came. "Hanna, what's wrong?"

"Just tired," she said.

"How is it going with your client and the Lacroix case?" he asked, trying to get to the root of her mood.

"I'm afraid we're putting the girl in terrible danger."

Alex had been briefed by Sharron Fairfield on the plans to tap phones and record a scheduled meeting with Lacroix's men. "She'll have plenty of protection tomorrow."

"What about the day after that and next week?" he heard her say, the concern in her voice clear. "These people get even, Alex. You know that."

"We need to get Lacroix and his network off the street. This is our best chance."

"And who gets sacrificed in the process is worth the risk?" Hanna said.

"They killed her father, Hanna."

"She thinks they did!"

"Now it looks like Remy Dellahousaye is the scumbag we thought he was all along," Alex said. "We can't figure out if he's working alongside Lacroix, behind the scenes or if the two of them are trying to carve out their own piece of Asa D's network."

He waited for Hanna to respond but there was only silence on his phone. Finally, he heard her say, "Can you make sure your team and the Charleston PD are doing everything possible to keep her safe?"

"Their very best people are on this, Hanna, but I'll check again in the morning."

"Thank you."

"Can I see you tomorrow?" he asked.

"You tell me."

"What?"

"You seem very busy and I understand you need to help find this girl, but..."

"Let me bring you that coffee you like in the morning. One pump of vanilla, right?"

"It has to be early. I need to be in my office by seven."

"I'll be there."

Hanna hung up the phone and placed her cell on the nightstand. She was feeling guilty for being so abrupt with Alex, but she couldn't get over the conversation she'd had with Sharron Fairfield about her earlier relationship with her new fiancé. She knew it was part jealousy. She was a very attractive woman and the thought of the two of them together was difficult to deal with.

She was aware Alex had seen other women in the years after his divorce from the crazy Adrienne. *Of course, he had.* She had not dated after her husband's death but was coming around to considering it when she and Alex suddenly moved beyond cop and victim, to friends... then lovers.

It was continuing to nag at her that Alex had chosen not to tell her about Sharron. The more she thought about it, he had never talked about any of the other women in his life, except Adrienne, and maybe he just put Sharron in that same category. The woman was so assured and confident, it just galled Hanna she had been caught unaware earlier in the day when she learned about their relationship. She didn't think Fairfield had any malicious intent. *She just assumed I knew about the two of them, right?*

Chapter Thirty-four

Lobbyist and potential Senate candidate, Jordan Hayes, Jr., sat with his father, the disgraced former Senator from South Carolina, over a cup of coffee in his well-appointed office down the street from the Capital Building. The two men had been on the phone several times since their son and grandson had been implicated as a *person-of-interest* in the disappearance of Ida Dellahousaye. They had already dispatched a team of attorneys to South Carolina to represent *JH the third*, as he was called by the family.

The elder Hayes took another sip from his coffee, then said, "You know this is politically motivated, right?"

JH Jr. shook his head. "I can't believe the Dems could pull this off so quickly. How could they get one of the kids at the party to make the accusation against Jordan, then leak it to the press?"

"You're kidding, right?" The defrocked Senator stood and walked to the window looking down Pennsylvania Avenue from the third floor of the office building. The past year had taken its toll on him. His fall from grace after being linked to the Asa Dellahousaye scandal had been quick and devastating, both professionally and personally. He had been lucky to stay out of prison. "This whole damn incident played right into their hands. They've been looking for something against you for months since you announced your interest in taking my seat." He turned to look back at his son. "I've already got people with contacts at the Justice Department and the FBI working to put a lid on this nonsense."

Jordan Hayes III had barely slept through the night, the booze and weed he'd consumed doing little to provide an escape from the spotlight he now found himself. The national and local media trucks and news crews remained camped in front of his fraternity house. They were demanding another statement or interview about his involvement in the Dellahousaye case.

The lawyers who had descended on Clemson, SC, at the request of his father and grandfather had insisted he remain secluded. Their designated spokesperson had repeatedly confronted the media outside to refute earlier claims that Jordan had suspiciously left the crowd at the beach for a significant time after Ida Dellahousaye had left the beach party. The three lawyers were all huddled in a room in the basement of the fraternity house where they had set-up a temporary office. They had warned Jordan he would have to ultimately make another statement, but they were still working on his response with guidance from his father and grandfather in Washington.

He got out of his bed and slowly walked to the window looking out over the street in front of the house. He parted the curtain just enough to see all the media trucks were still there. There may have even been one or two more, he thought.

His head was on fire from the previous night's excesses and his stomach was on the verge of full revolt. He looked back at the bed and saw the sleeping form of Jennifer Wallace. She had sneaked in the back of the fraternity late last night and come up to his room to *"be here for you"* as she had said. After a couple of beers and a joint, she had ended up spending the night. The lawyers had not been pleased when they discovered she was there.

His stomach churned again when images returned of Ida Dellahousaye being thrown into the trunk of the car down at the beach and driven away.

Chapter Thirty-five

Alex pressed the button for the bell on the front of Hanna's house. He heard the intercom box on the brick wall buzz and then Hanna's groggy voice, "Is that you?"

"Good morning." The electric lock on the door slid open and he balanced the two cups of coffee in his hands to go inside. Hanna met him at the open door at the top of the stairs to the small apartment she'd lived in after selling her house on South Battery following her husband's death over two years ago. She was already dressed in her typical casual business attire, khaki slacks and a sleeveless white blouse. Her sandy hair was still wet from the shower and combed straight back.

Alex handed her one of the coffees and leaned in to kiss her on the cheek. "Morning."

"Thanks for the latte," she said, moving aside to let him in and then closing the door behind them.

He walked into the kitchen and took a sip from his own coffee. Alex said, "I've already spoken with both my FBI team and with Beatty down at the Charleston PD. They assure me they have sufficient back-up today, discreetly placed so as not to compromise Christy during this meeting with Lacroix's goons." He could see in her expression that he was doing little to boost her confidence.

"People who go up against the mob end up either dead or in Witness Protection for the rest of their lives," she said, putting two pieces of bread in a toaster.

"I understand your concern, but otherwise, we just let these people squeeze her for her family's money and maybe even get away with the murder of her father. Is that a better choice?"

"If anything happens to this girl..." she began.

"Hanna, these people know what they're doing," he said, while immediately thinking how unconvinced he was about Christy Griffith's fate if Lacroix discovered she was setting them up. He watched Hanna move over to sit on a stool at the center island, looking down at her coffee cup she held tightly in both hands. He sat beside her, sensing the tension still lingering between them. "What else is going on?"

She looked up at him and he saw how tired and drawn her face appeared. She shook her head slowly, then said, "I don't know. I guess it's everything right now. Jonathan and school..."

"He's a good kid. He'll work through this," he said, trying to reassure her. Hanna stared back for a moment, searching his eyes.

"Is it the DC thing?" he asked. "I know how hard this would be for you to move..."

Her expression flared, "Of course it's going to be hard. I have to drop everything to move to a place where I don't know a soul."

"It won't be forever." He reached for her hand, but she pulled away and stood beside him.

"I had an interesting discussion with your partner yesterday," she finally said.

"Partner?"

"Sharron Fairfield."

He felt his heart quicken. "Sharron?"

"She was in the meeting with my client down at the police precinct."

He watched her pause and stare back at him. He knew what was coming and cursed himself silently.

"Why didn't you tell me about the two of you?"

Alex took a deep breath. "What did she tell you?"

"That you were a couple... that you got together after working on Ben's case."

"It was over long before you and me..."

"That's not the point!"

He held up his hands. "No excuses, Hanna. I should have told you, particularly since you know Sharron and have been working with her."

"Yes, you should have." She walked to the sink and poured the coffee out. "I need to get to work."

"Hanna, I'm sorry you were surprised by this. I really wasn't trying to hide anything, I just..."

"Just what?"

"I thought with me working more closely with her now at the Bureau you would be worried about the two of us together."

"Should I be?"

"No, of course not!" he said quickly. "It was a long time ago and it was never serious." He saw her face twist in exasperation.

"So, it was just sex," she snapped.

"Hanna, please..." He walked over to her and she reluctantly let him take her in his arms. "I love you, Hanna Walsh. I may be an idiot at times, but I love you." He felt her body soften into his and she placed her face on his shoulder. He sniffed in the scent of her shampoo and pulled her closer. They stood together, holding each other, the morning sun sparkling through the trees outside the kitchen window.

An hour later, Hanna hung up the phone in her office and sighed. Her calendar was full of appointments and she wasn't sure how she was going to balance everything in front of her on her desk. She knew she had to get a call out to her son before things got any more hectic. He picked up right away.

"Hey, Mom," he said, his voice breathless. "I'm on my way to class."

"Are you riding your bike?" she asked, imagining him dodging traffic and other students, trying to talk on the phone while riding.

"Just pulled over. What's up?"

"Tell me you've changed your mind about school next term," she asked, knowing full well her headstrong son was not going to reconsider.

"Mom, look..."

"I know, but listen to me," she said cutting him off. "I talked to my partners at the law firm out on the island. They need an intern for the summer. You can get paid and get some good experience for your law school application." She waited for his response, looking out over the deeply wooded back yard through the window.

Finally, Jonathan said, "You know, that could be great. Thank you!"

"If you're not going to be in school, at least you can get some valuable experience."

"Sure," he said. "I need to help Elizabeth find something. We both want to put some money away."

"And why is that?"

She heard some hesitation in his voice. "Well, I haven't asked her yet, but we want to be together... we want to get married someday."

Hanna's spirits lifted some as she thought about how much she loved his girlfriend and how good they were together. "That's terrific, honey."

"So, it's okay if we stay out at the beach house for the summer?"

"Of course. Let me think about other contacts we have out there who might have some work for Elizabeth."

"Thanks, Mom."

"Are you sure everything else is okay down there?"

She grew concerned again when he hesitated. "We just need a break. This has been a long haul and we need to catch our breath."

Hanna remembered her time in school and prepping for law school, the stress and exhaustion. "Well, you two need to take care of yourselves and..."

"Mom, we'll be okay. Thanks again for helping with this job."

She ended the call with an update on his grandfather's planned retirement and then placed her phone down. She thought about Jonathan being out at Pawleys Island all summer with his girlfriend and how nice it would be to have them so close. *But, I may well be in DC by then*, she thought, shaking her head and staring down at her phone.

Chapter Thirty-six

Remy Dellahousaye watched the early buzz of activity in the park along the Battery as he sat in the back of his car. Vincent was driving him downtown for an update meeting with the FBI and police teams working to find his daughter. During a call with his CFO earlier in the morning, he had confirmed steps were nearly complete in arranging for the wire of $5 million to the offshore account of Ida's captors. The thought of it again made his anger burn deep inside. He would pay the money to get his daughter back, but he would also find out who was responsible and there would be nowhere on earth they'd be able to hide from his vengeance.

He had a private detective agency following every move his wife, Jillian, was making. The thought of her and his rival, Xander Lacroix, together as lovers wasn't as infuriating as the likelihood they were behind his daughter's disappearance.

After his father's death, he had made overtures to work with Xander as he moved quickly to stabilize and then control Asa Dellahousaye's vast criminal network and wealth. It soon became apparent that Lacroix had no intention to allow the dead gangster's son to retain any level of involvement. The two had nearly come to blows on several occasions as they met to work through their many issues. Remy had continued to keep the charade of his cloak of legitimacy with his own business enterprise, but his links to his father's world were quickly being cut off as Lacroix ascended to his position of power. Support from the New York crime syndicate for Lacroix's efforts had been the final sign that Remy was being pushed out of the family business once and for all.

Now the sonofabitch is screwing my wife and probably behind the kidnapping of my daughter!

He seethed with a fresh wave of fury, gripping the plush leather seats of his big Mercedes as they drove along. He met the gaze of Vincent's eyes in the rear-view mirror.

"What is it, boss?"

Remy looked out again at the passing bikers and joggers in the park, then said, "Get hold of Lacroix's people. Tell them I want to see him this morning after we're done with the cops. I'll go to them."

"You sure that's a good idea?" Vincent said, tentatively.

"Just do what I tell you!"

Chapter Thirty-seven

The Dellahousaye twin who was still walking free knew it was time to end the charade. *How many times had she and her sister traded places?* No one had ever discovered their deceptions. It had become a regular part of their lives and there were times their personalities blended so completely, they found it hard to remember who was who. They both found a thrill in living each other's very different lives. It had become an obsession with them. They typically spoke at least daily to share the day's events and make sure they were knowledgeable and consistent with those around them when they took on their sister's alternate lives. Their looks were so identical, their own parents had never been able to tell them apart.

The real Ida slowed her morning run to a walk, catching her breath slowly, the sweat from the early morning heat and humidity pouring down her body and stinging her eyes. Seabirds along the break wall squawked and jockeyed for position as they hovered over the water. The morning sky out to the east was tinged in brilliant shades of orange and red across the low clouds.

They all think they're looking for Ida, she thought. Knowing her sister as well as she did, and how could she not, she was sure Ophelia had fallen deep into her twin sister's identity, as she always did, and probably couldn't separate fact from illusion. It would often take her days to come back mentally to her real identity when they switched again. She was even seeing a shrink to deal with her psychosis.

Playing the role of her wilder sister, Ophelia, these past few days had been a roller coaster of drinking, drugs and sex with Ophelia's *love couple* and then her father's man, Vincent, yesterday. She shuddered as she thought about the thrill of the excesses she longed for in her twin's life. It was always such a marvelous break from her often-boring existence at school and with her barely tolerable boyfriend, Jordan Hayes. She knew she had to end that relationship as soon as she returned to school and her real life as Ida.

She had found little sleep the previous night after her sister's lovers, Josh and Susanna, finally left her alone and fell asleep.

She couldn't calm her fears for her lost sister. *Has she really been abducted? Did she run off with someone else?* It wouldn't surprise her, she thought, if Ophelia in her altered state would take off on some wild adventure and not tell anyone. *She must be seeing the news coverage, though, and know everyone is looking for her, right?*

She was certain her parents would be furious with them. Of course they would, but if it will help find O, she knew she needed to see her father and finally tell him about the long deception of the Dellahousaye twins.

Chapter Thirty-eight

The hot humid air of the morning hit Hanna like a steaming wet blanket in a sauna as she walked down the back steps of her office. The early sun relentlessly pressed through the heavy canopy of trees above her. A small ripple of breeze rustled the leaves but offered no relief.

She looked at her watch. It was just a few minutes before ten and she needed to get to Christy Griffith's office before the police came to set up the wire for her meeting with Lacroix's people. As she approached her small Honda sedan, she looked in her bag for her keys. She was still searching when a strong arm gripped her from behind and a hand pressed tightly against her mouth. She let out a muffled cry of surprise and fright, but the man held her tightly against him. She felt his breath on her neck as she heard his low voice say, "Counselor, tell your client she'll end up like her father if she goes forward with the cops."

Hanna struggled to free herself and turn to see her attacker, but he held her close.

"Are we clear on this?" he whispered.

Hanna nodded, all her fears and nightmares coming back from her abduction by Asa Dellahousaye and his men. Then she felt the hand come away from her mouth. She was about to scream for help when the sharp steel edge of a big knife was laid across her cheek.

"You're going to lie down and face the ground. If you look up, I will come back and use this. Again, are we clear, Counselor?"

Hanna nodded, looking away over the roof of her car and the back yard of her house. She felt herself being pushed down and got to her knees, then laid prone on the ground, the hard cement of her driveway scratching at her chin and nose. She sensed the man moving away and willed herself not to look up. *I need to get to Christy!*

She continued to lay there, trying to catch her breath, trying not to let her panic overwhelm her. A sound from behind startled her and she rose to her hands and knees.

"Hanna!" a voice yelled out.

She knew it was her assistant, Molly, who came running up and knelt beside her.

"Are you okay?"

Hanna sat down on the ground and fell back against the door of her car.

Molly saw the blood on her face and gasped. "Ohmigod, what happened?"

Hanna, still stunned, looked over at the face of the young woman but couldn't respond. She scanned the parking area for any sign of her attacker, but he was apparently gone.

Molly said, "I came back to look for you in your office and then saw you lying out here through the back door."

Finally, Hanna said, "I'm okay."

"You don't look okay. Did you fall?"

Hanna thought for a quick moment, then decided she didn't want to alarm her assistant. "I must have tripped on something." She started to get up and Molly helped her stand and then lean against the car. She picked up Hanna's bag on the ground and handed it to her.

"We need to get something for your face."

Hanna touched the painful scrapes and then looked at the blood on her fingers. She reached for some tissue in her bag and then dabbed at the wounds.

"No, really," Molly said. "Let's get you inside and get those cleaned up."

As Hanna walked with her up to the back porch of the house, all she could think about was her client and the dangerous path she was about to go down.

Hanna found Christy in the kitchen of her restaurant working with the chef on the day's menu. She saw the surprise in the woman's expression when she saw her lawyer's face, still showing the panic from the earlier attack and two Band-Aids on her chin and cheek.

"Hanna, what happened?" Christy said, coming around the steel prep table. "Your face is still bleeding!"

She touched at her chin and her hand came away with a smear of blood.

The chef looked on in astonishment, rubbing at the gray stubble of his beard.

"What in the world...?" Christy began.

"You and I need to talk," Hanna said, still breathless.

Christy led her into the small private office and closed the door. "Let me get you something for your face." She pulled a small first aid kit off a shelf and rummaged for clean bandages. She removed the two blood-soaked Band-Aids and opened a disinfectant pad to clean the scratches. "Are you going to tell me what's going on?"

Hanna took the pad from Christy and held it to her chin, then sat in a small metal chair next to the desk. "Lacroix knows you're working with the authorities."

The look of surprise and fear was immediate on the girl's face. "How would they know?"

"Either they've been following you, or someone has tipped them off. Either way, they jumped me just a few minutes ago and threatened you if you go forward with this."

Hanna watched the girl's face pale, then quickly gain a sense of resolve. "Really, they'll kill me, too?" She started pacing in the small space of the office. "We can't let them get away with this, Hanna!"

"Christy, sit down and please listen to me."

The girl sat down next to Hanna, pulling a pack of cigarettes from her purse, but her hands were shaking too much to light one. She threw the pack and lighter on the desk and looked up at Hanna. "They killed my father, Hanna!"

"You don't have to tell me how dangerous they are. I know these people. They have no moral compass."

"I'm not going to let them intimidate me," the girl said, breathing deeply.

Hanna heard her words, but her mind was locked on the reality of dealing with the ruthless Dellahousaye and now Lacroix crime syndicate. She knew, only too well, these people live in an alternate reality of power over weakness, violence over reason, death over disobedience.

"Christy, please. You need to hear what I'm saying. I've personally looked down the gun barrel of these monsters. They will not hesitate to pull the trigger or kill you in some other gruesome way. Either way, you will be dead, and they will still have control. I'm sorry, but your father obviously made a grave mistake bringing them in to his business." She hesitated and threw her head back in exasperation.

There was a knock at the door, and it opened a few inches. Her chef, Richard, peeked in. There are a bunch of very serious people with badges here to see you."

"I'll be out in a minute," Christy said. Richard backed out and closed the door.

"We have to find another way," Hanna said.

Christy and Hanna sat at a six-top table in the main dining room of the restaurant in the dim light before opening across from Nate Beatty and his surveillance tech from Charleston PD, and Sharron Fairfield from the FBI. Before they could begin, Hanna said, "This whole operation has been compromised."

Hanna went on to share the news of her attack from the unidentified assailant at her office and the threats he had laid out against her client. Watching as the law enforcement representatives paused to consider this new development, she couldn't help but look at the attractive and immaculately attired Special Agent Sharron Fairfield. She knew she needed to focus on her client and the real danger she now found herself in, but images of this woman with Alex kept creeping into her mind.

Fairfield broke the silence. "We obviously need to regroup on this. Nate, do you agree?" she said, looking at the police detective.

"Unfortunately, yes," Beatty said. "They will obviously check you for wires when you meet so that's off the table."

"You already have the wiretaps in place on the phones?" Hanna asked.

"That's right," Fairfield answered. "They will have no way of knowing their phone calls to Christy will be recorded, but I'm quite certain they will expect that to be the case."

Beatty said, "So, where the hell are we?"

Hanna had a sudden realization. Thinking out loud, she said, "Both Xander Lacroix and now Dellahousaye have a lot of complications in their lives, at the moment. Obviously, Remy is totally caught up in the search for his missing daughter. After yesterday's informant came forward, Dellahousaye is jockeying for a leadership role in his father's business network. He and Lacroix have to be dealing with some serious issues. Don't you think Dellahousaye could use some leverage on Lacroix about now?" She looked around the room, her client and the law enforcement officials' faces staring back with questioning expressions.

Hanna continued. "What if we feed Dellahousaye with details on what we know about Lacroix's role in Christy's father's death and efforts to extort money from her business?"

"We're not in a position to do that," Fairfield said, "even if we thought Dellahousaye could somehow squeeze Lacroix and get him to back down."

"Nor are we," Beatty said.

Hanna considered their position for a moment. The thought of approaching another Dellahousaye on this sent a chill of apprehension through her, but she also knew she couldn't stand by and let these thugs get away with murder and extort her client. "You see any reason why I can't have a word with Mr. Dellahousaye?" she finally said.

Fairfield and Beatty exchanged glances, then both shook their heads *no*.

"You're putting yourself in a very dangerous position, Hanna," Beatty replied. "Getting in the middle of these two is a high risk move."

"I can't let you do that," Christy said.

She knew they were all right in their fears about this, but in her heart, she knew she had to do something.

Chapter Thirty-nine

Alex watched the face of Remy Dellahousaye as his colleague, Will Foster, concluded the latest briefing on the search for the man's daughter. They were sitting in Foster's office around a small conference table. The panorama of downtown Charleston shining in the bright morning sun through the windows.

Basically, nothing of substance had turned up yet. Curiously, the man didn't seem overly concerned. *How can a man facing the disappearance of his daughter for nearly two days now, not be more upset at the lack of progress in finding her?*

"Thank you for your ongoing efforts," Dellahousaye said, his voice low and restrained. None of his previous anger and frustration with Alex apparent as he stood to leave. "You will, of course, call me if anything else develops?"

"Certainly," Foster said.

When Dellahousaye left the room and closed the door behind him, Alex said, "What was that all about?"

"I have no idea," Foster answered, shaking his head.

"Have you lost your mind?" Alex barked into Hanna's phone.

"So, your *friend*, Sharron, has already filled you in?" Hanna returned.

"She's not my friend..."

"I'm sorry," Hanna said, regretting the cheap shot. She was back in her office and about to call Remy Dellahousaye. She was almost nauseous at the prospect of meeting with him and conveying information he could use against his rival. Hopefully, information that would get Lacroix to back off

Christy Griffith and give them all more time to build the murder case against the man.

"Hanna, I don't have to tell you the type of people we're dealing with here. I heard one of them already went after you this morning. Are you okay?"

"Just a little shaken up, but I have to do something."

"The best thing you can do right now is keep your nose out of this. If Lacroix finds out you leaked information to Dellahousaye…"

When he didn't finish the thought, Hanna said, "I'm going to do this, Alex. I was just about to call Dellahousaye."

"Hanna, please…"

"I need to help this girl," she said with an urgency that her mind was having trouble accepting.

"Dellahousaye just left here," Alex said. "We just had a very strange discussion. After we told him we were still nowhere in the investigation, he took the news surprisingly calmly."

"Do you think he might know more than he's letting on?" Hanna asked.

"We were all just discussing that possibility."

"If she's truly been kidnapped, maybe Dellahousaye's been approached about the ransom."

"It's the only thing that makes sense," Alex replied.

She looked at the clock on the wall. It was nearly noon. "Look, I need to go."

"Please tell me you're not going to meet with Remy Dellahousaye."

"I'll call you later," she replied and ended the call.

Chapter Forty

When she had finally reached Dellahousaye on his cell, he had been under-standingly curt and direct. *"I'm a bit busy at the moment, Ms. Walsh,"* he had said when she introduced herself and asked for some time to meet with him this afternoon.

"Yes, of course, I'm very sorry about your daughter. I just need a few minutes."

He had hesitantly agreed to a quick conversation at his office at 2:15.

She stood in front of the grand house on the Battery now, just two blocks down from her old home along the park overlooking the bay. She walked through the ornate black iron gate and up the stone walk to the front veranda of the house. She pressed the bell and within moments the door opened and a man she didn't recognize stood facing her, a very serious expression on his face.

"I have an appointment with Mr. Dellahousaye."

"Yeah, come on in. He's expecting you." He showed her into a large gathering room to the right furnished with plush chairs and a sofa around a big fireplace. "He's finishing up a call. Have a seat. Can I get you some coffee or something?"

"No, I'm fine."

He left her there and she walked over to a wall of framed family photos. There were several of the Dellahousaye twins at various ages. She thought it remarkable how truly identical they were. As she looked through the many images, she thought it odd there were none of the girl's mother. She knew Dellahousaye was divorced, but still?

The pictures of Remy Dellahousaye revealed a handsome man with looks that reminded her too much of his father, memories she would still rather not revisit.

The man came back into the room. "This way please, ma'am."

When she walked into Dellahousaye's office he stood from behind his desk and came around to meet her. "Hello, Ms. Walsh." He extended his hand and she felt a firm but sweaty grip. *He must be as nervous about something as I am in being here*, she thought.

"It's Hanna," she replied.

He nodded and looked to his assistant. "Vincent, did you offer Hanna something to drink?"

"I'm fine, Mr. Dellahousaye."

"Please, sit down." He motioned to a grouping of couches in the corner. The man named Vincent left the room and closed the door. Dellahousaye was dressed in gray suit pants and a white dress shirt with the collar and tie loose at the neck.

"I'm very sorry about your daughter," Hanna began. "Has there been any news?"

She watched him hesitate a moment, then say, "I'm afraid nothing yet."

She was tempted to remind the man his own father's people kidnapped her son and later abducted her in an attempt to get to Alex, but then thought better of it.

"I really am quite busy..." he said.

"I understand." She took a deep breath, trying to remain calm. "I'm an attorney..."

"Yes, I know who you are," he replied quickly.

Of course, he does! "I'm here representing my client, Christy Griffith and her deceased father, Charles."

"I'm sorry, Hanna, I don't know these people..."

"Please, let me get to the point."

"I wish you would."

"Let me be very frank," she said, trying to keep her breathing measured. "It's been all over the news that you have interests in your father's businesses..."

His face immediately shifted from calm to anger. "That's none of your...!"

Hanna jumped in, leaning forward for emphasis. "We are also aware a man named Xander Lacroix is moving quickly to control those interests."

Dellahousaye stood. "We're through here...!"

Hanna stood and faced the man. "I have information on Lacroix I think you should be aware of."

His expression softened. "What is this all about?"

"Lacroix and his organization may well have killed my client's father, Charles Griffith. They are also pressuring his daughter to sell their family restaurants and return money they've invested at exorbitant terms." She watched Dellahousaye staring back at her, considering her revelations.

He nodded, his gaze intense. "And why is this my business?"

Hanna didn't hesitate. "There may be some advantage in you sharing your knowledge of this with Mr. Lacroix, some leverage, so to speak, in your ongoing... negotiations with the man."

Dellahousaye shook his head and turned to go back behind his desk. He looked back at her. "You think I can get him to back off this girl?"

"I think it would be in both our interests for you to do so."

He placed his hands down on his desk, obviously thinking through the situation. "How much do you have on Lacroix? Why hasn't he been arrested for this supposed murder?"

"The police are still building their case, but they're close."

He looked at his watch. "I'll give this some thought."

"Thank you..."

"You know, if Xander Lacroix knew of your role in this..."

She felt her chest tighten. "I hope I can trust in your discretion."

Chapter Forty-one

Ophelia Dellahousaye, her mind lost in the tangled delusion she was actually her sister, Ida, tried to stand in the small cabin of the boat. The wind and waves had risen through the day and her seasickness was adding to her confused and weakened state. The boat lurched and she fell back onto the bed, wet with her sweat and stinking of her vomit.

Another wave of nausea swept over her and she fell back, covering her eyes. "Oh god, please no!"

She willed her stomach to calm and tried to focus on her situation. She knew it had been nearly 48 hours since she'd been taken at the beach. Her captor had remained a faceless and terrifying presence outside the door of the old cabin and now the boat these past hours. He had pushed in food and water, but she'd had no appetite. Her helplessness and terror were overwhelming, and she stood now and began pacing. She'd tried to open the door on many occasions and didn't care if they knew she was trying to get out. *What can they do?* She stumbled to the door again and began pounding.

"Dammit, I'm sick. Let me out of here!"

She kept pounding and yelling, and finally she saw the door open. The large man with the Halloween mask on again pushed her back. "Lay the hell down and shut-up or..."

With all her remaining strength, she kicked out as hard as she could and caught the man square in the crotch. She saw him fold over in pain and grunt, "Shit!"

She rushed by him through the door into the galley of the boat below the main deck. She stumbled up the stairs as the big boat rolled in the surf. The vast panorama of the Atlantic Ocean stared back at her, then turning, she saw the distant horizon of land in the other direction. Without hesitating, she ran to the rear of the boat and climbed up on the rail, balancing precariously in the heavy seas. She could hear the man coming up the steps.

"Get down from there, you stupid bitch!"

In her mind, she was certain she would die if she didn't get away. She dove out into the air and felt the cold shock of the water as she splashed down into a large swell in the blue ocean. She came up choking, thinking she would be sick again, but started stroking, desperate to get away, willing the pain throughout her body away.

"Get back here!" she heard the man yell behind her.

She kept trying to swim, the heavy surf buffeting her and keeping her from making much progress. She was tiring quickly but pushed on. The engine of the boat roared to life behind her and her spirits sank even more deeply. *They'll never let me get away!*

She had been swimming, but more like thrashing through the water for what seemed forever. Actually, it had only been a few minutes when the boat came alongside her, just far enough away that she wouldn't be sucked under the hull and chopped up by the prop.

The man yelled down to her, "You won't get far..."

A painful jerk on her right leg made her scream out in surprise. She stopped struggling to swim and came up in a crunched position, trying to keep her mouth above the waves. There was a stabbing pain in her leg, and then she saw the blood in the water. *It's my blood!*

She looked up and saw the boat was at least ten feet away. Then she saw the fin of the big shark.

The deafening crack of a rifle blast caused her to jerk, and she fell below the surface. She saw the blurry dark shadow of the shark just feet away, then it turned as a second muffled shot could be heard above water. She came back to the surface and lay on her back. The rolling waves washed over her, the taste of her own blood and salt in the water she was trying to spit out. She was completely exhausted, and the terror of the big fish had taken any further will to escape. *Get me back on the boat!*

The real Ida Dellahousaye sat across from their friends, Josh and Susanna, in a small diner down the block from her apartment. Her sandwich remained untouched in front of her. She felt Susanna's hand on her arm and looked up.

"Lose your appetite, O?" the woman asked.

Ida had been tempted all morning since returning from her run to finally expose the charade she and her sister had been playing for years, but something was keeping her from it. She knew she had to go to her father, though. When she called him earlier, he told her he was too busy to talk and that he'd get back to her... still no word about her sister.

Without warning, she suddenly cried out.

Josh and Susanna looked back in surprise. Susanna reached for her hand. "You okay?"

Ida's heart was racing, and she was suddenly finding it hard to catch her breath. A cold chill came over her. *Ophelia!*

Chapter Forty-two

Jillian Dellahousaye sat in a comfortable lounge chair on the sprawling deck of her husband's beach house and fought the urge to call Xander Lacroix again. She applied another layer of sunscreen on her deeply tanned skin and took a sip from the Bloody Mary on the table beside her. She'd been trying to reach Xander all day, but he wouldn't pick up her calls. Before he'd left the beach house that morning, he'd promised to keep her informed about his plans to deal with her husband.

She still couldn't believe how Remy had attacked her the previous day when he confronted her about the disappearance of Ida. Their relationship had been strained at best these past months, but she had never seen this violent side of the man. She shuddered as she remembered the ferocity of his assault.

He obviously knew about her relationship with Xander and of course, their marriage was over. It was just a matter of time before she was out on the street again, just as she'd found herself in her previous marriage to the wealthy investment banker from New York. He'd thrown her out with virtually nothing and his lawyers made sure her indiscretions during their marriage supported their case for her paltry settlement. That money was nearly gone when she had met Remy Dellahousaye in a hotel in Vegas when he was visiting on business. She was close to considering becoming a paid escort when all other options seemed out of reach. She had seduced Remy that first night after several drinks in the hotel bar. He was coming out of his own failed marriage and was an easy mark.

Their courtship was meteoric, and she quickly found herself the new Mrs.

Remy D, comfortably ensconced in beautiful homes, access to a private jet, a very generous monthly stipend and at least for the first couple of years, a reasonably healthy relationship with her new husband. Despite his twins attempts to reveal her past and sour their relationship, she had prevailed until just recently when Remy had discovered her infidelity with one of their friends from a local club, and most recently, with the gangster, Xander Lacroix.

Xander would hopefully be her new lifeline, though she found the man barely tolerable. He was unattractive, unexciting in bed, totally bereft of any social graces. He did seem to have incredible wealth and he was desperately smitten with her. *Or, is he just using me to get at Remy?*

This nagging thought had become more troublesome over the past couple of weeks as the rivalry between the two men became more evident in their open attempts to control the crime network of Remy's late father, Asa.

As always, she did have the ultimate trump card. She had been able to survive and take care of herself all these years by always having one more card to play.

Chapter Forty-three

Patience was not a virtue Xander Lacroix had any hold on. His rise to power in the Asa Dellahousaye organization had been accelerated by his decisiveness and ability to move quickly and assuredly when opportunities presented themselves.

He was surprised when Asa D made a fatal miscalculation in dealing with the cop, Alex Frank, who had killed him the previous year during the questionable abduction of the man's lawyer girlfriend and the wife of their former associate, Beau Richards. He had tried to counsel his boss, but the man wouldn't listen. Fortunately, he had been able to stay away from the mess that ensued and the ultimate death of Asa D.

With adversity comes opportunity, thought Lacroix as he paced in his kitchen in the palatial home he owned on Sullivan's Island outside Charleston. Over the past year, he had been able to solidify his position of power, and with the support of the prominent New York crime family as his benefactor, he was close to removing all the final hurdles to fully assume control of the Southern network of illegal businesses and enterprises. He knew he would be under the thumb of the Italians in New York, probably for the rest of his days, but he had determined it was his best play.

Remy Dellahousaye continued to prove troublesome. His ridiculous attempts to appear above the fray of his father's illicit business had now been exposed, thanks to a distant associate Xander had paid to blow the whistle. Remy would be distracted for months, if not years, by the Feds and his daughter's disappearance would also keep him off his game just long enough for Xander to completely take him out.

He walked to the living area across the back of the house looking across a vast expanse of marsh back to the mainland. The horizon of land shimmered in the intense heat of the afternoon. His long boat pier stretched out into the channel. A large sailboat was motoring past on the way out to the bay.

Danny Wells came into the room. He knew the stupid sonofabitch was on the pad with Remy Dellahousaye, but as they say, *keep your enemies closer.* He was looking forward to the day he could personally take this bastard off the board.

Wells said, "Just got a call from one of Dellahousaye's guys."

Of course you did, you measly prick!

"He wants to meet."

This caught him off guard as he quickly tried to think through Remy's intentions. "When and why?"

"Didn't say why but wants to come out here this afternoon."

"Who'd you talk to?" Lacroix demanded.

"His flunky, Vincent."

It was nearly five in the afternoon when Lacroix heard Dellahousaye's car pull into the drive along the back of the house. He'd been sitting at his desk for the past hour trying to think through all the moves Remy was plotting and what he was trying to accomplish with this meeting. There had been times he'd been tempted to just arrange a convenient death for the bastard to get him out of the way, but the right opportunity hadn't presented itself. Screwing the man's crazy wife had given him some satisfaction in the meantime.

There was a knock on the door and Wells leaned his head in. "You ready, boss?"

Lacroix just nodded and stood as his rival walked quickly into the room. The two men stood facing each other without speaking. Lacroix had always thought Remy weak and inferior to his father on most counts. Today, he saw a fury on the man's face he had never seen before.

Finally, Lacroix broke the silence between them. "What is it, Remy? I'm a busy man."

Remy Dellahousaye stood and stared at Xander Lacroix, trying to throttle his impulse to kill him with his bare hands. When Lacroix finally spoke, Remy took a deep breath and said, "I know about you and my worthless wife and frankly, I couldn't care less. You're welcome to her. What I *do* care about is my daughter."

"I was sorry to hear about that," Lacroix said, his tough expression seeming to soften. "Any news?"

Remy struggled to remain calm, his fists clenched at his side, the heat in his face rising. "You think the money means anything to me?" He saw the look of confusion on his rival's face.

"What are you talking about?" Lacroix asked, stepping closer.

"You think $5 million can take me down, get me out of the way? Does Jillian get half?"

Lacroix didn't answer and just stood there staring back for a moment.

"I think you and my wife know where my daughter is and I'm not leaving this room without you telling me."

He watched as Lacroix smiled and then turned to walk back behind his desk. "You've lost your mind, Remy. I heard you were under a lot of heat, but this is crazy, man."

Remy felt a circuit in his brain break loose and enraged, he rushed the man. Before Lacroix could react, he had him by the neck and threw him up against the window behind his desk. He squeezed until he thought he felt cartilage breaking, the man's face going red as he struggled to get away.

The door behind them flew open and he felt two men pulling him away and then holding him.

Lacroix stood gasping, holding his neck and spitting blood on the floor.

"Let him go," Lacroix rasped.

Danny Wells and the other man stepped back.

"Get out of here!" Lacroix yelled to his men and both reluctantly backed out of the room and closed the door again. "You've lost your goddamned mind, Dellahousaye!"

Remy stood there, trying to catch his breath and calm his impulse to tear the man apart. "So help me, Lacroix..."

"Remy, you're way off base here."

"Tell me where she is!"

"I've got nothing to do with your daughter and you best get this out of your mind right now or you may not leave this property alive. Do you understand?"

Remy watched as Lacroix opened a desk drawer and pulled out a black semi-automatic pistol. He chambered a round and laid it on the desk. It wasn't an unexpected move. Remy doubted the man would shoot him in his own house. The first threads of doubt began to cloud his thinking. *Am I wrong about this bastard and my whore of a wife?*

"You need to get your shit together, Remy." The man coughed up more blood and spit into the waste basket next to his desk. "Look, you need to know our friends in New York are growing tired of your act, too. They're strongly suggesting I encourage you to get the hell out of the way and stop complicating things."

Remy listened to this latest threat but knew the risks he'd been taking in trying to keep his hold on his father's business. In desperation, he thought about his discussion with the lawyer and her client Lacroix was trying to move in on. "I think *your* days are numbered, Lacroix," he said. "I personally know you're about to get taken down for the murder of this Griffith guy. The Feds have their case..."

He stopped when Lacroix managed a hoarse laugh. "You're reaching now, Remy."

"No, I don't think so. Neither does the Charleston PD and the FBI. They have you directly in their sights and it's just a matter of time until they show up at your front door."

"And why is this your concern?" Lacroix asked, his hand resting directly beside the gun.

"Only to let you know I'll be doing everything in my power to assist with their investigation to take your ass down!"

Lacroix rubbed at the bruises on his neck but smiled back at Dellahousaye. "How did you even learn about this?" he asked.

Remy didn't hesitate. "When the so-called *informant* came forward yesterday, I'm sure one of your own people, it quickly became clear you and I had a connection and common interests."

"So, the Feds put you up to this?"

He didn't answer the question, instead, "I'm in a position to make this go away."

"You think I'm worried about this?" Lacroix asked. "I know what you're talking about, but I'm so far removed from small stuff like this, no one would ever work this back to me."

"Don't be so sure. The daughter has seen you personally meeting with her now deceased old man. The goon you sent to rough up the lawyer today will also be easy to trace back to you."

"What are you after?" Lacroix said, picking up the gun, clearing the round in the chamber and ejecting the magazine.

"I need my daughter back by the end of the day. If it's not you, I want your help in getting this done. You better pray hard I don't find out you're involved."

"Remy, back off already!"

"We also need to come to an agreement on my old man's interests." He could see Lacroix's expression change and he was doing a very poor job of appearing open to compromise.

Chapter Forty-four

Alex came back to his cubicle at the FBI offices. The clock on the wall read a quarter past five. He rubbed his eyes and took a deep breath. It had been a frustrating and unproductive day in the search for the missing Ida Dellahousaye. He sat at the desk he'd been assigned and checked his cell for phone messages and emails.

He felt a hand on his shoulder and turned to see Sharron Fairfield standing behind him. She let her hand linger a moment then stepped around to sit on his desk, pushing papers and files aside. It seemed one more button than necessary was undone on her blouse, and he purposely kept his gaze up to her face.

"Long day," she finally said.

"Probably a longer night ahead," he answered.

"Why don't we take a break, get a bite to eat and something strong to drink," she said.

Alex pushed his chair back and stood. "Sharron, this isn't going to happen."

"Alex..."

"No, you need to listen to me. What we had was a long time ago and it's over."

Her expression didn't change. She just kept staring back at him as if her overtures were no big deal.

"Hanna and I are going to get married and nothing is going to come between that. Clear?"

Sharron stood and now seemed irritated when she said, "I don't know what you think, but I'd just like to get some dinner before we get back to work on this tonight."

He shook his head slowly. "I just had a sandwich down at the deli."

She smiled, then said, "Really, Agent Frank, don't get the wrong idea here."

"Right."

Chapter Forty-five

Brenda Walters, the former Mrs. Remy Dellahousaye, stared out the window of her hotel room, the vast expanse of Charleston Bay teaming with commercial vessels and sailboats making way on the west wind. She let the curtains fall back and sat at the small table arrayed with her room service dinner. Pouring another glass of wine, she looked at her cell phone and thought about her last conversation with her ex-husband earlier in the afternoon. There were still no leads on finding their daughter. Remy had been typically curt and emotionless as he brought her up to date on the search.

She thought back to their early years together. They met in school at the university in Columbia. She knew he was the son of a mobster. Everyone did, but it held some thrill for her as they became lovers and then married soon after graduation. Remy had been determined to chart his own course and build a legitimate career. Very soon he discovered he would need the support and financial backing of his corrupt father to accomplish his dreams. His success was quick to come as his business empire expanded in real estate, banking, manufacturing, hotels and even more offshoots than she could remember or knew about.

Their relationship had been wonderful in the early years despite his time away with business. They had tried for several years after their marriage to have children. They were never certain what the problem with getting pregnant was, but it just wasn't happening. She finally became pregnant eight years into their marriage, but they were devastated when the pregnancy ended in an early miscarriage. Still dealing with the grief of their loss,

Remy had raised the prospect of adoption one evening. Through high-level business contacts in Russia, they were connected to an agency who had twin girls available for adoption. Within months, they brought home the one-year-old twins.

Ida and Ophelia became the center of her world but as hard as she tried, the loss of her own child continued to haunt her, and she struggled to forge the kind of maternal bond she had hoped for. As much as she hated herself for it, her inability to build a true loving relationship with the girls escalated to the point that the nannies they hired became far more important in the twin's lives than their own mother. They had never told the twins about their true heritage and few people knew about the adoption.

Brenda was certain her eventual split with Remy was as much about her detached relationship with their adopted daughters as it was about his reckless attraction to other women. *Maybe that's what really drove him away,* she thought.

She sipped at her wine and put the lid back on her untouched food. *What is it about the men in my life?* She knew her current husband was having an affair and it was just a matter of time until she'd be cast off again. *The bastard isn't even trying to hide it anymore.*

She thought again about her adopted daughters... the prim and dedicated Ida, now missing over 24 hours, her father on a desperate search with the authorities. The "wild child" Ophelia, still running down a typically irresponsible path. She was over the guilt in her distant relationship with either of the girls. Neither had ever embraced her occasional attempts to build a real mother-daughter relationship. It seemed they somehow knew she wasn't their real mother.

Chapter Forty-six

Hanna realized she'd been dozing and sat up suddenly, yawning and trying to shake off the exhaustion she was feeling. Light was still shining in the window of her office and she saw the clock on her laptop... just past six.

The stress of the afternoon confronting Remy Dellahousaye had taken its toll, combined with the workload in front of her she felt she would never catch up with. She thought about Dellahousaye again and wondered if he would truly use his new knowledge of the Griffith situation to put heat on Lacroix to back off her client. She couldn't read the man when they were meeting. She had a sick feeling things still weren't headed in the right direction.

She heard her door open and was pleasantly surprised to see the face of her fiancé. Alex walked in with a paper bag in his hand. He held it up, "I brought tacos from down the street. Thought you'd probably skip dinner again."

She stood and walked over to him, wrapping her arms around him and leaning into his hug. "Thank you, I knew I always loved you for your tacos."

He lifted her chin and kissed her, first on the lips and then gently on the bruise and scratches on her face. "I grabbed a sandwich down at the office an hour ago and I need to get back. I just wanted to check in on you."

"I actually just woke up from a great nap right here at my desk. God, I need to get a good night's sleep."

"Maybe I can help with that later," he said, smiling.

She pushed him away, "I said, I need some sleep."

They both sat at her conference table and she looked into the bag of food, pulling out one of the foil-wrapped tacos and a napkin.

"Sure you won't join me?" she asked.

He shook his head. "How'd you and Remy D get along?"

She frowned then took a big bite of the food. Alex kept staring back at her while she chewed and swallowed. "I wish I knew. Hard to read the man."

"We still don't have anything on his daughter. Did he give you any indication he knows more than he's letting on?"

"No, but something's not right."

"Any idea how he's going to move forward with Lacroix?"

"No. I tried to convince him the Charleston PD and your office are building a strong case against him in the Charles Griffith death and that it won't help for him to be aggressively shaking her down."

"You need to let me know if you get any push-back from either Della-housaye or Lacroix," he said, his gaze intent on her eyes. "I don't want you dealing with these assholes any more than necessary, and not at all if things go south."

"I understand."

He stood. "I need to get back. You're sure you don't need some help falling asleep later tonight?"

She looked back at him and smiled. "Probably a good idea."

Alex walked down the shaded street back toward his office, thinking about Hanna Walsh. He was truly concerned for her safety but knew she would always do what was necessary to help her clients. Lacroix had already sent one of his goons to lean on her this morning. Dellahousaye tried to put on a civil front, but Alex knew in his gut, the man was dirty and dangerous.

His thoughts shifted to the brief encounter earlier with his former flame, Sharron Fairfield. There had been no lead-up to her sudden flirtation. It had caught him completely off guard. If Hanna knew, she'd be furious. *No more secrets. I'll tell her tonight and assure her nothing is going to happen.*

Chapter Forty-seven

Willa James tried to ignore the make-up kid applying the last layers as she readied herself to go on-air for the 6 p.m. news broadcast. Her assistant came into the studio and handed her a final note which she glanced at quickly as the producer barked in her ear... *ten seconds!*

As the show's intro video wound down and the announcer introduced her as the night's broadcast host, Willa began, "Good evening. I would like to start with an update on the still mysterious disappearance of the daughter of businessman and as we've learned recently, aspiring crime boss, Remy Dellahousaye. According to spokespersons for both the FBI and the Charleston Police, there are still no solid leads on the whereabouts of 21-year-old college student, Ida Dellahousaye, missing now for almost 48 hours. Of further interest, is the earlier account of an anonymous informant that Remy Dellahousaye is embroiled in a struggle to retain control of his late father's crime syndicate. According to a source close to Mr. Dellahousaye, he is in a bitter dispute with known crime figure Xander Lacroix, a rising player in efforts to control the void left with the death of mob leader Asa Dellahousaye a year ago.

"Dellahousaye refused to be interviewed for this broadcast but issued the following statement... *Our efforts are focused entirely on the safe return of my daughter, Ida. We ask anyone with knowledge of her whereabouts to contact the information hotline set-up by the FBI. We are offering a significant reward for assistance in this matter. Beyond that, any reports of my connections with my late father's enterprises are patently untrue. I ask that you respect our family's privacy during this difficult time.*"

"Not surprisingly, we are still unable to reach Mr. Lacroix for comment."

Willa looked earnestly into the camera. "Let's begin with the missing Ida Dellahousaye. Our contacts tell us there is no evidence to date to suggest foul play. If this was an abduction, there has been no ransom demand, at least that the authorities are aware of. There was no evidence of violence or injury at the scene of the disappearance. Again, according to authorities at the local, state and federal level, there is no evidence to refute the possibility that Ida Dellahousaye simply walked away from a college beach party two nights ago."

"We must say we find it odd timing that the bitter rivalry between the girl's father and rising crime figure, Xander Lacroix, surfaces at the time of Mr. Dellahousaye's daughter's disappearance."

The 800-number set up to take calls in the missing girl's search scrolled across the bottom of the screen.

Willa James concluded her report. "If you have information regarding the disappearance of Ida Dellahousaye, please call the number below. The family has offered a reward of $50,000 for information leading to the safe return of Ms. Dellahousaye."

Adjusting her page notes in front of her, she said, "In other news..."

Chapter Forty-eight

Ophelia lay back on the bed in the dank cabin of the boat, an arm across her eyes as she winced at the pain in her leg. The shark had done considerable damage to her lower right leg in its quick attack.

Her captor had initially carried her back down into the cabin and cuffed her to the bed before wrapping her shredded and bleeding leg in a towel. In his frantic efforts to get her back on the boat and away from the shark, he had shot two times. The mask he had been wearing to hide his identity had fallen off. *Ida* did not recognize the wide face of the man, black hair cropped short, eyes a soul-less dark brown.

The captured twin had nearly passed out from the excruciating pain and had been screaming frantically from not only the extreme discomfort but also the trauma of her near deadly encounter with the shark.

After some delay, another man came into the cabin with a doctor's bag. He had a ski mask over his face and began administering to her wounds. He first gave her a shot that she almost immediately felt quell the pain. She didn't watch as the man cleaned the wound and proceeded to stitch and bandage. When he was finished, she drowsily watched both men conferring in the corner of the small cabin and then leave, the door locking behind them.

The real Ida Dellahousaye rang the bell on the front veranda of her father's house on the Battery in Charleston. Her nerves were raw as she prepared to speak to her father about the deception she and her sister had played upon everyone for the past many years.

The door opened and her father's bodyguard and assistant, Vincent, stood smiling at her. He stood aside as she walked in and then pulled her quickly into a gathering room and tried to pull her close. "Hey, *sweet cheeks*," he whispered.

She roughly pushed him away. "Leave me alone! Are you crazy?"

"Papa's on a call," Vincent said, leering. "We've got a few minutes to play." He tried to herd her into a corner, but she pushed him again.

"Enough, already!"

She saw a frown appear on his face. "I know you, O. I know you want me."

"This is not the time! Just tell my father I'm here or I swear I'll tell him everything."

Vincent just laughed. "You would never let Daddy know what a bad little girl you are."

"Just tell him!"

"You and I need to talk," he said.

"About what?"

She heard her father's voice yell from down the hall. "Vincent!"

Her father's office door was open, and Ida walked in to find him sitting at his desk, looking through some papers. He looked up when he saw her, rising to come around to give her a tentative hug. She could always tell the difference in how he treated her when she was herself, or like now when she had taken on the persona of her twin, Ophelia. His expression was strained, and he looked exhausted.

"I'm really busy, O. What is it?"

No, how are you Ophelia? No, how are you holding up, dear? He rarely did little to hide his disappointment with his wayward twin daughter.

She felt her knees quivering and a chill raced through her as he returned to sit behind his desk. He motioned for her to sit across from him.

"Still nothing on Ida?" she asked.

Surprising, he didn't answer right away, just staring back at her. Finally, he said, "I've received a ransom demand for the release of your sister."

Her first reaction was a mix of surprise, relief and then dread as she thought about her sister being held captive. *At least she's alive!*

"We're making preparations for the exchange."

"So, she's okay?"

"As far as we know."

"And the police think they'll return her unharmed?" she asked.

"They don't know and we're not going to bring them in on this. There's too much risk."

She sat, staring back at him, trying to gather the courage to confess the Dellahousaye twin's deception.

"Really, O, I need to deal with a few things here. What is it?"

She took a deep breath and then just plunged forward. "I'm not Ophelia."

She watched him squint his eyes and look back at her with a surprised and then very angry expression. "What the hell...?"

"O and I changed places before she went on this spring break trip." They've got Ophelia, Daddy."

She watched him rub his face and look away out the window, obviously trying to process what she'd just revealed. After a few moments, he turned back and asked, "Who else knows about this?"

"No one has ever known."

"This isn't the first time?"

She shook her head *no*.

"How long?"

"Since we were little girls."

"I can't believe this!" he erupted. "Even your mother doesn't know?"

Again, she shook her head.

"I always thought you were the sane one, the one I could trust."

"I'm sorry, Daddy..."

"Sorry!" he said, pushing away from his desk and standing, leaning toward her with both hands down to steady himself. "All these years you've both been lying to us."

"Daddy..."

"So, my daughter, Ophelia isn't the only crazy one. You've both lost your minds."

"Daddy, I just want to help get O back."

"The best thing you can do is get the hell out of my sight!"

She cringed and shrank back at his blistering disgust. "You need to know..."

"What else?" His face was red with fury. "What else have you been lying about?"

"Ophelia has a problem."

"She has a lot of problems!"

"Sometimes, when she switches to become Ida, she really thinks she's me. It's some kind of personality disorder. We've both seen a shrink together. He thinks it's some form of psychosis or schizophrenia. We've done this for so many years, living each other's lives, that sometimes she can't tell the difference."

Her father sat back down, shaking his head. "I can't believe this."

"You just need to know that O may really believe she's me right now. I don't know how this will help, but you needed to know."

"I needed to know a long time ago, dammit!"

Ida stood and walked around the office for a moment, then said, "There's something else." She stopped and looked at her father, who was staring back at her with an incredulous look on his face. "You probably know that twins can sometimes sense each other's feelings, share each other's thoughts. We've told you about it a few times over the years, right?"

Her father nodded.

"I've had moments where I could feel Ophelia's fear, even her pain." She paused, then continued, "I think she's hurt, Daddy."

He came over and took her by the arms, holding her close. "How can you be sure?"

"I'm as sure as if I was there... I think she's on a boat."

Remy Dellahousaye ended the call and placed his cell on the desk. His daughter, Ida, had left a few minutes ago. His head was still spinning with her news about the twin's dual lives. He had been trying to think back over the years for any sign of their crazy deception, but nothing came to mind. They were certainly identical physically, and somehow had managed to keep the details of each other's lives straight when they were changing places.

He had reached the FBI office downtown to share their suspicions that his daughter might be held captive on a boat and to alert local authorities and the Coast Guard. He had not shared the news of his daughter's charade.

He had just finished a call to let the girl's mother know he was sending Vincent over to the hotel to pick her up. He hadn't revealed why he needed to see her.

Since returning from Xander Lacroix's house, he had been struggling with how to proceed with the ransom demand for the return of his daughter, who he now knew was really Ophelia. The money was staged to be wired to the offshore account he'd been provided by her captors. He still wanted to give Lacroix time to come forward and either admit his involvement in the kidnapping or help in finding her. He had little confidence the man would help. His leverage on Lacroix was thin, but he knew he needed to give this possibility some time.

The kidnappers had set a deadline of midnight for receipt of the money and made it very clear his daughter would otherwise not survive the night.

"They what?" said Brenda, having just listened to her ex-husband explain the long game their daughters had been playing. "It's not possible."

"Apparently it is," Remy said. "So, it's Ophelia who's been taken and it's very likely she really thinks she's Ida."

"I can't believe this!" Brenda gasped, laying back into the pillows on the couch of his office. "I always knew the girl had issues, but..."

"Ida wouldn't tell me who the shrink is, but we'll find out."

Remy came over and sat beside her, not touching, but leaning in close. "I know you've always struggled with the adoption."

"Remy, please, let's not..."

"No, hear me out." He reached for her hand. "I'm going to get O back, tonight."

Brenda looked back, confusion on her face.

"They will need both of us to work through all this. They need their mother."

She pulled away and her anger and frustration boiled over, "I've never been their mother!"

Chapter Forty-nine

As the sun slipped lower to the west over the roof of the beach house, Jillian Dellahousaye pulled on a t-shirt to cover her swimsuit and shivered in the growing shadows. She rubbed at the goosebumps on her tanned arms and nestled back down into the soft cushions of the lounge chair next to the pool. Xander had called 30 minutes earlier to tell her he was coming over. He had been vague and detached, and she was wondering what he had to share with her.

Latching on to Xander Lacroix had, at first, seemed a desperate move and granted, she had been quite drunk the first night they were together. But, as time progressed, she realized the man presented an ideal opportunity to create a more than comfortable lifestyle into the coming years. *God knows how long it will last...!*

A girl has to take care of herself these days, she thought, smiling and watching the day fade away out across the vast expanse of the Atlantic Ocean. The running lights from a boat far offshore caught her eye, blinking through the low haze on the horizon.

Ophelia Dellahousaye jolted awake, the pain in her leg suddenly flaring hot and sharp. She realized she had been dreaming. It was a dream about being back at school, about her boyfriend Jordan... *the loser.* It was one of those dreams she often had about missing too many classes and being behind just before a big exam. Jordan had been laughing at her for being so worried about it.

She looked down at the wrapped bandages around most of her lower leg.

She cringed when she thought again of the big shark grabbing her by the leg with deadly jaws, jerking her hard beneath the surface, then coming back to finish her off. She realized she must be on some sort of pain killer. She felt drowsy and confused, and the pain in her leg was a dull ache, just barely tolerable.

When she tried to sit up, her left arm was held fast by the handcuff attached to the bed. She jerked on it several times, crying out as it cut into her wrist again.

She had given up on being rescued and resigned herself to the fact these people would ultimately kill her. *It's been too long. No one is coming!*

Xander Lacroix opened the door and got out of the back seat of his BMW. His driver and bodyguard looked back at him through the open driver's window.

"I'll be a while. Go down to the guest house and let me know if you hear anything, but only if it's important."

"Sure," the man said, closing the window and pulling away.

The door to the house was open and he walked through the opulent living area of the beach house. He could see Jillian sitting out near the pool. As he walked down the back steps to the large lounge area around the pool, she heard him coming and got up to greet him. He felt her slide into his arms, the smell of vodka and suntan oil overpowering. He rubbed his hands up under her t-shirt as they embraced.

"Hello, darling," she said in a low whisper in his ear.

Their coupling was frantic and rough, and both were soon on their backs panting, naked on top of cool sheets in the master bedroom of the house.

Jillian reached for his hand and let out a long breath. "That was crazy, babe."

Xander heard her but didn't respond. His thoughts had quickly turned from sex to the challenge laid down by Remy Dellahousaye. He had set wheels in motion before leaving his house, but he still had doubts on how best to proceed.

Remy Dellahousaye sat seething in the back of his car. Vincent sat in front, driving him out to the beach. His people had tipped him off that Lacroix had come over to see Jillian again. *It's time to bring this to a head!* He'd been waiting nearly two hours to hear back and nothing.

When they pulled up to the gate at the beach house, Vincent let his window down and punched in the security code on the keypad. The heavy black metal gate groaned on its hinges then parted in the middle and slowly opened to both sides.

"Hurry up!" Remy demanded. He felt the big sedan speed up. Vincent expertly navigated the tight turns through the woods on the long twisting drive out to the house.

Remy reached down and lifted his pant leg. An ankle holster held a 9mm semi-automatic Ruger pistol, loaded with a full magazine of 15 rounds. *Lacroix won't pull a gun on me again and hope to live,* he thought. He held the gun up and slid a round into the chamber. He saw the look of surprise on Vincent's face in the rear-view mirror.

He was out of the car almost before it came to a stop. He heard his man yell out, "Wait, boss!"

He saw Lacroix's car parked over near the garages and guest house, and his anger burned even hotter. He ran up the steps and through the front door, the gun in his right hand. He stopped in the foyer and listened, trying to calm his breathing. There were low murmurs of conversation coming from the bedroom. Without caring what noise he made, he rushed down the long hall and pushed open the door. In the low light of a lamp beside the bed, he saw his wife and Xander Lacroix lying naked together, side-by-side, holding each other's hand.

Jillian sat up in surprise, not bothering to cover herself. "Remy!"

"Get some clothes on!" he yelled as he watched Lacroix slowly slide back and sit up against the headboard, a thin smile on his face.

"Evening, Remy."

His smug attitude sent Remy over the edge, and he lifted the gun up into firing position aimed directly at Lacroix's face.

"Easy now, Remy," Lacroix said calmly, still smiling.

Jillian had reached down for a t-shirt and was pulling it over her head. "Remy, for god's sake!" she pleaded.

"Shut-up!" He looked back to Lacroix who sat with his arms crossed now.

"So, you're going to shoot me here in your own bedroom... a crime of passion, huh?" He started laughing and shaking his head.

The first round exploded with a roar in the confines of the room and hit two inches to the side of Lacroix's head.

"Jesus!" Lacroix yelled out, recoiling and turning to get his legs on the floor.

"Stay where you are," Remy yelled out. "Where's my daughter, you sonofabitch?"

"I told you I had nothing to do with it, but I put some feelers out, goddamit! I've got people working on it."

Remy turned when he heard someone running down the hall. He figured it was Vincent, coming to check on the gunshot. Down the hall he heard Vincent yell out, "Stop!" and then two gunshots echoed out.

Remy flinched, then ran to the door. Vincent stood looking at the prone body of Lacroix's man, Danny Wells, his own informant. Two bullet holes in his back were starting to leak a steady stream of blood on his white shirt. A gun lay a few feet from his outstretched arm.

"Sorry, boss," Vincent screamed. "I couldn't stop him."

Remy started to turn and heard Jillian yell out just as he felt the sharp blow of a hard object on the back of his head. He fell to his knees, the pain intense, his senses fading. He looked up and saw the naked form of Xander Lacroix standing over him, his gun in his right hand. Two more gunshots fired before he lost consciousness and fell to the floor.

Chapter Fifty

Sharron Fairfield came rushing up to Alex's desk, a flushed look on her face. "We need to go."

"What?" he asked, standing in surprise.

"The Coast Guard has a boat offshore from the bay that satellite records show has been drifting near the same position most of the day," she said. "They have a boat and chopper ready to go check it out. We're going to be on the chopper."

When their office received the call from Remy Dellahousaye regarding the anonymous tip he received that his daughter was being held captive on a boat, alerts had immediately gone out to all local and state law enforcement and the Coast Guard. They put little hope in the opportunity, knowing there were a huge number of boats of all shapes and sizes along the South Carolina coastline. But, with nothing else to go on, it at least gave them some slim hope.

Dellahousaye had also had second thoughts about revealing the ransom request he had received. FBI analysts were attempting to track the bank wire information, though that was typically a stone wall with Cayman banks. They all knew that a midnight deadline was now at stake for the safe return of Ida Dellahousaye.

As Alex rushed out of the office, he glanced at his watch... 8:05 pm.

Hanna was startled by someone knocking on the front door of her offices. She looked up from her work and saw the day's light fading out the window. She knew her assistant, Molly, and the rest of her staff had left long ago.

She walked hesitantly down the hall toward the front of the old house. A porch light outside illuminated the face of her client, Christy Griffith. She breathed a little easier and increased her pace to the door. *Why in the world didn't she call?*

Hanna noticed the fearful expression on the young woman's face as she was opening the door. It was too late to react when a big man stepped out from the side and pushed Christy into the office, almost knocking Hanna to the floor. She caught her in her arms and they both stumbled back into the reception area of the office.

"Hanna, I'm so sorry!" Christy wailed.

Hanna saw the man close the door behind them. He was broad and muscled, a neck thicker than she'd ever seen. His shaved head glistened with sweat from the humid night outside.

"We need to have another talk, Counselor."

She recognized the voice right away, the man who had assaulted her out back.

Christy was in tears, barely able to speak. "He grabbed me from my office."

"What do you want?" Hanna said defiantly, feeling less assured than her voice would indicate.

"I thought I made it clear to you to back off, lady."

Hanna didn't respond but moved to stand between her client and the looming figure of the man.

"This didn't have to be difficult," he continued. "The lady here sells her business, pays us back and everyone's happy. Life goes on."

"We called off the surveillance of your meeting..."

"You also went to Remy Dellahousaye..."

Christy cried out, "I'm sorry, Hanna. He made me tell him."

"You've made my employer extremely unhappy," the man said, lifting his shirt and showing a handgun holstered on his belt.

"Xander Lacroix, you mean," Hanna said, trying not to let panic take over.

"Let's just say, our investor."

"Like I said, what do you want!" Hanna yelled out.

He took the revolver out and spun the chamber for effect, then looked back at Hanna and her client. "My employer insists we give you both one final opportunity to do the right thing. I tried to convince him there was an easier solution." He smiled and put the gun back on his belt. "We want Ms. Griffith to take immediate steps to sell her restaurants, returning our investment at the terms agreed to as soon as possible. If you have other options for raising the five hundred grand, plus the interest due, that would be acceptable. My employer is no longer interested in the restaurant business. Is this clear to both of you?"

Hanna's head was swirling with anger and trepidation this goon would change his mind and do something stupid. "You need to leave now!" she managed. "I will consult with my client and we will share our plan when we are ready."

"No!" the man screamed. "You will provide proof tomorrow that a broker has been engaged to sell the business or you have another way to raise the cash."

Hanna stared back, breathing deeply, holding her client behind her. She was tempted to raise the issue of the murder of the girl's father but knew there was nothing to be gained and much to lose.

"Just leave!" Hanna shouted.

The big man laughed and started to back away toward the door. "You're a brave bitch, aren't you?"

Hanna watched him go out the door and down the steps. A car was waiting at the curb and they drove away. She turned back to Christy Griffith who had fallen to the floor, holding her face in her hands crying. Hanna knelt beside her and put her arm around her shoulders. She took a deep breath to let out the tension of the moment. "We'll figure something out. We'll figure something out."

Chapter Fifty-one

Ophelia was riding in a smaller boat, still under the delusion she was living the life of her twin sister, a cloth bag over her head and her hands zip-tied together behind her, despite her cries of pain. The boat lurched through the rolling swells of the ocean. They had come for her about half an hour ago and lowered her down from the bigger boat she'd been held captive on.

Is this the end? she thought as she struggled to keep from falling to the deck of the boat as they crashed ahead. *Are they going to dump me out here?* The pain in her leg was excruciating from the shark attack. She laid her head back to the heavens, the dark cloth of the bag masking her view. *Please God! I just want to be back at school. I just want this to be over!*

The Coast Guard chopper made it to the boat before the patrol boat. It approached at the lowest altitude possible from the west, bright spotlights illuminating the boat in the fading light. The prop wash of the chopper consumed the boat in a swirl of wind and blown water. No one could be seen onboard and only a dim light was on in the lower cabin. No running or navigation lights were on.

The commander of the helicopter spoke into the loudspeaker system. "This is the United States Coast Guard. Please come up on deck."

Alex looked down through the large rescue opening in the chopper with Sharron Fairfield and the flight commander, a Captain Harrold. He glanced toward the mainland and saw the shadowed form and lights of the Coast Guard cutter rapidly approaching.

The chopper stayed overhead as the boat arrived and came alongside the big cruiser. Four Coast Guard sailors boarded the ship with guns drawn. Within a minute they came back on deck and reported on the radio the boat was abandoned.

Alex and Fairfield had been lowered to the deck of the boat and were standing in the lower cabin in a small berth with a bed and blood-stained sheets and blood drops all over the floor. Alex heard Fairfield on her phone, "We need a crime scene team out here now!"

Coast Guard Captain Harrold came into the crowded cabin. "We checked the registration of the boat. It's owned by a retired couple who are already home in South Dakota for the summer. They didn't know their boat had apparently been stolen."

Alex knew they had no real evidence that the missing girl, Ida Dellahousaye, had actually been here, or that this was her blood. It would take some time for the crime scene technicians to determine that, but they didn't have time. It was now past 9pm. The colliding sequence of information and events would give them some sense the girl had been held here, but it did them little good at this point.

"We need to get back," he said to Fairfield as she ended another call.

Alex was getting off the helicopter at the Coast Guard station when his cell rang. He saw Hanna's ID on the screen and pressed down to take the call. "Hanna..."

"Alex!"

He could hear the alarm and fear in her voice. "What's going on?"

"Lacroix's man was just here at the office. He brought Christy. He threatened both of us to back down and play ball with them. I swear the guy was going to shoot us!"

Alex threw his head back in frustration. He knew this was all going to end badly. He quickly thought through his current situation and Hanna's plight. "Are you okay?"

"We're fine, now, but..."

"You're at your office?"

"Yes, I'm here with Christy."

He knew he had to stay with the team working on the leads to find the Dellahousaye girl. "You need to get somewhere safe until we get this all sorted out."

"We could go up to Pawleys Island," he heard her respond.

"No, they'll know you have a house there, or it won't take them long to figure it out." *Dammit, I need to be with her!* A sudden thought came to him. "Can you get up to Dugganville? Stay at my dad's place. I'll call him."

There was a pause on the line, then she said, "Okay, tell Skipper we're coming."

"If Lacroix figures it out, at least my old man has an arsenal to protect you."

"That's reassuring," Hanna said.

"You need to watch to make sure you're not being followed," Alex warned.

"I'll make sure."

"You sure you're okay?" he asked again.

"Yes... you can't get away?" Hanna asked.

"We finally got a solid lead on the Dellahousaye girl, but we were late to the scene. There's a midnight deadline."

"Deadline for what?" he heard Hanna ask.

"There's finally a ransom demand. We don't have much time."

Chapter Fifty-two

Remy Dellahousaye shook his head and tried to lift himself up. A deep pain shot through the back of his head and he slumped back to the floor lying flat on his stomach on the thick rug of his bedroom at the beach house. He turned his face to the side and saw the lifeless form of a man lying just outside the door in the hall. Fragments of the earlier events of the evening began coming back to him... confronting his wife and Xander Lacroix in bed... his man, Vincent, shooting Danny Wells, who appeared dead in front of him on the floor.

He managed to get up on his hands and knees and felt like he might pass out again from the pain in the back of his skull. He lifted up on his knees and looked around the room. Lacroix and Jillian were not there. Wells was apparently dead. His own gun was lying a few feet away on the floor. He reached back and felt the wet blood from the wound in his hair. He looked at his hand and could see it was still bleeding. He struggled to get to his feet and looked around again at the big bedroom. The bed was a mess of tangled sheets from his wife's and Lacroix's tryst. He stumbled over to the door to the hall and jerked back when he saw another man lying past Danny Wells. It was Vincent, and he lay sprawled with limbs splayed at awkward angles, blood pooling around his face.

"Oh shit!"

He leaned against the wall to steady himself, then looked around again. A light was on in the bathroom and he made his way along the wall to the door. When he looked in, he recoiled in shock. His wife, Jillian, lay on the floor, multiple gunshot wounds bleeding through her gray t-shirt and from the back of her head onto the white tile floor.

He sunk to his knees, holding one hand on the bleeding cut on the back of his head. Jillian's face was staring back at him, lifeless. He crawled back out of the doorway, then looked around and saw his gun on the floor. He made his way over and picked up the weapon, still hot from recent rounds fired. *I didn't shoot this gun!*

Xander Lacroix drove slowly back to his house on Sullivan's Island. *The last thing I need is to get pulled over for speeding away from the Dellahousaye house,* he thought.

He grinned in the dim light of the car, the sun setting behind the line of trees along the road. The mess he had left behind would have Dellahousaye tied up with investigations and criminal charges for years. *They'll never believe his claims I was there.* He had already made a call to arrange for his alibi. One of his associates was prepared to swear he had been with Xander all night at his house. He had also taken the laptop that had the security system footage on it. He would dispose of it later.

He had used Dellahousaye's gun to take out his own man, Vincent, when he came in after him.

And then there was Jillian... he thought.

She had totally freaked out with all the shooting. He couldn't calm her down and she wouldn't leave with him. He remembered the moment of clarity when he knew she *couldn't* leave. Of course, she couldn't leave. She had seen it all. He could never trust her to hide what had come down.

He had followed her into the bathroom when she thought she was going to be sick. She went down with two shots through her chest. A third in the back of her head made sure she was finished and no longer a threat. A momentary wave of regret came over him, but he quickly thought about how fortunate the evening's events had turned out. *Dellahousaye might even get the needle for the multiple murders.*

I need to get away!

As his mind raced through the implications of the mess all around him,

Remy Dellahousaye fought to calm himself. Leaving the scene of these multiple homicides seemed the only solution. He would never be able to explain what had happened here. How would he ever prove Lacroix had even been here? *I need to get my daughter back!*

The ransom deadline for Ophelia, more than anything, convinced him he needed to leave immediately, get back to Charleston and continue to work with the authorities to either find his daughter or send the ransom as a last resort. The bodies at the house might not even be found until morning when some of the help arrive.

He walked quickly around, looking for any evidence he had been here when the shootings went down... obviously his gun. He needed to lose the gun. *Ballistics would show shells from an undiscovered weapon... a shooter who left the scene. That's okay... more confusion.*

The laptop for the security system was gone. *Lacroix!*

Within minutes, he was out of the house and driving back to town. The images of the three dead bodies in his house continued to flash in his brain. He tried to think through all he would need to do to protect himself.

The fact he had just seen his wife lying brutally murdered seemed only a complication. He felt no sense of loss. He pushed aside thoughts for the moment of Xander Lacroix, Jillian's real killer. *We'll deal with that later. We need to get Ophelia back!*

Chapter Fifty-three

Jordan Hayes watched through the window of his fraternity house as his father's lawyer again took questions from the media mob that had descended upon him. The news and several law enforcement agencies were still pursuing him as a *"person of interest"* in the Ida Dellahousaye disappearance.

He had been interrogated twice earlier in the day. His lawyers had been present and his answers to police questions had been carefully rehearsed.

He felt a queasy churn in his gut when he remembered, again, the two details he had yet to share with anyone. He *had* left the fire when Ida walked away. He *had* seen her abduction, the man who threw her in the back of a car and drove away.

He hadn't revealed this to police because he knew he might be partly to blame.

His father had called days earlier to ask him to take a call from a woman who wanted information on Ida. His father was adamant he take the call. He apparently owed the woman a favor. His father had also insisted again he break off his relationship with Ida, but he hadn't committed. *Is there any connection to all of this? Did I somehow help in Ida's abduction?*

Chapter Fifty-four

Alex drove as Sharron Fairfield updated Will Foster and the rest of the team by phone back at the FBI Charleston offices. He was thinking about Hanna and her client and furious that Xander Lacroix was threatening them. He was tempted to track the man down tonight and have a serious *discussion* but knew he needed to stay on the Dellahousaye case. The midnight deadline was fast approaching, and they had little to go on since finding the possible crime scene on the boat offshore.

He heard Fairfield end the call. She put her phone down and turned to him. "So, what do you think?"

"I think we've got nothing," Alex said, keeping his eyes ahead into the glow of the headlights on the road back to Charleston. "Dellahousaye needs to release the ransom money. He needs to let us help with the exchange to get the girl back safely."

"He wouldn't even tell us about the ransom until he was desperate."

"Can you blame him?"

They continued on in silence for a few moments.

Fairfield's phone buzzed. She answered and said, "Yes, Mr. Dellahousaye. We found the boat. There was clearly a crime committed onboard, but no one was there. The boat had been abandoned."

Alex listened as Dellahousaye's muffled response came through on Fairfield's phone.

"No," she answered. "There was no direct proof your daughter had been there." She didn't mention the blood. "We have a crime tech team headed out there to find everything they can."

Fairfield held the phone away from her ear as Dellahousaye yelled back. Alex could hear him fuming about their handling of the case and failure to get to the boat in time.

"Sir, where are you now?" she asked.

"We can be there in ten minutes. We need to talk to you about next steps. You need to seriously consider sending this ransom payment. We don't have other options at the moment, and you're of course aware of the deadline." She listened to his response, then, "We'll talk to you about it in a few minutes."

She ended the call and turned back to Alex. He nodded his head, turning at the next light to go to Dellahousaye's house.

They rode in silence for a while, then Fairfield said, "I need to apologize about that thing earlier."

He looked over at her and didn't respond.

"I shouldn't have said anything," she continued. "It's just... I never thought we really ended things. Suddenly, you and Hanna started getting closer and we just let it all slide."

"Sharron..."

"No, I'm not trying to start this again. I just want you to know that I'm sorry. It won't happen again. I want you and Hanna to be happy. The last thing I want is for this to come between us at work."

Remy slammed his cell down on his desk, feeling helpless and outraged at the same time. The FBI had a solid lead and they'd been too late. He pressed thoughts away of the carnage he'd left out at the beach. *There will be time for that later.* They had less than two hours until the midnight deadline to pay the ransom... $5 million to get his daughter back. Again, it wasn't the money, it was the fact someone had this edge on him, was playing him for a fool, was threatening to kill his daughter. It all swirled in his brain like a haunting dream sequence.

His head was pounding with pain from the blow from Lacroix. When he had returned to the Charleston house, he had done his best to clean the wound. He had changed clothes and had a ball cap on now to hide it. The thought of Lacroix almost sent him into a total rage again, but he placed his palms down on the desk, took a deep breath and then stood, walking to the liquor bar on the side wall. He poured a whiskey straight up and threw back the drink. *I need to keep a clear head, but...*"

Alex watched Dellahousaye sit behind his desk. He and Fairfield took chairs across from him. Alex smelled the liquor on the man as they came down the hall to his office. He also seemed unsteady and confused. *Understandable*, Alex thought, pushing the thoughts aside as Fairfield recounted the little they had found out on the abandoned boat. Again, she didn't mention the blood.

"What the hell took you so long?" Dellahousaye demanded, squinting and seemingly in pain. He gathered himself and said. "Why are you still on this case, Frank?"

Alex stared back, their eyes both locked on the others. "I would think you'd want all available resources working to find your daughter."

Dellahousaye rubbed his forehead, looking down at the desktop. "What can we do now?" he finally asked.

Fairfield said, "We have a team going over the boat to look for anything that will help."

"We've got barely more than an hour," Alex said. "You need to seriously consider meeting their demands and sending the money."

"How do I know they'll even give us my daughter back?"

"You don't," Fairfield said. "But, what other options do we have at this point?"

Alex watched the man processing this.

"I have no way to contact these people," Dellahousaye said, desperation coming through in his voice now. "Only the wire transfer instructions for the money they gave me. My financial guy is on standby. Isn't there any way you can trace the wire?"

"We'll try," Fairfield said, "but it's quite likely they have a sequence of blind transfers set up that will quickly lead to a dead end."

"So, I tell my guy to send $5 million out into the dark web and then what happens?"

"We have to assume they're monitoring the account and will contact you about Ida."

"And if they don't?" Dellahousaye demanded.

"We're not giving up until we find her, Mr. Dellahousaye," Fairfield said.

Alex watched as the man slowly laid his head back, his eyes seemingly squeezed in pain again.

"What is it, sir?" Fairfield asked.

Dellahousaye stood suddenly, seeming to gain some sense of resolve and purpose. He picked up his phone and started bringing up screens. "I'm calling my guy."

Chapter Fifty-five

Hanna knew the route out to Dugganville and drove almost on instinct, her mind full of conflicting thoughts about the safety of her client, Christy Griffith, sitting in the seat beside her, Alex's search for the missing girl, the latest developments in their own relationship... *engagement, a wedding, moving to Washington!*

She glanced again in the rear-view mirror of the Honda sedan as she had every few minutes since leaving Charleston about a half hour ago with her client. There was no sign of any car appearing to be following them. She certainly wasn't a trained surveillance professional, but she felt confident she would be able to spot a vehicle obviously staying close enough to be following her. She had pulled over into a convenience store and then a fast food restaurant and again, nothing suspicious.

Alex had texted her a few minutes earlier to let her know he had reached his father, Skipper Frank, and he would be waiting for them in Dugganville. She knew it was smart to get Christy out of town until they could come up with a plan of action to confront Lacroix. Alex and the FBI and the local Charleston PD were all neck-deep in the search for Ida Dellahousaye.

While she didn't know the girl, her heart went out to her as she thought about how terrified she must be. *A midnight deadline!* she thought. The clock on her dash said it was 11:15.

Lacroix's man, a hood named Joey Grant, drove one mile behind Hanna. He was far enough back she would never see him, particularly in the dark and it would allow him time to pull over if she stopped anywhere. On his phone, he watched the GPS map location from the tracker he had placed on the lawyer's car. She had been foolish enough to think he would trust them to move forward with Lacroix's demands. Instead, the lawyer and the girl were running. He wasn't certain where. Somewhere north out of town. He knew Hanna Walsh had a house on Pawleys Island and it was beginning to look like that's where they were headed.

Xander Lacroix was not an understanding type and Grant knew his ass would be fried if he screwed this up.

Hanna turned off Highway 17 onto the road to Dugganville. She looked over to her client who had been silent for most of the trip. "You okay?"

"These people are scaring the crap out of me!" Christy said. "Why can't the police stop them?"

Hanna wished she had a better answer, but said, "There isn't enough evidence yet to tie Lacroix to your father's death."

"But they attacked you and how many times have they threatened us?"

She couldn't tell the woman the Dellahousaye case seemed a far greater priority for law enforcement at the moment. "We need to get out of town, let the police do their work."

"I have restaurants to run... a business to take care of!" Christy said.

"I know... I understand," Hanna replied, thinking about the many demands and commitments in her own life that would go unattended. "Let's give it until morning and see where we are. You'll love Skipper and his wife, Ella. They're quite a pair."

Joey Grant saw the blue dot on the GPS screen on his phone take a right turn up ahead. He used his fingers to make the map wider on the screen and saw the town of Dugganville a few miles out at the end of this road. He knew the little shrimper town on the river. *What the hell?*

Hanna pulled the Honda off the road onto the shoulder in front of Alex's father's house. Lights were on in the house up in the trees. Memories of her visits here with Alex came back quickly... memories of Skipper Frank facing murder charges for killing a rival shrimper just down the river... memories of Alex's crazy ex-wife and her almost successful deceit to get him back.

She got out of the car and heard the screen door on the porch open. The wide form of Skipper Frank stood shadowed against the light from behind in the house.

"Hanna, that you?"

"Hey, Skipper," she yelled back. "We'll be right up." She looked back in the car and in the light from the overhead, she saw Christy looking up, hesitantly. "Come on, we'll be safe here."

Grant drove down through the main street of Dugganville. He had been up here on a few occasions on business, back when Asa Dellahousaye had Beau Richards and his kid, Connor, working for him. He pulled over to the curb in front of an old diner and parked. He rubbed his broad shaved head and looked at the GPS screen again. The woman had stopped just a few blocks from here at a house on the river. He would give her some time and then drive by to check it out.

Ella and Skipper Frank met them at the door. Both made a big fuss about hugs and kisses, and then the introductions to Christy Griffith.

"What the hell's goin' on?" Skipper asked when they were in the kitchen. Ella was pouring hot water for tea for the women. Alex's dad had a can of *Bud Light* in his hand.

"What did Alex tell you?" Hanna asked.

"Only that you and Ms. Griffith here have got that snake Xander Lacroix on your asses," he started, sipping at his beer again. "I thought we were through with that Dellahousaye bunch."

Hanna told Skipper and Ella about Christy's father and Lacroix's attempts to steal her blind with their extortion.

"Same rotten apple from the same tree," Skipper said when she was through.

"We got the guest rooms... Alex and Bobby's rooms made up for you," Ella said, her voice a bit slurred from her evening cocktails with her husband.

"Thanks Ella," Hanna said. "I'm sorry…"

"Don't think nothin' of it," Skipper said. "You're damn family now and you're always welcome here."

Hanna leaned over and hugged the man. "Something about the Frank boys, I just love!" she said, trying to lighten the mood.

Skipper blushed and Ella laughed.

"Any of them Dellahousaye or Lacroix boys come 'round, they gonna find some buckshot up their ass," Skipper said, making a mock toast with his beer can and then taking a long swallow.

Hanna was starting to feel a little nervous about the readiness of her security detail, but she knew the Skipper would die for her if it came to that.

Joey Grant parked his black SUV three doors down and across the street from the Honda the Walsh woman had driven out to Dugganville. The house he was parked in front of was dark and there seemed no one around. The nearest streetlight was at the end of the block and he felt confident he was in a good position to remain unseen. The river snaked by to his left and he saw several large commercial boats tied up at piers. He was thinking through all the possibilities of her decision to bring the Griffith girl here. Maybe they were just taking a night away from town to think through how to proceed with the demands his boss was placing on them. *Maybe they were trying to hide!*

Ella Frank pulled Hanna aside when she came back from the bathroom. "I'm so excited 'bout you and Alex," she said, her eyes at half-mast from the drinking. "You two are gonna be great for each other and I can't wait for the wedding. What's the latest?"

"Haven't had time to even think about a date yet, Ella."

"That boy too busy with the FBI?"

"They've got him working on the Dellahousaye kidnapping."

"Been watchin' that on the TV," Ella said. "Poor girl. Too bad her old man is such a crook."

Grant had made two passes on the house he was watching. He pulled the address up on the internet on his phone. When the name of the owner finally came up, he cursed to himself. *It's the cop's old man.*

He knew he couldn't sit out here on the road all night. It was just a matter of time until some neighbor got suspicious and called the sheriff's office. There was a small roadside motel on the way into town. He pulled away to go get some sleep and come back early in the morning. *These women are really starting to piss me off!*

Chapter Fifty-six

Alex listened as Remy Dellahousaye ended the call to release the $5 million ransom. "Call me as soon as it's done!" Dellahousaye put his cell down on the desk, his face a stoic mask of fatigue and defeat.

Agent Sharron Fairfield said, "You're doing the right thing."

He looked back at her with a doubting gaze. "I swear, if anything happens to Ida..."

Alex said, "Sharron, I can stay here to monitor any callbacks from the kidnappers. You can get back down to the office to see what they're finding on the boat."

Fairfield stood and said, "I expect you'll hear from these people very quickly. Alex will be here with you to help with next steps."

Dellahousaye looked about to protest, then said, "Fine, but get your people moving on any evidence they pulled from that boat."

"They're all over it, sir," she replied. "Alex, can I have a word?"

He walked out into the hall with her. She said, "I know the two of you have a history, with his father and all. I don't need to tell you..."

"Sharron, it's not a problem."

She looked back at him for a moment, seeming to think through the wisdom of leaving him here with Remy Dellahousaye. Finally, she said, "Keep him away from the booze."

Alex nodded.

Thirty minutes later, Alex stood in Dellahousaye's kitchen pouring another cup of coffee for himself and then for Remy who was sitting at the island counter. There had been no contact from the kidnappers and the man was growing more agitated by the moment.

"Goddamit!" he suddenly yelled out. "Can't you people do something?"

Alex tried to remain calm. "The Bureau has every resource working on this, as do the state and local cops."

Dellahousaye looked back at him. "I will hold you all personally responsible for the safe return of my daughter. You've done nothing but screw this up..."

Alex jumped in, "That's enough!"

Dellahousaye stood quickly, the stool he was on falling away across the floor. He came quickly around the island. Alex didn't back away as the man grabbed him by the shirt with both hands. With his face inches away, he yelled, "Why aren't you doing something?"

Alex pushed him away and watched as he fell back against the counter. "Everyone is doing all they can. You need to keep your shit together."

This seemed to make Dellahousaye even more angry. He came at Alex again but stopped a step away when Alex held up a hand with a menacing look on his face. "Sit your ass down, now!" Alex said. "None of this will help get your daughter back any faster. Do you understand me?"

Dellahousaye glared back, his eyes intense on Alex's face. "My old man should have finished the job on you."

"What!" Alex was stunned.

"I still can't believe you and that pissant Sheriff up there got the jump on him."

Alex couldn't control his anger. "Your old man was a murdering sonofabitch who kidnapped and threatened to kill two women..."

Dellahousaye came at him so quickly, it was all Alex could do to grab him by the arms as the man crashed into him. They both went down hard on the floor. Alex felt the full weight of the man crush down on him. His head hit hard on the tile floor, and he felt the wind get knocked from his chest. Dellahousaye went for his neck. Alex rolled hard to his left and threw him off. He lay there dazed for just a moment before struggling to get to one knee. Dellahousaye lay on his back, breathing hard and staring up at the ceiling.

The cell phone on the island buzzed. Both men got to their feet. Dellahousaye staggered over to his phone, looked at the screen, then answered the call.

"Hello... who is this?"

Alex signaled for him to put the call on speaker. He watched as Della-housaye pushed the button on his phone and placed it down on the granite counter. A muffled voice said, "You did the right thing, Dellahousaye."

"Where's my daughter?" he yelled out.

"You need to call off the cops."

He looked up at Alex, then yelled again, "Where the hell is Ida?"

Alex drove while Remy Dellahousaye sat beside him in his own Mercedes, the two-lane road out of town dark with only a few approaching headlights. Neither man had spoken of their quick and violent encounter earlier before the call had come in. Dellahousaye seemed to have gathered himself and was now intent only on retrieving his daughter.

The caller had indicated a remote location out near the shore, south of Alex's hometown of Dugganville. Dellahousaye had been instructed to come alone, but Alex had finally convinced him to allow the authorities to at least be nearby. He had called the office and alerted agents Foster and Fairfield of the location. They were all going to meet five miles away and finalize plans to get the girl back. Sheriff Pepper Stokes had also been alerted but asked to have patrols stationed at a distance from the pick-up location with an alert to keep an eye for suspicious activity.

Alex looked over at Dellahousaye who was checking his phone. He noticed Alex's gaze and looked up, then turned away, peering out to the dark roadside racing by. "Look, I'm sorry about earlier," he finally said. "This is all been a bit much..."

Alex said, "Let's just focus on Ida."

"Right."

Twenty minutes later, Alex pulled the car into a convenience station off Highway 17, just before the turn out to the location the kidnapper had given Dellahousaye. His two FBI colleagues were standing by their car in a dark corner of the parking lot. He pulled to a stop beside them, and he and Dellahousaye got out.

Will Foster said, "We've been monitoring traffic in and out with the Sheriff's Department patrols discreetly placed since the call came in. There has been no further traffic out that way. We suspect they had already dropped your daughter."

Sharron Fairfield jumped in. "We don't want you going out there alone."

Dellahousaye started to protest, but she held up a hand. "We'll have Alex low in the backseat in case they have someone watching. We want you to have backup in case there is any trouble."

Dellahousaye considered the approach for a moment then nodded in agreement. "Let's just get going. We need to get Ida."

Fairfield continued, "You got confirmation the wired money was received?"

"Yes, can your people start tracing it?"

"I'll make sure," Foster said and reached for his phone, stepping away.

Alex considered the plan. He couldn't imagine the kidnapper would try anything stupid at this point. They had the money. "I have the location in my GPS," he said.

"Okay, let's get going," Fairfield said. "Will and I will stay positioned here. Keep in touch on your cell."

Alex nodded.

Alex sat low on the back seat of Dellahousaye's Mercedes sedan, watching the back of the man's head as they bumped along on a remote dirt road through the marshes. He looked down at his GPS screen on his phone. "Stay to the left at this next fork," he said.

They drove on for another mile, then Alex said, "Slow down, the road ends just around this next bend."

He peered up as high as he could to look out through the front window without being seen. The car's headlights illuminated the deep and nearly impenetrable woods off to the right and as they came around the turn, the broad expanse of the marshlands out to the distant shore to the east, barely lit in the dark night.

Dellahousaye screamed out, "Oh shit!"

Alex lifted up higher in the seat and in the glare of the headlights saw the form of the girl lying on her side in the sandy rut of the old two-track road. She wasn't moving.

Dellahousaye slammed on the brakes and started to get out.

"Wait... just a minute!" Alex said, reaching over to grab the man's shirt collar. He scanned the dark around the car for any sign of danger. Only the screech of tree frogs split the silence of the night. Dellahousaye pulled away and was out of the car before Alex could stop him. He watched as the man ran toward his daughter, then knelt beside her. His voice screeched out into the night, "Lord, no!"

Alex made an instant decision to reveal himself and ran from the car. When he got to Dellahousaye's side, he was whispering in his daughter's ear. "Ophelia, wake up."

Alex could see the girl was dressed only in the bottoms of a swimsuit and a torn and dirty college sweatshirt. One of her bare legs was heavily bandaged. He knelt down and saw her legs were held together with a zip tie. He pulled out a pocketknife and cut the plastic. Then he heard a low moan.

Dellahousaye pulled his daughter close in his arms, "Honey, I'm here!"

Alex watched the girl begin to respond, her arms coming up around her father, then pulling him tight.

"Daddy?" she whispered weakly.

Alex looked around and saw no immediate threat. He pulled out his phone and pressed the number for Fairfield. "We have her. She's okay, but we need to get an emergency crew out here!"

"Is the area secure?" he heard Fairfield ask.

"Yes, but we need an ambulance, now!"

Ida Dellahousaye woke with a start. As the fragments of the dream, no the nightmare, quickly began to fade, she knew she had just seen the face of death... *her sister's face!*

Chapter Fifty-seven

Hanna was having trouble sleeping again, another night with too many thoughts of sons, lovers, clients and past trauma racing through her brain. She checked the time on her cell and moaned softly when she realized it was only two o'clock.

Alex had texted about an hour earlier that they had found the Dellahousaye girl. She had some injuries and was very shaken up, but she would be okay. Hanna felt a great sense of relief the girl had been returned safely. Her own haunting memories of kidnappers and abduction were coming back again.

She had sent a quick note back to Alex they were safe at his father's house, and she would contact him in the morning.

She thought again about her client, Christy, hopefully sleeping in the next room. The young woman found herself in the line of fire of one of the most dangerous crime elements in the country. They had already likely killed her father when he threatened to reveal their extortion. *Was there a safe path for her in all this? Is she better off selling her father's company, paying off the gangsters and moving on with her life?*

In the short time she had come to know Christy Griffith, she doubted that was an option she would consider. The girl was scared, as she should be, but she was also a fighter and wanted justice for her father's death.

Hanna's senses went on full alert when she heard a hard object fall on the deck outside her window. She sat up and listened, the silence in the house cut only by the sound of crickets and a persistent bird who wouldn't call it a day. There was no other sound out of place and she convinced herself she was hearing things.

Lying back down on her pillow, she stared up at the white ceiling of the room Alex had grown up in. As she struggled to clear her thoughts, she tried to imagine Alex Frank as a young boy. She knew he and his brother had been good athletes and had worked hard on their father's shrimp boat, the *Maggie Mae*, docked down at the river. She also knew the boys had lost their mother in a tragic car accident that Alex still had trouble dealing with.

These last years with Alex had been some of the most challenging in her life, but also some of the most loving and intimate. She was grateful he had come into her life. Their love for each other was real and she felt blessed they had found each other.

Now, another challenge lay ahead. Uprooting all she had built in South Carolina would need to be put on the shelf if she moved to Washington to be with Alex. *And for how long? And what if she didn't go? Could they survive further time apart?*

As Hanna finally drifted off into a restless sleep, her last conscious thought was the look on Alex's face, the look of expectation as he knelt before her on the deck out at Pawley's Island, the ring in his hand, reaching out to her.

Chapter Fifty-eight

The paramedics were still working on the Dellahousaye twin on the gurney next to the ambulance. The red and yellow flashing lights of the vehicle illuminated the trees and heavy brush behind them. The sparkle of distant house lights across the marshes toward the coast lay below a dark sky filled with stars and a bright moon.

Alex watched Remy Dellahousaye standing beside his daughter, holding her hand as the paramedics continued to make sure the girl was stable before transferring her to the nearest hospital.

She had obviously experienced considerable trauma and injury. The wound on her leg looked very severe. She hadn't spoken and was not fully conscious, despite her father's attempts to talk to her.

Dellahousaye leaned in close to his daughter and said, "I'm here, honey. I'm here, O."

Alex was caught off-guard and moved closer. *He's calling his daughter, O? I thought this was Ida Dellahousaye. Is O the other twin, Ophelia?*

He felt a pull on his arm and turned to see Will Foster. "We need to talk."

Alex followed him back to their cars parked a short distance away. Fairfield was there talking on her cell as they came up. She ended the call and put the phone in her pocket.

"That was the police department out on Isle of Palms," Fairfield said. "They were patched through to me after calling the office downtown."

"What's going on?" Foster asked.

"Security out on the island was called to investigate what sounded like gunshots at Remy Dellahousaye's house earlier tonight."

192

"Gunshots?" Alex said in surprise.

"It's apparently a *shit show* out there. Three dead bodies, including Dellahousaye's wife. Multiple gunshot wounds."

Foster whistled and they all looked over at Dellahousaye, still standing with his daughter. "Who are the others?" he asked.

"A man named Vincent, Dellahousaye's main security man and driver, and one other man, a name I didn't recognize."

Foster said, "Alex, would you have him come over here."

As Alex stepped away to go over to Dellahousaye, his thoughts were sorting through the shocking news of multiple murders at the man's house. He tried to piece together the timeline of the past night and where Dellahousaye might have been before he went to see him at his house leading up to the midnight deadline to get his daughter back. The man's demeanor was certainly strained when Alex had arrived at his house. He had attributed it to the stress of his daughter's kidnapping.

The paramedics were lifting the girl into the back of the ambulance as he came up. Dellahousaye was starting to follow them up into the vehicle to accompany his daughter to the hospital.

"Wait," Alex said.

Dellahousaye turned. Tears streaked his face in the strobing lights from the ambulance. "I'm going to stay with her," he said.

"We need a word first."

"No, I'm not leaving her." He continued to climb up into the ambulance.

Alex reached out and grabbed his sleeve. "You need to stay here with us. We have some news about your wife."

Dellahousaye looked back, seemingly confused.

Alex pulled him back more forcefully. "Come with me. We'll get you down to the hospital as soon as we can."

Dellahousaye looked back at his daughter, still barely conscious on the gurney. "You'll be okay, honey. I'll be down there with you soon." He stepped back.

Alex led him over to Foster and Fairfield.

"What the hell's going on?" Dellahousaye demanded.

Sharron Fairfield stepped forward. "Mr. Dellahousaye, security was called to your house out on Isle of Palms a short while ago."

"Security?"

"Neighbors reported hearing gunfire," she continued.

"Gunfire!"

"Sir, I'm sorry to tell you, your wife was found shot and killed."

Alex watched the man's reaction closely. At first, he just stared back without responding, then his eyes squinted as if he was trying to make sense of what he had just heard. He started shaking his head. "There must be some mistake."

"I'm afraid not, sir," Fairfield said. "Two other men, including your driver, were also found dead."

"Vincent?"

"Yes sir."

Dellahousaye seemed to lose his balance and stepped back. Alex reached out and grabbed his arm to steady him.

"We're going to have to ask you some questions," Foster said. "We can start here or take you back to our offices in Charleston."

"What?" Dellahousaye said, dazed and confused. "No, I need to be with O."

"O?" Alex asked, confused again.

"I need to be with my daughter."

"That will have to wait, sir," Foster said.

"Forgive me," Fairfield said, stepping over in front of Dellahousaye. "You don't seem very upset about the death of your wife."

"What? Where is she?"

"The crime scene is still being processed," she said. "The victims will be transported to the morgue in Charleston when that is finished."

"The morgue," Dellahousaye repeated. "Oh... what happened?"

"We don't know yet," Fairfield replied.

"Who did this?" he demanded, pulling his arm away from Alex.

"We don't know, sir," Fairfield replied.

"When were you last out at the beach, Remy?" Alex asked.

He turned and looked back at Alex, a distant and confused look on his face. "I... I don't know... earlier today."

"When was that?" Foster asked.

Dellahousaye shook his head, "This is all too much. I need to get to the hospital."

"That will have to wait," Fairfield said.

Alex followed the car with his two FBI colleagues leading the way back to Charleston. Remy Dellahousaye sat in the seat beside him. His head was down. It appeared he might even be sleeping. He hadn't said a word since they'd started back to town.

Alex was processing the man's reaction to the death of his wife, and his earlier behavior when they were together at the house in Charleston. He had obviously been drinking and was understandably stressed about his daughter.

"Remy," he said, trying to get the man's attention.

No response.

"Remy!" he said louder and reached over to push on the man's shoulder.

Dellahousaye seemed startled and looked up and then over at Alex. In the dim light of the car interior with few headlights passing, Alex saw a man seemingly in total disarray. His normal composed and commanding presence was nowhere to be seen. His hair was mussed, and he sagged in the passenger seat like he might sink to the floor if the seatbelt didn't hold him up.

Alex looked back at the road ahead and the taillights of his co-worker's car. "You might want to call your lawyer."

"What?"

"Do you have any idea what's going on here?" Alex asked.

Dellahousaye just stared back at him, a vacant gaze for a moment, then a look of tentative resolve seemed to return to his face. "You don't think...?"

"Think what, Remy? That you killed your wife and two men earlier tonight before I met you back at your house?"

Alex saw anger now in the man's expression. For a moment he thought

Dellahousaye was going to attack him again. He sat up defiantly in his seat, his fists clenched in his lap.

"Where were you tonight, Remy?"

He didn't respond, then reached into his pocket and pulled out his phone. After a few moments, he said, "Meet me downtown at the FBI offices." A pause, then, "Now!"

Chapter Fifty-nine

The other Dellahousaye twin, the real Ida, sat with her sister's friends, Josh and Susanna, in the apartment in Charleston. Both of them were passed out on the couch across from her after a long night of wine and weed. Ida had not partaken and was still waiting anxiously for word of the safe return of her sister.

When her phone finally rang, she saw the time was a little after 1:30.

She answered the call tentatively, "Hello?"

"Ophelia, this is your mother."

"What have you...?"

"She's okay. They have her back."

Ida felt a flush of relief and sagged back in her chair; her head thrown back. "Oh, thank God! Where is she?"

"I just spoke with your father. They found her out by the marshes, east of town. They're transporting her now to the hospital on the north side of Charleston. They should be there anytime."

Ida thought for a moment then said, "Why are they taking her to the hospital?"

"I guess she's pretty shaken up. He wouldn't tell me anything else. Can you pick me up?"

"Of course, I'll be there in a few minutes."

Ida saw her mother waiting under the covered drive at the front of the hotel. She pulled up and waited for her to get in. As usual, there were no pleasantries in the woman's greeting.

"It's the hospital off the interstate up on the north side," she said.

Ida sat staring at her mother for a moment, the icy cold façade she always put up was there again, even in a time like this when mother and daughters should share real love and emotion. There were few times in their past she could remember that had ever happened.

Ida pulled out into traffic, then asked, "What did Dad tell you?"

"The kidnappers left Ida out on a deserted road leading to the marshes. They found her laying by the side of the road, still tied up."

"Oh no…"

"She was barely coherent…"

"What!" Ida jumped in, looking over at her mother.

"Your father was very brief on the phone. He was with the FBI and local authorities. That's all I know."

They continued on through the dark streets of Charleston, little traffic out so late. Ida's hands fidgeted on the steering wheel. She tried to calm herself. *Ophelia is okay. They found her. She's going to be okay.*

Her mother broke the silence in the car. "I called her boyfriend, Jordan, up at school."

"I'm sure he was very relieved," Ida said, a hint of disgust in her response. She sensed her mother staring over at her but didn't respond. They drove on for a few minutes without conversing, Ida's mind filled with relief for the safe return of her sister and anxiety about the long deception the twins had perpetrated on everyone in their lives. *Tonight, it has to end*, she thought.

Ida took a deep breath, then began, "Mother, we're not going to see Ida tonight."

Again, she sensed her mother staring over at her as she kept her eye on the road ahead.

"It was Ophelia who was abducted, Mother."

She waited for her response, but there was only silence for a few moments, then, "Your father told me earlier today. I'm still trying to understand how the two of you…"

"I'm sorry," Ida began.

"Sorry?"

"It started so many years ago as just a game we played, and then it eventually got out of control."

"Do you have any idea..." her mother began.

"I can't explain why," Ida interrupted.

They drove on for several blocks without speaking, Ida's thoughts jumping from relief at her sister's safe return to her continuing fear of not knowing who was behind the abduction and were they all really out of danger now.

She heard her mother break the silence. "So, you've been with those horrible people your sister has taken up with?"

Ida let the comment pass.

"And this has all been going on for how long?"

"It started when we were little, maybe five or six, a game between us to see if we could fool people. Then it became more."

"More?" her mother asked, totally incredulous.

"More like an obsession. We both could escape our own lives for a while, get away and play the game."

"I still can't believe this."

Ida hesitated to continue, then said, "For O, it's become even more, I'm afraid." She looked over at her mother who was staring back, her mouth open and a stunned expression clear even in the dark light of the car.

"O has a hard time now distinguishing..." She paused, not sure how to explain.

"What are you talking about?"

"We've gone to a therapist together."

"A therapist?"

"O has some kind of personality disorder... maybe even schizophrenia. It's been getting worse. When we switch, she truly thinks she's me. It sometimes takes days for me to bring her back."

Her mother reached over to hold Ida's arm, a rare show of affection and concern.

"I'm sorry..." Ida began.

"Why? Why do you keep doing this?"

"I told you, it's become almost an obsession, particularly with Ophelia.

Both of us need a break every now and then and..."

"And no one else knows?" her mother asked, more anger in her voice now.

"Only you and Daddy."

"And no one's ever suspected?"

Ida shook her head.

Ida was sitting in the waiting area of the Emergency Room of the hospital with her mother, waiting to get in to see her sister. The nurse said they were evaluating her condition and treating some injuries. She wouldn't elaborate but assured them Ophelia would be okay.

Her mother had been silent, for the most part, since she had shared the deception the twins had been playing for much of their lives. They were both surprised when they arrived that her father wasn't there. Both had tried to reach his cell but there had been no answer yet.

Ida looked up when the nurse came back through the swinging door. She and her mother stood.

The nurse said, "We're moving her up to a room on the third floor. Give us a few minutes and you can see her."

"Thank you," Ida said.

She reached for her mother's hand, but the woman pulled away and started toward the elevator.

Ophelia Dellahousaye lay apparently asleep in the hospital bed as Ida and her mother came into the room. Both walked up on opposite sides of the bed and stood staring down at the silent twin. Ida winced as she saw the bruises and scratches on her sister's face and arms. Her hair was a terrible mess, matted back and wet, her skin pale and mottled.

Ida reached down and took her hand and was startled at how cold it felt. "O, it's me. It's Ida."

No response.

"Ophelia, we're here," their mother said softly.

Ida felt a faint squeeze in her hand and reached down to brush some hair away from her sister's forehead. "O, you're back. You're going to be okay."

Her sister's eyes fluttered, then opened tentatively. She looked up at both her sister and mother and then scrunched her eyes closed again, shaking her head slowly.

"Ophelia!" Ida said, more forcefully, trying to jolt her sister back.

Her eyes opened again, and she stared up at Ida's face, a weak smile beginning to show. "Ida, what's...? She couldn't continue, looking over at her mother and then back to Ida. "Where are we?"

"You're okay, honey," Ida said. "You've been away. You've been hurt, but you'll be okay."

Ida watched as her sister squeezed her eyes shut, seemingly in pain, and reached below the sheet. Their mother pulled back the sheet and they saw the dressings on her leg. Ida looked down, shocked. "What happened?"

Ophelia continued to have a look of confusion and even fear on her face. "I don't know. I don't remember."

Chapter Sixty

Xander Lacroix sipped at the 12-year-old bourbon in his glass, the ice cubes shimmering in the low light on his desk. He let the whiskey slide over his tongue and down his throat, then set the heavy glass tumbler down, his hand trembling slightly. He felt exhausted and drained as the clock on his wall edged past two. The adrenalin rush from the night's events had faded, and now he felt only a persistent sense of dread. His earlier comfort in thinking Dellahousaye would surely take the fall for the three murders out at the beach house was diminishing. He kept thinking through all the scenarios and how he would be able to protect himself as the investigation into the deaths proceeded.

Remy Dellahousaye was the only living witness to what had actually gone down. *I should have taken him out when I had the chance*, he thought. *Made it look like a suicide after killing the other three.*

His cell buzzed on the desk and he saw the caller ID for Joey Grant.

"What?"

"The Griffith girl and the lawyer are out here in Dugganville with Alex Frank's old man, the shrimper."

"What the hell?" Lacroix said.

"Not sure what they're planning to do, but I think I put a pretty good scare in them last night."

Lacroix sat thinking for a moment, then said. "We need to clean this up."

"What do you want me to do?"

"The last thing we need right now is for this thing to linger on and the cops getting back into it."

"You want me to make it go away," Grant asked.

"No, you idiot! We'll never get our money back."

Lacroix took another sip from his drink, then continued. "Get her ass back to Charleston, tonight! She needs to know we're losing our patience with this thing. I may have a new investor who can take over the restaurants and cash us out. I want her there in the morning to meet with this guy. I'll call back to confirm but get her back to town!"

"No problem," Grant said.

Skipper Frank's house was dark, not a single light on in the little ranch that sat up in the trees from the street.

Joey Grant was parked in front of the house next door. He got out and quietly closed the door. He pulled the pistol from the shoulder holster he was wearing. He ejected the clip and confirmed it was fully loaded with 15 rounds. *Just in case.* He had to assume the old shrimper had weapons in the house.

He put his gun back and reached for his phone in his jacket pocket. Pulling up the number for Christy Griffith, he sent the call. There were three rings before a groggy voice answered.

"Who is this?"

"Your best friend," Grant said quietly. "I thought we had an understanding."

There was a pause while he waited for the woman to respond.

"You and I need to get back to town," he said.

"How did you find us?" he heard the woman ask, her voice unsteady.

"We need to get back to Charleston, now!" he hissed.

There was silence on the phone for a few moments, then, *"But Hanna..."*

"She's not going anywhere. Get your ass out here or I'm coming in to get you, and I don't care who gets in the way."

"You're outside?"

"Just get out here and be quiet about it."

No response. He saw the call end on his screen. He continued to watch the house from behind his car. Several minutes passed. Looking in both directions down the street, there was still no sign of neighbors or approaching cars.

Grant was just putting his phone back in his pocket when he felt cold steel against the back of his neck.

"Do not move asshole, or this 12-gauge takes your head off."

Despite the warning, Grant turned his head far enough to see Frank's father holding the shotgun aimed at the back of his head. He was dressed in plaid boxer shorts and a sleeveless t-shirt.

"You're making a big mistake, old man," Grant said, starting to turn.

"Do not move!"

This is starting to piss me off! thought Grant, thinking through how Xander Lacroix was going to react. *Not well! Enough of this bullshit!*

Grant spun suddenly, without warning, knocking the barrel of the shotgun away with his forearm. He watched Skipper Frank fall back and stumble against the car. He launched a savage kick into the man's groin and saw him fall to his knees, a low groan breaking the stillness of the night. The gun fell to the ground and Grant reached down for it, pointing it now at the man's head.

Frank was bowed down, holding himself, obviously in serious pain. Grant had had enough. He turned the shotgun, gripping the barrel with both hands and swung the wooden stock out hard catching Frank on the side of head. He watched as the man crumbled to the ground and then lay still.

Grant looked back up to the house. There were still no lights on or signs of movement inside. He laid the shotgun on the roof of his car and then reached down and grabbed Skipper Frank's lifeless body under both arms. He pulled him around the car and left him lying in the grass away from the street.

Retrieving the gun, he started up to the house, cursing silently to himself. *Let's get this bitch and get the hell out of here!*

He got to the porch and walked up the steps, opening the screen door. He walked the three steps to the front door and turned the knob... *not locked.* He stepped cautiously inside with the gun pointed to the floor in front of him. His eyes were adjusted to the dark and he saw a small living room and a hallway where he assumed the bedrooms were.

He took one more step and then heard a scream behind him just as a heavy blow struck him across the back of the head. The pain was intense, and he fell to his knees, the gun falling from his hands. He turned enough to see the woman lawyer standing there with a large cast iron skillet in her hands. He couldn't react in time before she swung it again and caught him across the side of his forehead. He wasn't able to keep himself from falling and saw the floor coming up to catch him as his last conscious thought faded. *Lacroix!*

Chapter Sixty-one

Hanna stood over the big man, trying to catch her breath and calm herself. She threw the heavy pan down on the floor and heard movement behind her. A light came on and she saw Christy Griffith standing with Ella Frank.

Ella held a hand in front of Christy, her eyes wide in surprise. "Holy shit!"

Hanna reached for her cell phone in her pocket and dialed 911. When the dispatcher answered, she said, "We have an intruder down at the home of Skipper Frank in Dugganville! Please get someone over here!"

After ending the call, Hanna reached down for the shotgun and handed it to Ella. "Don't let him get up! I need to go find Skipper."

She ran down the front steps and saw the car parked next door, the body of Skipper Frank lying beside it in the low light from the streetlamps. She ran over and knelt beside his lifeless form. *Oh, please no!*

"Skipper!"

No response. She could see blood leaking from a cut on his forehead. She reached for her phone again and was asking the 911 operator to also send an ambulance when Christy Griffith ran up beside her.

"Oh, Hanna, no! I'm so sorry!"

Sheriff Pepper Stokes had his deputy take the handcuffed and still groggy Joey Grant away to a patrol car parked out on the street. The scene was ablaze in the flashing red and blue lights of two police cars and an ambulance. He followed the officer out of the house and down to the paramedics working on Skipper Frank.

Hanna Walsh stood beside them watching them assess Alex's father, sitting on the back opening of the ambulance.

Stokes placed his hand on her shoulder, and she turned to him.

"You okay?" he asked.

She shook her head. "Just a little jumpy still," she said. "I thought I might have killed him. I hit him so hard the second time."

"He's gonna have a hell of a headache," Stokes replied. "How's the Skipper?"

"I'm fine, dammit!" Frank yelled out. "The sonofabitch got the jump on me!"

The paramedics were trying to clean the headwound and get a temporary dressing on it.

"Who was this guy?" Stokes asked.

Hanna said, "The goon Xander Lacroix put on my client. They've been squeezing her for money from her dead father's business after they killed him. He followed us up here tonight from Charleston and was trying to take Christy back.

"Had the bastard in my sights," Skipper Frank growled. "Should have taken his head off."

"It's okay, Skipper," Hanna said. "He won't hurt anybody now."

The sheriff looked around for a moment, then said, "After we get you cleaned up, I'll need to get a statement from everyone.

"What!"

Hanna listened to Alex's frantic reaction on the phone as she described the takedown of Lacroix's man.

"And you're sure Skipper is okay?" he asked.

"They decided to take him out to the hospital," she said. "He's probably got a bad concussion."

"And how about you?" she heard Alex ask.

"I've been better."

"I wish I could get up there," Alex said. *"At least we got the girl back."*

"Yes, thank God. Is she okay?"

"Pretty shaken up and a few wounds the doctors are working on right now."

"Any leads on the kidnappers?" she asked.

"Nothing yet. We do have multiple homicides, however, out at Remy's house."

"Who?"

"His wife and two men who work for Lacroix and Dellahousaye."

"Really!" Hanna said, astonished. *What next?* She looked back and saw Ella Frank standing beside her husband as he was loaded on a gurney and then into the back of the ambulance. Hanna walked over and put her arm around the woman's shoulder. "You should go," she said. "I'll come down as soon as I can. Alex wants to talk to you for a moment." She handed the woman her phone and stepped back.

Christy Griffith came up beside her. "Hanna, I'm so sorry about all of this."

"You have no reason to apologize."

"I shouldn't have gotten all of you involved."

Hanna could tell the woman was on the verge of a total meltdown. She reached out and pulled her into a tight embrace. She felt her shudder and then start to cry. "We'll get these guys," Hanna said, trying to calm and reassure her.

Ella came over and handed the phone back. "Alex?"

"I'm sure Pepper will need some time with all of you," Alex said. *"Can you get back in the morning?"*

"As soon as we can," Hanna said.

"We've got the Charleston PD out to bring Lacroix in tonight. Dellahousaye's telling us he was having an affair with his wife. I can't imagine he'll send anyone else out there after you, but please be careful. I've warned Pepper."

"Thank you," Hanna said. "You think Lacroix was involved in the murders?"

"We're going to find out."

Chapter Sixty-two

Ophelia Dellahousaye lay back on the hospital pillows, groggy now from the painkillers the hospital staff had given her. The cuts and scrapes on her leg and her swollen and broken wrist were still throbbing and sore despite the meds. She felt exhausted and drained, still not remembering the events of the previous night. Her sister had shared what little she had been told about an abduction, a ransom demand, the call that led to her being found out on a deserted road by the marshes.

Ida had tried to make her remember they had switched again. She had been taking Ida's place with her friends from school out at a beach house for spring break. None of that was coming back to her yet. It always took her time to piece everything back together after they switched. Sometimes it took longer than others. She closed her eyes and tried to pull the random thoughts and images in her mind into focus.

"O?" she heard her sister ask.

She opened her eyes and looked over at her twin, the identical face she had lived with since her earliest memories. She shook her head and in a weak voice said, "This can't be happening..."

Ida looked back, doubt and concern in her eyes.

Ophelia blinked and looked away. "I just don't remember..."

"It's okay," she heard her mother say.

She looked over at the woman, sitting on the other side of the bed. As usual, she was dressed immaculately and made up like she was going out on the town. The look seemed so out of context in the stark hospital room.

Her mother continued, "Ida told me about your *game*... your game of switching."

Ophelia looked back at her sister who nodded.

Her mother said, "I still don't understand how you could have kept this deception from us for so many years, but we need to put all of that behind us. You need to rest. You need to remember. You need to help us find who is responsible."

Chapter Sixty-three

Alex sat facing Remy Dellahousaye across a table in a small interrogation room in the downtown precinct of the Charleston Police Department. Agent Will Foster was beside him. Sharron Fairfield was with the police detail sent out to bring in Xavier Lacroix. Dellahousaye's lawyer had been waiting for them when they got downtown and now sat beside his client. Nate Beatty, the police detective assigned to the case, was standing at the head of the table and got everyone's attention by saying, "Okay, let's get started."

He sat down and placed his hands on the table. "We'll be recording this discussion, Mr. Dellahousaye."

The man looked over at his lawyer who nodded.

"Fine," Dellahousaye said, "just tell me what happened to my wife."

"That's what we intend to find out," Beatty replied.

Alex watched Dellahousaye's face, looking for any sign that would betray his claim of being nowhere near the house when his wife and the others had been murdered.

"Have you brought Lacroix in yet?" Dellahousaye asked.

Beatty said. "We're here to talk about you, sir."

"Goddamit! The man's been banging my wife and she ends up dead along with one of my employees..."

"And one of Lacroix's men," Beatty cut in.

Will Foster said, "Tell us about that wound on the back of your head, Remy."

Alex watched the anger continue to grow on the man's face, now red and flushed.

"That has nothing to do with this!" he shouted back, defiantly.

"You're going to need to calm down, sir," Beatty said. "Let's walk back through the events of the evening."

"I've already told you. I was at my house here in Charleston all night until we got the call about my daughter. Frank and I went to meet the team sent to pick her up."

Alex said, "Was there anyone at the house before I arrived that can confirm this?"

Dellahousaye hesitated, then said, "I don't remember when the cook left. She was there earlier."

"Does she often stay late into the night?" Beatty asked.

Dellahousaye shook his head, seemingly confused and struggling to respond.

The lawyer was a man named Stuart Cox. He was an older man, near seventy, Alex guessed. Deeply tanned, his hair and eyebrows were silver gray and bushy. He was dressed in jeans and a white dress shirt with a blue plaid sports jacket. He jumped in, "My client is obviously in shock from the news of his wife's passing and the stress of his daughter's abduction these past couple of days. I really think we should table this until he can get some rest and gather himself."

Alex was impressed with the man's smooth demeanor. Obviously, Della-housaye could afford the best to represent him.

"We have a triple homicide here," Beatty said, impatiently, standing again and pushing his chair back. "When was the last time you saw your wife?"

Dellahousaye looked down at his hands folded in front of him on the worn surface of the table. He took a deep breath, then said, "I saw her earlier in the afternoon. I already told you that. I went out to the island to talk to her about Ida's abduction."

"And what time did you leave your house out there?" Beatty asked.

He turned to his lawyer. "Stuart, really, do I have to go through this all again? I need to go to my daughter!"

Beatty held up a hand. "We'll be here all night if we have to. The sooner you share everything we need to know, the sooner you can leave."

Alex sat back and listened to Dellahousaye and his lawyer dodge and obfuscate around nearly every question Beatty and Will Foster offered up. Clearly, he knew more than he was letting on and may have possibly been the gunman.

His thoughts strayed to Hanna and his father and their run-in with Lacroix's man up in Dugganville. His temper simmered as he imagined the scene. His father was lucky not to be in the morgue and Hanna... he cringed when he thought about how badly it might have gone for both of them.

Sharron Fairfield had texted them a half hour ago that Xavier Lacroix had agreed to come down to the station without incident. He was down the hall in another interrogation room going through the same line of questioning with another team.

His phone buzzed and he saw another text from her. *Meet me in the hall.*

Fairfield was waiting for him when he and Foster came out. "Lacroix has an alibi for the whole night. He's laying it on Dellahousaye. He admits to the affair with the wife but says her husband has been abusive and has threatened to kill her several times."

"What was his guy doing out there?" Alex asked.

"Says he was there to pick up Mrs. Dellahousaye and bring her into town. Apparently, the Dellahousaye's have been estranged for a while, and the wife has been spending time with Lacroix out at the beach house, here in town at his house and a few select hotels around town."

"Busy couple," Foster said, shaking his head. "You think you can get any more out of him tonight?"

"No, and there's nothing really to hold him on."

"Someone checking on the alibi?" Alex asked.

"Done," she replied. "Seems solid."

"What do the locals think?" Foster asked.

"We're on the same page," Fairfield replied.

"Did you ask him about the Griffith girl's claim about her father."

"Said he didn't have a clue what we were talking about."

"Sure," Alex said in frustration.

"Any progress with Remy?" Fairfield asked.

"He can't account for his time when the shootings went down. He was a mess when I went to see him at his house just before we got the tip on his daughter. I stacked it up to him being upset about the kidnapping, but he was really distracted and a little drunk."

"He's also got a serious wound on the back of his head," Foster said.

Beatty came out of the room. Agent Fairfield briefed him quickly on their progress with Lacroix.

The detective leaned against the wall and crossed his arms. "Dellahousaye really stinks for this, right?"

Alex nodded.

Foster said, "I agree, but we clearly don't have enough to bring him up on charges yet. Nothing really ties him to the crime scene until we get more from the techs.

A door opened down the hall and Alex watched as Xander Lacroix came out, talking with his attorney. Both men turned and walked toward them. Alex had never met the man but as they made eye contact, Lacroix smiled and locked his gaze on him. Alex was struck by the intensity in the man's eyes. As the two men passed, Lacroix looked only at Alex and just nodded as he continued on and walked through a door at the end of the hall.

Alex felt his temper flare again and he started off after Lacroix. The firm grip of Will Foster on his arm stopped him.

"Let it go, Alex," he heard Foster say. "Let it go."

Chapter Sixty-four

Hanna sat with Ella Frank at the 24-hour clinic on the outskirts of Dugganville. Skipper Frank had been with the doctor for almost an hour. The doc had stepped out a few minutes earlier to assure them there were no serious injuries, but he was still going through the concussion protocol, which looked likely.

"He's going to have a killer headache for a few days," the doc told them.

Hanna looked over at Ella and couldn't help but think back when the woman's daughter, Adrienne, had come back to Dugganville to try to win Alex back after her many affairs and their failed marriage. Unlike the daughter, Ella seemed to have a true and kind heart. She drank too much and that usually led to a short fuse for whoever crossed her, particularly Skipper Frank, but she was a saint compared to her daughter.

Ella was clearly stressed and upset about her husband's run-in with the man sent by Xavier Lacroix to keep tabs on them. Hanna reached over and put her hand on the woman's knee.

Ella turned and smiled. "Thanks for being here with me, dear," she said. She ran her other hand through her dyed red and auburn hair, traces of gray showing through at the roots. "Still can't believe that low-life got over on the Skipper."

"He's a professional, Ella," Hanna replied. "Probably a hired killer if what we hear about Lacroix is true. We're lucky this all didn't turn out much worse."

Ella leaned into Hanna and spoke in a whisper. "Aren't you afraid about these bums coming back after you?"

Hanna felt a chill rush through her and thought of her past run-in with the mob toughs linked to Asa Dellahousaye, and then the old gangster himself. She tried to keep a strong face for Ella. "Alex and the Feds have all these guys in their sights. Hopefully they'll be able to take them down soon."

The doctor came out from the exam room and walked over. Hanna stood with Ella as he said, "Here is a list of warning signs for concussions I want you to keep an eye on."

Ella reached for the piece of paper.

The doctor continued, "He seems to be doing pretty well. His head wounds are superficial. I've given him some good pain medication to get him through the rest of the night. You can get this prescription filled tomorrow. He needs to rest for a few days. Keep him off the boat. Don't want him knocking his head again."

"That's gonna go well," Ella said. "I can hear the bitchin' already."

Hanna couldn't help but smile. *The two of them are quite a pair.*

It was past three in the morning when Hanna got them both back to the house in Dugganville. She was exhausted and didn't think she could keep her eyes open a moment longer. Ella had taken the Skipper to bed. Christy Griffith was waiting for them, and she and Hanna sat at the island in the kitchen, both sipping on a glass of red wine from a bottle they'd found in the refrigerator.

Christy was understandably still upset about the earlier encounter and all the trouble she had brought down on Hanna and now Alex's family. Trying to hold back tears, she said, "This has to end. I have to get them the money and get away from all this. I know my father would want to keep the business going, but I just can't do this anymore."

Hanna reached over and placed her hand on the woman's arm, squeezing it softly and looking for words of encouragement, but none would come.

"I'll do whatever they say, Hanna. I just want all of this over with."

Chapter Sixty-five

Somewhere in his drowsy consciousness, Alex tried to catch up with Hanna on the beach. She was running out ahead of him, her hair blowing in the early breeze off the ocean, the sun just coming up on the far horizon. His words seemed muted as he called out to her. She kept running and the harder he tried to catch up, the further she distanced herself.

A final cry out into the hazy mist of the morning finally brought him out of his restless sleep. He opened his eyes to see the first signs of light in the small bedroom of his apartment. He shook his head and turned on his side, trying to recall the random fragments of the dream, but it all quickly faded.

He looked over at the clock on his nightstand. In two minutes, his alarm would go off at 6 a.m., another early call to get back down to his office. The events of the past night quickly clouded his thoughts of Hanna and the troubling dream.

The Dellahousaye twin was safe, but her father's possible role in the death of three people, including his wife, at his home on Isle of Palms would now guide the day's events. Remy D had been released just hours earlier at the police precinct but warned to stay in town and available for more interrogation.

His last conversation with Hanna had given him little comfort she was out of danger in her attempts to help her client stand-up to the treachery of Xander Lacroix. The thought that Lacroix's man had nearly killed his father and put Hanna in harm's way again sparked a new slow burn of anger as he turned to get out of bed.

He remembered the brief exchange with Lacroix earlier that morning down at the police precinct, the mocking look as he passed in the hall. As he walked into the kitchen to put coffee on, he vowed to himself to make a personal visit with Xander Lacroix a top priority for the coming day.

His phone pinged on the counter. A text from Hanna said, *Headed back to town. Skipper is home and resting. Call you soon. H.*

Hanna pulled to the curb in front of Christy Griffith's condo building on the west side of town. They had spoken little on the way back from Dugganville, both exhausted from a long, mostly sleepless night, and the frightening memories of the events of the previous night.

Hanna turned to Christy as she opened the door to get out. "Detective Beatty has assured me they are doing everything they can to protect you."

Christy looked back, the doubt clear in her expression.

"They want to talk to both of us this morning," Hanna said. "All of this will help build their case against Lacroix. Try to get some rest."

"I have to get down to the office," Christy said. "The work has to get done."

"I'll call as soon as I hear from Beatty."

Christy nodded, then stood to get out. She turned and looked back into the car. "The guy last night..."

Hanna nodded.

"He said I needed to get this over with."

"Right."

"I'm going to do it, Hanna. I'm sure there will be nothing left after Lacroix gets paid back. I may even have to go into debt to cover some of the loans my father has on the business, but I can't do this anymore. I don't want anyone else to get hurt."

Hanna listened but couldn't respond. She knew her client was probably right, but the thought of letting Lacroix off the hook just wasn't sitting well. "We'll talk."

"Okay, call me."

Hanna watched as she walked up the sidewalk and into the main entrance of her condo building. She looked around, up and down the street behind her car. She couldn't shake the feeling they were still being watched or followed.

As she pulled out from the curb, her cell phone buzzed. She saw Alex on the caller ID. "Good morning."

"Hey, you back?" she heard the familiar sound of his voice ask.

"Just dropped off my client."

"Dumb question, but how are you doing?"

"Well, considering I almost killed a man with a frying pan last night... not bad."

She waited for Alex to reply. There was a pause, then, *"I'm sorry I couldn't be up there with you."*

"I know."

"Skipper's doing okay?" he asked.

"He was still sleeping when we left this morning, but the doctor reassured us there shouldn't be any long-term complications."

"He has to be spitting mad about that guy taking him down."

"That's putting it mildly," she said. "What's happening with the Dellahousayes?"

"The girl is recovering, although banged up a bit. The ransom has been paid and we're trying to track it down, but something strange is going on with this whole thing and I just can't tie it down."

"What?" she asked.

"I don't know. Something just isn't sitting right."

"And what about the three dead bodies out at Dellahousaye's house?" she asked, slowing for a stop light.

"We'll bring Dellahousaye in again this morning."

"And what about Lacroix?"

"Seems to have a solid alibi...."

She waited for him to continue, then, "Alex, what is it?"

"When I get a break today, Xander Lacroix and I are going to have a chat."

"Alex, don't..."

"This has to stop, Hanna... after last night."

"Let the police take care of it."

"I am the police."

She started off again with the green light, now just around the block from her offices. "When can I see you?"

"I'll try to come by at lunch. You'll be around?"

"I should be. Alex please don't try to handle Lacroix on your own. You know what these people are capable of."

"Trust me, I know…"

Chapter Sixty-six

Remy Dellahousaye had never found sleep. His lawyer had dropped him back at his house after the long night. His relief at the release of his daughter was tempered by the overwhelming weight of concern about the murders discovered at his beach house. The sight of his wife lying brutally murdered on the floor of the bathroom was seared into his brain. He knew he had no solid proof or alibi to exonerate him in the murders.

He had been trying to think through all the possible evidence the investigators would be able to bring forward. He had thrown his gun deep into the marshes on a deserted road coming back to Charleston the previous afternoon. Only a few alligators or snakes would ever happen upon the area.

Certainly, his prints and DNA were all over the house. *He lived there, for God's sake!*

Before leaving the house, he had checked the security system. The laptop for the system was gone. Lacroix, or someone, had obviously taken it.

The cops had insisted he be available for further questioning, and he expected their call at any time. His attorney had not been particularly comforting in his parting comments. "Just keep your mouth shut," was his final piece of advice.

He walked into the kitchen of his house on the Battery, quiet now in the early morning light. He placed a coffee pod in the Keurig and listened to the familiar gurgle of the machine coming to life. His head ached from the tall glass of whiskey now sitting empty next to his bed.

His thoughts turned to his daughter and the sight of her lying lifeless on the old marsh road. He thought she was dead when he first saw her. He sat down on one of the barstools around the big island and hung his head, grimacing at another round of pain shooting through his brain.

At least she's back safe, he thought. *And what's this with O and Ida switching places?* He still couldn't get his mind around how long this deception had been going on. He searched for any clues in his past memory with the girls that would betray their crazy charade. He had always believed he had at least one sane daughter, but now..."

And who's responsible for Ophelia's abduction? There seemed no clue and $5 million of his money had disappeared out into the air. *I will find these sons of bitches!* he cursed silently.

His thoughts were interrupted by a knock at the back door. He looked up and saw a familiar face staring back through the window of the door. Alarms went off in his brain, but he knew there was nowhere to run. Trying his best to control the rising panic racing through his body, he got up and walked toward the door.

Xander Lacroix had actually slept quite well. He had always been an easy sleeper and usually woke as he had today, well-rested and eager for another day. He sipped at a cup of coffee in his den as he watched the morning news on the television mounted to the wall. The local reporter was giving an update on the safe return of the Dellahousaye twin.

He shook his head, grinning and took another sip from his cup.

Chapter Sixty-seven

Alex listened to the talk around the table. He sat with Sharron Fairfield and Nate Beatty in the same Charleston Police interrogation room they'd had Remy Dellahousaye in late last night.

Beatty said, "Let's get him back down here. Ballistics show at least three weapons and only two accounted for on the two bodyguards. Great job they did, by the way."

Fairfield asked, "Did you see Remy with a gun any time yesterday?"

Alex shook his head *no*.

Beatty stood. "I'll have them get Dellahousaye back down here. How long can you stay?"

Sharron looked at Alex, then said, "We'll set up here until we get another pass at Remy. Nothing new back at the office on the kidnapping. The girl is back safe. The money is long gone."

Beatty nodded and left the room, closing the door behind him.

Alex was thinking about the weapons report. *Certainly, Dellahousaye could have taken another gun out to the house.*

"What's on your mind?" he heard Fairfield ask.

He looked up and took a deep breath. "Nothing else yet from the crime scene guys putting Dellahousaye there at the time of the shootings, right?"

"Right."

"And the security system computer is missing?"

She nodded back.

"I've got this nagging feeling I can't quite put my finger on."

"Where is that going?" she asked.

Alex hesitated a moment, trying to pull his thoughts together. "There's something off about this abduction."

Fairfield stared back, waiting for him to continue.

"The twins... Remy called his daughter *Ophelia* when we found her."

"I thought it was Ida that was abducted."

"So did I," Alex said. "Remy wouldn't explain." He scratched his head and thought for a moment longer. "I also can't square with the timing of all this. Dellahousaye's daughter goes missing... his wife and bodyguard are murdered."

"Seems a bit much all at once," Fairfield added. "So, you think it's all connected?"

Alex nodded his head without answering, still trying to piece together the events of the past days.

Hanna was stunned when she walked into her office and saw her son sitting at her conference table, looking down at his phone. He stood when she walked in.

"Jonathan! What..."

He came to her and pulled her tight in a hug. "Sorry to surprise you."

She looked up at his face. "What's going on?"

"We need to talk."

A mother's sense of dread rushed through her. "Sit down, tell me what's going on."

Her son sat across from her at the small table, looking down and fumbling with his phone.

"Jonathan?"

He looked up, tears starting to flood into his eyes.

Hanna reached across and held his hand. "Jonathan, please..."

Her son looked up, wiped at his eyes, then began, "I have a problem... we have a problem."

Hanna just stared back, squeezing his hand tighter.

"It's about school..."

"We've already agreed you can take a break," Hanna said.

"That surgery I had last fall when I hurt my knee in the bike crash?"

Hanna nodded.

"There was a lot of pain... it wouldn't go away. The drugs I was taking were barely cutting it, so I kept taking more."

"Oh, Jonathan..."

The tears were flowing now. "I couldn't stop, Mom. When the doctor wouldn't renew the prescription, I..."

She waited for him to continue, but he lowered his face into his hands.

A sinking despair came over her. "You're not hooked on something?"

He looked up at her. "One of my friends had a bottle of something. It took the edge off for a while, then I just needed more."

"You're using an opioid?" she asked, not wanting to hear the answer.

Jonathan nodded, looking back with desperation and sadness on his tear-streaked face.

"Where are you getting them?" she asked.

"They're everywhere on the street. It's no trouble getting them... I just can't stop!"

Hanna stood and came around the table. She leaned down with her arm around his shoulders and her face close. "We'll get you some help, honey."

He turned to her. "I'm not going to pass this semester. I've already stopped going to class. There's no point. I'm too far behind."

She took a deep breath and stood up, then walked over to her desk, taking in all her son was sharing, trying to remain calm.

Jonathan continued, "I thought if I took a summer away, I could deal with this... get it behind me."

"We'll deal with it... we'll get some help."

Chapter Sixty-eight

Ida Dellahousaye woke with a start, a pain in her neck causing her to groan as she sat up and realized she'd fallen asleep in a chair in the hospital room with her sister. She looked over and Ophelia was still sleeping. Her mother must have stepped out.

Ida stood and tried to stretch the soreness away. She looked out the window across the parking lot of the hospital and saw the early morning light shining through the palms and live oak. She walked over and put her hand on her sister's forehead. It felt warm and damp. She brushed some hair away from her face and leaned down and kissed her on the cheek.

Thank God you're back, she thought, as she watched her sister's eyes flutter, then open.

Ophelia put an arm over her eyes as the morning light poured in. "What the hell..." she said in a low raspy voice.

Ida pulled a chair up close and sat beside the bed, taking her sister's hand in hers. "You're back, O. You're going to be okay." She watched as her sister turned and stared back, a confused look on her face.

Ophelia squeezed her eyes closed then looked back. "I was up half the night trying to think back on what happened. It's all just a jumble. The last thing I really remember is meeting you in the coffee shop in Charleston. When was that?"

"About a week ago. You were there to switch with me to go out to the beach with the college friends for spring break."

Ophelia shook her head, "And I actually went?"

"Yes, and on the last night, someone took you. You've been gone for two days. You still don't have any memory of that?"

Ophelia shook her head in frustration. "And that's where I got all banged up?"

"Apparently."

Their mother came back into the room. "Well, good morning everyone. She had a cupholder with three steaming cups of coffee. "The best I could do here in the hospital." She handed the cups to her daughters. "You're looking a little better this morning, O."

"I feel like I was run over by a train."

Ida said, "They say you're going to be fine. Just need a little time to heal."

Ophelia blew on the hot coffee, then took a sip.

Ida watched as a strange expression came across her sister's face as she looked away out the window. "What is it, O?"

"Honey?" her mother asked.

Ophelia continued to stare out the window, seemingly lost in thought and oblivious to their concern.

The youngest Jordan Hayes lay awake in bed in his fraternity room, drenched in sweat despite the A/C running through the vents. He looked over at the empty beer cans on his nightstand and the half-smoked joint in an ashtray. He knew he had his first class soon, but he was in no mood to confront the army of news people camped in front of his house.

There was a knock on the door.

"It's open."

His best friend in the fraternity, his nickname Rover, leaned in. "They found her, buddy."

Jordan sat up, then winced at the pain in his head.

"Is she...?"

"She's okay. They found her early this morning. They're reporting she'd been kidnapped, then returned after her old man paid the ransom."

"Ransom..."

"Ida's okay, man. Some of the news trucks have been packing up."

"Thank God for that."

"A couple still want a final statement. Pretty crazy, huh, man?" Rover pulled the door closed behind him.

Jordan lay back on the pillow, a tentative sense of relief washing over him. That quickly went away when he thought again about the strange call he'd taken as a favor for his grandfather. The woman had wanted information on Ida. The sick feeling of complicity returned, though he really had no idea if any of this was related to Ida's disappearance.

Pulling his feet over the side of the bed, he stood and walked to the window. Pulling the curtain open a crack, he was reassured when he saw only two media trucks still parked in front.

He found his cell on the nightstand and pulled up his father's number. The call went quickly to voicemail and Jordan listened to the familiar formal greeting from his father and invitation to leave a message.

"Dad, it's me. I heard Ida's back." He paused, then said, "We need to talk."

Ophelia Dellahousaye lay back on the pillows of her hospital bed and closed her eyes, the chatter between her sister and mother drowned out by her thoughts.

There was one memory that was coming back more clearly now, and it made her stomach turn in a queasy rumble.

Chapter Sixty-nine

Sharron Fairfield came back to the interrogation room at the police precinct. She and Alex had set-up their laptops and had been trying to stay on top of things for the past hour, waiting for the return and further questioning of Remy Dellahousaye. Alex immediately saw the look of concern on her face.

"What?" he asked.

"Dellahousaye isn't answering his cell or his home phone," she answered.

Alex thought for a moment. "You don't think he's running?"

"I don't know what to think. Beatty and I are going over to the house with back-up. You want to join us?"

Alex stood, closing his laptop and putting his phone in his pocket. "Did they call out to the beach house?"

"Another crime tech team is out there. No sign of him," she said.

Alex drove with Fairfield in the seat beside him. Beatty was in a Charleston PD unmarked car in front of them with his partner. A patrol car was close behind. Alex saw Dellahousaye's big house on the Battery coming up on their left.

The three cars pulled into open spaces along the curb fronting the park on the bay. They all regrouped on the sidewalk under the shade of tall oaks.

Beatty assigned the two uniforms to go around back while the rest of them would start at the front door. Alex followed the officers across the street. Beatty's partner stayed at the iron gate at the sidewalk, and Alex followed Fairfield and Beatty up the walk and onto the big verandah of the front porch. The two uniformed officers disappeared around both sides of the house.

Beatty rang the door chime and Alex could hear muffled sounds inside. After a few moments, Beatty pushed the button again. When he started knocking hard on the door, Alex heard a loud message coming over Beatty's police radio from an officer in the back.

"The back door's unlocked."

"Wait there," Beatty answered back. "He turned to his partner out on the sidewalk. "Keep an eye out here." The man nodded.

Alex stood aside to let Beatty lead them down the steps and then along the side of the house. When they got to the back, one patrol officer was standing back from the door, his gun drawn and pointed at the ground. The other was standing over by the garage.

Alex joined Fairfield and Beatty in pulling out their service weapons.

Beatty whispered to the young cop, "Wait here."

Alex and Sharron Fairfield followed Beatty into the house. They stepped into a large kitchen. A single cup of coffee was sitting on the long granite island countertop. All three had their guns up, covering each other in different directions.

Beatty broke the stillness in the house, "Mr. Dellahousaye! Is anyone home?"

No reply.

The piercing sound of a siren raced by out in front of the house, the fire truck blasting its loud horn as it approached a coming intersection. When the sounds subsided, the three of them continued deeper into the house. They separated and Alex took the hall toward the right that opened into a long dining room. He was just coming out through the opening into a living area when he heard Beatty yell out, "Shit!"

Alex kept his gun up on full alert as he made his way cautiously through to the other side of the house. He saw Fairfield coming back down the stairs from above. They both walked down another hall with a door on the right. Alex followed her in.

Beatty stood to the side, his gun now pointed down to the floor. Behind a large wooden desk, Remy Dellahousaye sat in a leather chair, his arms limp over the cushioned arms, his head to one side, eyes wide open. On the left side of his forehead, a large caliber entry wound was leaking a thin trail of blood. On the leather behind his head, a wide splatter of blood and brain matter was still dripping fresh.

As Alex came around the desk to get a closer look, being careful not to step on any potential evidence, he saw a 44-caliber revolver lying on the floor next to the chair below the lifeless right arm of Remy Dellahousaye. One expended cartridge was on the carpet a foot away.

Chapter Seventy

Hanna left her son in her apartment upstairs to try to get some rest. He had come from Chapel Hill early to make the drive down to Charleston. She walked down to her office, a heavy burden of fear and doubt bearing down on her. The thought of her son now a victim of opioid dependency was a frightening and overwhelming thing to process.

He's seemed so healthy... and normal!

She had been hearing for many months how pervasive the epidemic was growing in the country. Even Alex had been dealing with an addiction to pain meds up until last year from his past wounds in Afghanistan and then gunshot wounds in the line of duty since he'd been back.

Alex had been able to overcome the horrible dependency for the past year but was on constant guard about the temptation for a relapse.

She sat down heavily behind her desk, sinking back into the old leather chair, breathing hard.

We need to talk to my doctor. We need to talk about rehab. All these thoughts were spinning through her head when her assistant, Molly, leaned in the door.

"Alex has been trying to reach your cell. He's on your office line."

Hanna had seen his call come up on her screen, but she was too distracted with her son to answer.

She looked over at the blinking line on the screen of her desk phone.

"Alex, I'm sorry..."

She stopped as Alex cut in, breathless and hurried. "You're at the office?"

"Yes, what's going on?"

"We just left Remy's house down on the Battery. We found him in his office with a bullet through his head."

Hanna felt the air sucked from her lungs and stood unsteadily. "What happened?"

"It looks like he turned the gun on himself."

"He killed himself?"

"It looks that way, but... well, we're checking all possibilities. I just wanted to make sure you were back safe. I don't want you going anywhere near Lacroix or any of his people today. There's just too much crazy stuff coming down."

Hanna was trying to process what would lead a man like Remy Della-housaye to take his own life. *He just got his daughter back...!*

"Hanna!"

"I'm here," she answered, slumping back down into her chair. "What a terrible thing for his daughters."

"We're headed over to the hospital to inform the two girls and their mother," Alex said.

Hanna thought again about her own son. She didn't want to burden Alex with Jonathan's situation just yet. "I need to see you about something when you can break free."

"That sounds ominous."

She hesitated, then continued, "It's Jonathan. He's here. There are some issues. Can you come by later?"

"As soon as I can. Is he okay?"

Again, she hesitated. "No, we need your help. I don't want to go through it all over the phone."

"I have to go see the Dellahousayes and probably back downtown, but I'll call as soon as I can get away."

Hanna had already talked to her doctor's office and they had an appointment scheduled for the morning, the earliest she could get him in. She had been searching through drug rehab facility websites online and was becoming more frustrated and confused. Certainly, her doctor would have advice and referrals, but she wanted to deal with her son's issue now, not tomorrow!

She suddenly thought about Elizabeth, his girlfriend. *What does she know or not?*

She reached for her cell and found the girl's number in her directory. The phone rang twice. "Good morning, Elizabeth."

"Hanna, is Jonathan there with you? Is he okay?" Her voice was panicked and breathless.

"Yes, he's here," she answered, trying to remain calm. "He's trying to get some sleep."

"He left me a text he was going down to see you, but no reason why. He has classes and..."

"No, he's here," Hanna said, slowly. "So, you don't know about him dropping out?"

"What?"

"He told me he stopped going last week. He's too far behind."

There was silence for a moment, then, *"I know he's been struggling,"* Elizabeth said. *"We thought we could take a break this summer."*

"Yes, I know," Hanna said, deciding not to tell her about the drugs until she had spoken to her son. *Maybe she already knows, but I need to speak with Jonathan first.*

Chapter Seventy-one

Christy Griffith let her head fall back. She was sitting in her father's office chair behind his desk at the downtown Charleston restaurant. She had been using it since his passing and was struggling now to get through the demands of the coming day. She was exhausted from the past night and confrontation with Lacroix's *enforcer* in Dugganville with Hanna and the Franks.

Her latest problem was a workman's comp issue filed by one of her cooks who had cut himself badly in food prep the previous day. She turned to the cabinets behind her, still not able to find the personnel file she needed. One final cabinet door was locked. She spun back around to the desk and pulled open the center drawer and began rummaging through a mess of papers and office supplies. At the back of the drawer was a key ring she hadn't seen before with several keys of various sizes and shapes.

Turning back to the cabinet, she tried several of the keys before one actually worked in the lock. She opened the door and saw two sets of sliding shelves that could be pulled out, each loaded with file folders. She couldn't find what she was looking for in the top files and pulled out the lower drawer. As she sorted through the file labels nearly to the end, she came to one labeled *Transactions.* She was about to skip by it when she noticed it was heavier than the others for some reason. Pulling it open, there were several dozen documents as many of the other files had but also what looked like a cell phone at the bottom. She reached in and brought up what she immediately realized was a recording device.

Christy held it for a few moments, turning it in her hands, looking for the right way to operate it. Finding the power button, she saw a small screen come to life and then a menu of functions including *Files.* She clicked on the link and a series of a dozen file names came up. Pressing on the first, she immediately heard the familiar voice of her father. It quickly became apparent this was a personal note to himself regarding plans for purchasing a new restaurant in Columbia, South Carolina.

Over the next several minutes, she listened to more of the files which were similar "notes to self" her father had left. The sound of his voice was difficult to listen to and she wiped at her eyes as tears began to swell.

The last file was different. There were three voices in conversation... her father and two men whose voices she didn't recognize. The discussion seemed to be about future plans regarding her father's restaurant business.

When her father said, *"Mr. Lacroix"*, she sat up straight, and her breath caught in her throat. She continued to listen as her father restated terms for an investment in the business. The man, apparently named Lacroix, said, *"Griffith, I'm not sure what there is about our deal you don't understand. I'm tired of this bullshit!"* There was a pause and the recording picked up some shuffling sounds, possibly chairs being pushed away from a table.

The Lacroix voice continued, *"You're making a very big mistake if you think you can screw us on this and don't even think about going to the cops. You should be aware we have zero tolerance for shit like that."*

Christy thought she was going to be sick. She turned off the recording and sat back in the chair, trying to catch her breath. She put the recorder down on the desktop and pulled her hand back almost like it was hot or toxic. She sat staring at the device, her heart pounding in her chest.

She saw her phone lying to the side and quickly picked it up, scrolling through calls in her *Recents.* She pressed the number she wanted and waited three rings before she heard, *"Christy, what is it?"*

"Hanna, I need to see you... now!"

Chapter Seventy-two

"I told you, that conversation never happened!"

The youngest Jordan Hayes lay back on his pillow, his cell phone to his ear listening to his father. He didn't respond, trying to think through what his father was demanding.

"Jordan, are you there?"

"Yes..."

"Are we clear on this?"

"Clear?"

"We won't discuss this again, son."

"I need to know what happened," he finally blurted out.

"Nothing happened. A friend asked for a favor."

"A favor? What did any of this have to do with Ida's disappearance?"

"That's enough!" his father demanded.

Jordan pulled the phone away from his ear for a moment, his eyes squeezed shut. He sat up and pulled his legs around to stand. "She wanted to know where Ida and I would be during our break. She said she was just checking up on her."

"I said that's enough!" his father yelled again. "You need to forget this ever happened."

Ophelia was dozing in her hospital bed. As noise in the room started bringing her back from a restless sleep, she grasped to catch on to fading images of friends around a beach fire, a frightening ride in the trunk of a car...

"O, wake up."

She opened her eyes and saw Ida standing beside her. She wiped at her eyes and squinted at the bright sunlight in the room. Her mother was standing at the foot of the bed with a man and a woman she didn't know.

Ida said, "Ophelia, these are Special Agents Fairfield and Frank from the FBI."

She felt a sudden sense of apprehension and pushed herself up against the pillows and the wall behind her. "FBI?"

The woman, who had an FBI identification badge on a lanyard around her neck and a confused look on her face now, said, "We're glad you're back safely. How are you feeling?"

She didn't answer right away, trying to process what was going on, who these people were and what they were doing here.

"Ida?" the woman asked again.

She looked up at her sister who nodded, then back to the woman from the FBI. "I'm just a little tired... and I'm not Ida." She watched as the two agents looked at each other in surprise. "My sister and I had changed places before the kidnapping. This is Ida," she said, reaching over to take her sister's hand.

"Switched places?" the woman asked.

Ida jumped in. "We've been doing this since we were little girls. We should have said something earlier. I'm sorry."

The man with another FBI credential hanging around his neck made a step forward and placed his hands on the rail at the end of the bed. "Ladies, my name is Alex Frank. I've been working with the team to bring you home safely... Ophelia?"

"Yes, thank you," she answered back, tentatively.

The man continued. "I'm afraid we have some difficult news to share." He looked to her sister and mother and then back, pausing a moment before saying, "First, you need to know there has been an incident out at your father's house on Isle of Palms."

"An incident?" the girl's mother asked.

"Three people were found dead last night," Alex continued, "including your stepmother, Jillian."

238

Ophelia shook her head in disbelief. "She's dead?"

"Yes, I'm sorry," Alex said. "A man who worked for your father and another on the payroll for a man named Xander Lacroix were also found dead there."

"Who was that?" Ida asked, her voice weak and tentative.

"We believe your father's man was named Vincent," Sharron Fairfield said.

Ophelia exchanged a look with her sister. *Vincent!*

Ida turned to Agent Frank. "You said *first*. What else..."

Fairfield said, "We are sorry to tell you your father was found dead this morning at his house here in Charleston."

Ophelia closed her eyes as she heard Ida and her mother cry out.

Her mother's voice broke as she asked, "What in the world happened?"

Fairfield said, "It was a gunshot wound. It appears to be self-inflicted."

Ida sat down in the chair beside the bed, obviously stunned. "Appears to be?" she implored.

Fairfield said, "We're continuing to investigate the incident."

Ophelia watched both her sister and mother trying to deal with the devastating news, as her own emotions flared between shock and disbelief. She shook her head, "This isn't possible."

"I'm sorry," Agent Frank said.

Ophelia looked over at her mother whose face was now beginning to flush with tears. Ida had her head buried in her hands.

Frank continued, "Would you mind if we ask a few questions?"

Ophelia looked at her sister and then over to her mother who seemed in shock now, unable to respond.

Fairfield asked. "Are any of you aware your father owned a 44-caliber revolver?"

Ophelia looked at her mother again who was shaking her head *no*, trying to wipe at the tears streaming down her cheeks.

"He had a lot of guns in his collection," Ophelia said.

"Yes, we're aware of that," the man named Frank said. "We need to know about this specific weapon."

"I don't know," Ophelia replied. "He has so many."

Fairfield said, "We're sorry to burden you with this, I know..."

Ophelia heard her mother break in and looked over.

"Could I please have some time with my daughters."

"Yes, of course," Fairfield answered back. "We're so sorry for your loss. We will keep you informed of any developments in our investigation."

"Where is my father?" she heard Ida ask, looking up now.

Frank said, "He will be down at the morgue until the medical examiner's office completes its investigation. They will work with your family on the arrangements following that."

Silence hung in the air for a moment.

Her mother finally said, "Thank you for coming."

Ida felt the tears coming now with the devastating shock of her father's passing. *Self-inflicted? Why would he kill himself?*

She watched as the two FBI agents left the room, then stood to walk around the bed. Her mother was standing there in stunned silence and she took her in her arms and pulled her close. They stood there together, her mother shaking now and unsteady. She let her sink down into a chair then heard Ophelia blow her nose and looked over. The mirror-image of her own face stared back, awash with tears with a frightened and defeated look.

Ophelia whispered, "I can't believe any of this.... Daddy *and* Jillian?"

Both girls turned when their mother said, "Your father would never do this. He would never take his own life!"

Ida stared back at her mother, nodding in agreement, trying to make sense of the tragic news.

Chapter Seventy-three

Alex closed the door, placing the key in the ignition. He looked over at Fairfield. "They switched places. Are you kidding me?"

"I know," she said, shaking her head.

"Why are we just hearing about this now?"

"Exactly."

Alex started the car and pulled out of the parking space in the hospital lot. "And who knew about this?"

"Dellahousaye never said a word."

"Maybe he didn't know either," Alex said, trying to sort through all the confusing implications of this new revelation.

Fairfield's phone rang. "Yes." She listened for a few moments, then ended the call with "Okay, thank you." She turned to Alex. "The 44 was registered to Dellahousaye."

Hanna saw Christy Griffith come in the front door of the coffee shop down the street from her office. She came over and sat across from her at the table against a long red brick wall in the old historic building. Two cups of coffee sat between them and Christy reached out, her hand shaking. With both hands on the cup, she steadied herself and took a sip.

"Good morning," Hanna said. "Did you manage to get any sleep?"

Christy shook her head and took another slurp from the coffee, then placed the cup back down. Hanna could see the frightened look on her face.

"What's going on?" Hanna watched as she reached into a large leather bag on her lap and pulled out a thin silver electronic device and placed it on the table in front of her. Christy looked around the coffee shop, alert for threats or eavesdroppers.

"I found this in a locked file drawer in my father's office."

"What is it?"

Hanna leaned in to listen to Christy's hushed response.

"My father recorded a conversation with the men he made the loan agreement with. Xander Lacroix is on the recording."

"What!"

"There's no question." She paused, then continued, "The man makes it very clear what they'll do if he goes to the police."

Hanna looked back, stunned at the news, quickly thinking through how best to proceed. "We need to get this down to Beatty and the Feds."

"Do you want to hear this?" Christy asked.

"Not here." Hanna continued to think through their options. "Let me call Alex first." She reached in her bag for her phone and pulled up his number.

She heard him pick up the call and say, *"Hey, we're on our way back downtown. We just met with Dellahousaye's wife and the two daughters."*

Hanna put thoughts of the Dellahousaye twins aside. "I'm here with Christy Griffith. We're at the coffee shop down the street."

"What's going on?"

"She found a recording her father made."

"What kind of recording?"

"A conversation with Lacroix threatening him if he went to the police." There were a few moments of silence as she waited for Alex's response. She looked back over at her client who was waiting expectantly.

Alex continued. *"This is Beatty's case. He needs to hear this. Have you called him yet?"*

"No, I wanted your advice," Hanna said, a hint of irritation in her voice.

"My advice is to get down to the Charleston PD right now."

"Can they use this against Lacroix?" she asked. "It's an unauthorized recording."

"I'm not sure. We'll help you with this, but I'm not sure right now."

"Thank you."

"What's going on with Jonathan?" she heard him ask.

Hanna hesitated for a moment, not wanting to get into her son's problem in front of her client. "I'll tell you later."

"What's going on?" he demanded.

"I said, we'll talk later. Call me when you're free."

Hanna walked out of the coffee shop with Christy Griffith, the late morning sun blistering with little breeze to cut the heat. She wiped at her forehead that was immediately damp in the heavy humidity. The sidewalk was crowded with people rushing to their next obligation, hurrying to get back inside for relief from the heat. Traffic was building as the noon hour approached.

She had ordered an Uber car so they could get down to the police precinct quickly. Her phone showed the driver should be coming around the corner in just a few moments. Christy stood near the curb with her back to the traffic, holding her bag tightly under her arm with the damning recording safely secured.

"What do you think the police will do?" Christy asked.

"Alex wasn't sure exactly how they can use this evidence, yet." Hanna said. "Worst case, it should be enough to get Lacroix to back down, even if they can't use it as direct evidence."

Hanna watched as Christy looked down the street, clearly disappointed her discovery may not be enough to implicate the gangster in her father's death. She heard someone yell out behind her, *"Hey,"* then a scuffling sound. As she turned, a short man pushed through several people, one man lying on the ground behind him. He was running directly at them only a few feet away now. A gray hooded sweatshirt was pulled low over his face.

Instinctively, she reached out to shield Christy, but the man crashed between them, lowering his shoulder into Christy's midsection.

Hanna watched helplessly as the woman was hurtled backwards into the street. A horn blasted and tires screeched, and in a split second, she heard the sickening sound of Christy being hit by the front end of a big pickup truck. Hanna watched in horror as she flew through the air in front of the truck, limbs askew, others crying out in surprise and shock around them. Christy fell to the street and rolled several times before coming to rest, face down, not moving.

Hanna ran on instinct, yelling out, "Nooo!!!"

When she reached the lifeless body, she knelt down. The sound of cars screeching to a stop around her mixed with yells and screams from other people nearby. Hanna sensed a man kneel beside her as she gently rolled Christy over. Her face was masked in blood and a horrific wound across her forehead.

"Christy!"

The man next to her yelled out, "Oh God!"

Someone yelled, "Call 911!"

Christy Griffith never regained consciousness as the paramedics loaded the gurney into the back of the ambulance. Hanna kept close, trying to get some response from her friend and client, but the med techs kept pushing her back. The doors were closed, and the vehicle's siren blared as it pulled out into traffic and rushed away.

Hanna stood in the street, her pulse racing, her breath coming in ragged gasps. She looked around at the gathering of people, all with grave looks of concern on their face.

A policewoman came up. "Let's clear the street here," Hanna heard her say and started backing toward the sidewalk, numb and disoriented. She realized she had dropped her bag when she ran to help Christy. As she turned to look for it, a woman came up holding it out to her.

"Is this yours?" the woman asked.

"Thank you..." Hanna pulled it over her shoulder and then stepped up on the curb. Immediately, she thought of Christy Griffith's bag, the recorder inside. She looked around the street and sidewalk as the onlookers began moving away. *Where is it? Where is the man in the hooded sweatshirt?*

She couldn't remember if the paramedics had loaded the bag in the ambulance with Christy. She pushed through the departing crowd, looking everywhere. There was no sign of the man.

The bag was gone.

Chapter Seventy-four

Xander Lacroix sat beside his lawyer in the small interrogation room at the Charleston police precinct. He knew why he had been called back in, but the cops had yet to reveal anything. He had been waiting nearly thirty minutes when the door finally opened. Detective Ned Beatty walked in, followed by a man and a woman with FBI creds around their neck.

Lacroix watched as his attorney stood quickly, pushing his small metal chair back against the wall. "This is bordering on harassment!" the lawyer said, his face flushed with anger. Lacroix remained still, a calm look of defiance on his face, thinking, *these assholes have nothing!*

"Sit down, sir!" Beatty demanded.

"What is this all about?" the lawyer demanded, an immaculately dressed forty-something, all bluster and pretense.

"I said, sit down," Beatty repeated more calmly now. "We have a few more questions for Mr. Lacroix."

"We were here for hours last night and it was abundantly clear my client had nothing to do with the deaths at Mr. Dellahousaye's house."

"There have been some new developments," Beatty said. His words seemed to catch the lawyer off-guard. "Now, please sit down. These are my associates from the FBI, agents Sharron Fairfield and Alex Frank."

Lacroix knew of Frank from earlier encounters with Asa Dellahousaye, but he had never met the man. He also knew that Frank and the pissant local sheriff from Dugganville were the two who took Asa D off the board a year earlier in a bloody shoot-out. *I should thank the man for creating a new business opportunity*, he thought. *And he's dating the bitch lawyer who's been a pain in my ass!*

Beatty continued. "You may be aware, Mr. Lacroix, that your business associate, Remy Dellahousaye, was found shot to death in his home a few hours earlier today."

Lacroix stared straight back at the cop without reaction or change of expression.

"What are you implying?" the lawyer asked.

"I'm not implying anything. I'm asking your client if he was aware of Dellahousaye's death."

The lawyer started to respond, but Lacroix held up his hand. "No sir, I was not aware. I'm very sorry to hear that. I was close to Remy. As you know, I've worked for their family for many years. He's been through a lot lately. What happened?"

Agent Fairfield said, "We were hoping you could tell us."

Lacroix kept his temper in check, smiling back, then shaking his head. "And why would you think that, ma'am?"

Alex Frank leaned in. "It's common knowledge you and Remy were rivals in trying to secure control of the Asa Dellahousaye crime network. It is also known you were having a not-so-secret affair with his wife."

Lacroix locked eyes with Frank and didn't blink. He didn't respond.

After a few moments, Detective Beatty said, "Sir, we need to account for your whereabouts earlier this morning after you left the precinct."

"I went home and slept like a baby," Lacroix responded, again smiling back defiantly.

"And who can back up your presence there?" Beatty asked.

"I have a live-in housekeeper and cook. You can ask her yourself."

Lacroix watched as Frank leaned over and whispered something to the other two cops. As they looked back, he said, "How did Remy die? You said he was shot?"

Beatty looked back without answering at first, then said, "There is some indication the wound was self-inflicted."

"Then what in hell is my client doing here!" the lawyer said, indignantly.

Fairfield answered, "I assume then, your client will not object to us testing his hands for gunpowder residue?"

"Test away, ma'am," Lacroix said, thinking to himself, *Hell of a body for a Fed.*

Chapter Seventy-five

Ida Dellahousaye walked slowly with her sister, pushing a wheelchair as Ophelia was still struggling to overcome the pain in her leg from wounds she had yet to remember. They were walking along a paved path through the grounds in the back of the hospital. The midday sun was shielded some from the heavy cover of trees across the property, but the heat still simmered.

When Ida suggested a walk to get her sister out for some fresh air, their mother took the opportunity to go back to her hotel to rest for a while and get some fresh clothes. Despite her issues with their father and his new wife, she had seemed devastated by the news of their death. She had remained speechless through much of the morning, lost in her own thoughts about a relationship and family that were now a distant memory.

Ida continued to press Ophelia all morning for any details that may be coming back to her about her abduction, but still nothing.

The shock of their father's apparent suicide hung over them both like an unreal nightmare that would surely go away if they could just wake up.

Ida saw a small bench in the shade ahead and turned her sister in the chair to face her as she sat down. She saw some color had returned to Ophelia's face. The nurses had washed her hair and given her a dry bath. With no make-up though, her face still showed the trauma of her captivity with dark circles under her eyes and the cuts and bruises from her ordeal.

She placed her hand on O's knee beneath the hospital gown. Ophelia stared back with a sad, distant look, almost peering right through her.

"This makes no sense," she said, shaking O's knee gently to get her attention. When she looked back, in the moment now, Ida continued,

"There's no way he took his own life."

"But who...?" Ophelia didn't finish the thought.

"I don't know, but this is all just too much... your kidnapping, Jillian shot and killed... now Daddy."

She watched Ophelia's face as she processed all that she had just laid out. O finally said, "Do they think he was responsible for Jillian's death?"

Ida thought about it for a moment. There had certainly been some serious issues between her father and his second wife. Jillian's indiscretions were widely known. He was in the final stages of divorce proceedings, but killing her seemed a preposterous and completely unlikely notion. *But, if he was responsible, if he had somehow lost control of all reason... there was some logical explanation for a suicide.*

She looked up again into her sister's face and saw a strange expression of doubt and even fear.

Ophelia felt herself slipping away from the present, her sister sitting there on the bench in front of her, but not really there. Flashing images of faces and places kept coming back to her, but there was nothing she could connect to any recollection of the past few days.

The one nagging thought that had been able to break through as she recovered in the hospital came back to her again. Each time the memory surfaced, she had pushed it away, as if somehow reality could be relegated to some false narrative, too difficult to accept.

The girls' mother, Brenda, lay back in the tub, letting the hot water consume her. She let her face dip below the surface, the water still running and nearly splashing over the sides onto the tile floor in the hotel bathroom. She lay suspended beneath the water, eyes closed, a quiet hum ringing in her ears.

When her breath grew short, she rose slowly up and took a deep breath, wiping the water from her eyes and smoothing her hair back. As she thought about the body of her rival, Jillian, laying on the floor in a pool of blood in the palatial beach house, and her ex-husband with a bullet through his brain in his plush office on the Battery, a thin smile spread across her face.

Chapter Seventy-six

Alex drove and Sharron Fairfield sat in the passenger seat as they worked their way through heavy noon-time traffic to their offices downtown. Fairfield's phone buzzed.

"Will, we're on our way back. Let me put you on speaker so Alex can hear."

She pressed the button and they heard Foster say, *"Lacroix is clean... no residue from firing a handgun."*

Alex thought about it for a moment, then replied, "Not surprised. Hard to believe if this was a murder, Lacroix would do his own dirty work."

"Agree," Fairfield said.

"Lacroix left about ten minutes ago with his lawyer, who was threatening to sue everyone if we continued to harass his client," Foster said.

Fairfield held the phone closer to her mouth. "We met with the Dellahousaye twins and their mother to inform them of their father's passing and the mess out at the beach."

"How did that go?" Foster asked.

Alex slowed for a red light and turned toward the phone. "They're all very shook up as you can imagine."

"Strange thing, though," Fairfield began, "the twins switched places this past week. It wasn't Ida Dellahousaye we were looking for."

They heard Foster's surprised response, *"Switched!"*

Alex said, "Apparently it's a game they've been playing for years... assuming each other's identity."

"That's crazy!" Foster replied. *"And the real Ida was with us all the time we were looking for her sister and never said anything."*

"No one ever knew," Fairfield said, "even her parents."

"And now we have four dead bodies and nothing but more questions," Alex continued.

After he dropped Sharron Fairfield at the FBI offices, Alex drove to Hanna's office. His phone pinged and he looked to see a text from her.

I'm at the hospital downtown. There's been an accident. I'm with Christy now. Please come when you can. H.

There was a sick, empty feeling in his gut. He looked ahead and then in his mirrors. He made a sudden U-turn, heading back to the hospital.

Hanna was in the waiting room of the Emergency Room, her face in her hands. She didn't hear him come up until he sat beside her. Her face was flushed red and streaked with tears.

Alex put his arm around her shoulders and pulled her close, his face resting in her hair. "Tell me what happened?"

Hanna pulled back and sat up, gathering herself. "I told you we had the recording of Lacroix. We were meeting at the coffee shop down from my office to discuss it."

"You have a recording of Lacroix threatening Christy's father if he goes to the police?"

"We *had* a recording."

"What are you talking about?"

Hanna wiped at her face. "We were going to go down to the precinct to share the information with Beatty. We were standing on the corner waiting for a cab. A man ran up and pushed Christy. She fell into the street..." She paused for a moment and Alex saw the anguish on her face.

"What happened?"

"A truck... she was hit by a truck. I've never seen anything so awful. She just flew through the air."

"How is she?" Alex asked.

"They won't tell me anything."

"Someone bumped into her?"

"No, he pushed her! It was deliberate."

"You said you *had* Lacroix's threat recorded."

"It's gone... her bag is gone," Hanna said. "I looked everywhere."

Alex shook his head, scratching at his face trying to piece together all that was happening.

They looked up when a doctor in blue scrubs came through a door to their left. There were blood stains across his stomach and on his latex surgical gloves. He was pulling off the gloves as he walked up. Alex stood with Hanna, taking her arm.

The doctor whose name tag read, *DiMarco*, said, "I understand you're a friend of Miss Griffith."

Hanna nodded.

The doctor paused, then said, "I'm sorry, we weren't able to save her."

Alex reached around Hanna's back to hold her. She just stared back at the doctor, her eyes blinking slowly. He felt her take a deep breath and sink down into herself. He let her sit back down and did the same beside her.

The doctor said, "Again, I'm sorry. Can you help us contact her family?"

Hanna looked up, breathing heavily again. "Family?"

"Yes, ma'am."

Alex watched as she looked over at him, a helpless expression in her eyes. She turned back to the doctor. "No, her parents are gone. They're all gone now."

Hanna made her way unsteadily up the stairs to her apartment and unlocked the door. Alex followed her in, closing the door behind them. She saw her son sitting on a stool at the island in her kitchen, a glass of iced tea half gone in front of him.

"Mom... Alex!" Jonathan said, standing.

She walked over and hugged him.

Alex said, "How you doin'?" He came around and gave Jonathan a hug as well, then stepped back.

Hanna watched her son hesitate before responding, "Been better."

"Your mom told me about..."

CHAPTER SEVENTY-SIX

"About the drugs," Jonathan said, finishing his thought.

"I'm sorry," Hanna said, feeling guilty for revealing his problem without his permission. "I just thought... well, Alex has been through this before. He can help."

"I know, it's okay," Jonathan said. "I thought I could handle it, but the pain wouldn't go away and I needed more. Before I knew it, I was a damn junkie."

Hanna rushed to him. "No, don't say that."

"It's the truth."

She heard Alex respond behind her. "I *do* know what you're going through. I've been there... unfortunately, a few too many times. We'll get you some help."

She felt her son's chin on the top of her head as they embraced. A memory of him as just a small boy in her arms came back to her.

She heard Jonathan say, "Thank you... thank you. I'll do whatever it takes."

Chapter Seventy-seven

Ida left the cafeteria in the hospital with a cardboard tray filled with two steaming cups of coffee and two questionable blueberry muffins wrapped tightly in plastic wrap. Ophelia had turned her nose up at the food the hospital staff had brought in earlier. Ida had little hope this meal would pass inspection, but it was worth a try, she thought.

Her restless night sleeping in a chair beside her sister's bed had left her feeling dazed and exhausted. The last nurse she spoke with suggested Ophelia might be released later today. She was looking forward to a hot bath and a big hotel bed.

She came around a corner and bumped into a man coming the other way. She tried to catch one of the coffees knocked out of the tray but had to jump back as it fell to the floor and splashed all over her legs.

She looked up when she heard, "O!"

Jordan Hayes stood there, looking back in surprise.

Without thinking, Ida decided to continue the charade and not tell her boyfriend about their secret. She wasn't in the mood to try to explain.

"Jordan, what are you doing here?"

"I couldn't get through to Ida. I wanted to come down and see how she's doing."

Ida always traded cell phones with her sister when they switched, and she knew her phone had been found discarded in the dunes out at the beach.

"She's better," Ida replied, wishing he would just leave. Now was not the time for their inevitable break-up.

"I was headed down to her room," he said. "I heard she had some injuries."

"She'll be okay."

"I heard about your father on the radio coming down this morning," he said. "I'm so sorry."

Ida winced as she thought again about the shocking news she still couldn't get her head around. "Thank you."

A maintenance worker came up behind them and bent down to start cleaning up the spilled coffee. She handed Ida some paper towels to dry off her legs.

Ida thanked the woman and then said to Jordan, "Let me take you."

Ophelia had just dozed off again. The painkillers they'd been giving her made her extremely drowsy and she welcomed the chance to rest. She felt a hand on her arm and opened her eyes. The face of her identical twin looked down.

Her sister said, "*Ida*, you have some company."

As she stood aside, Jordan Hayes came into view. A glance back at Ida confirmed he was still unaware of the switch.

"Jordan!"

He came over and then leaned down to kiss her on the cheek. "Thank God you're safe," he said.

She watched as her sister walked around to the other side of the bed, the two exchanging knowing looks.

"I'll be fine," she said.

"What in the world happened?" he asked.

She paused a moment, trying again to bring together the random fragments of memory about her abduction. "I wish I knew."

"What?" he asked.

"I just can't remember much of anything before I regained consciousness here in the hospital."

The real *Ida* said, "The doctors say it's understandable for her to have blocked memories of such a traumatic event."

"What did they do to you?" Jordan asked, looking at the cuts and bruises on her face.

She shook her head. "I just don't remember."

"And the cops have no idea who did this?" he asked.

She hesitated, thinking again about the one memory that was continuing to come back to her. "No, my father paid the ransom. I don't know where the investigation stands."

"I just told O how sorry I am to hear about your father," Jordan said.

Ophelia didn't answer, the shock of her father's death still overwhelming.

"When are they going to release you?" she heard Jordan ask, still thinking about her father's suicide.

"Ida?" he asked again.

The real *Ida* said, "We may be able to get her out of here later this afternoon."

"Oh, that's great. Will you be coming straight back to school?"

Ophelia hadn't even thought about where she would be going... when they would put their latest switch behind them. "I don't know yet," she finally answered, looking over at her sister.

Ida just stared back.

Jordan Hayes unlocked the door to his car in the hospital parking lot. He left the room when Ida had started to doze off again with a promise to see her back at school. He had kissed her goodbye, then hugged Ophelia before leaving... *the crazy Ophelia.*

As he was walking down the hall to the elevator, his mind was sorting through all he had heard from the twins about the abduction. They seemed to know very little and he hadn't picked up any sense they knew anything about someone he spoke with prior to Ida's abduction. *Ida has lost all memory, even of the beach house and all their college friends there. Wasn't it just a matter of time, though, before she's able to start putting all the pieces together?*

His panic returned and despite his father's warnings, he was growing more concerned about the authorities discovering he had shared news of the beach vacation with an unknown caller that may likely have been involved with the kidnapping. The thought of being implicated in Ida's abduction continued to give him a sick feeling in his gut. His guilt continued to magnify and the sight of Ida in the hospital bed with all her injuries only made it worse.

As he started his car, he placed both hands on the steering wheel, closed his eyes and tried to push all the doubts and fear aside.

Chapter Seventy-eight

The man handed Xander Lacroix the thin recorder he'd taken off the Griffith woman. He was still seething mad the girl's father had recorded their earlier conversations. The tail he'd put on the girl overheard the conversation she had with her lawyer in the coffee shop.

When the call came in advising him of the situation, he hadn't hesitated. "Do whatever it takes to get the damn recorder back!"

The news of Christy Griffith's death was just coming across the local news on the television he was watching in his office. It was being described as an accident, a woman knocked off the curb by a passerby and then hit by a truck.

He looked back at the man in his office.

"Good work, Leo."

The man walked out and Lacroix picked up the phone on his desk and dialed his lawyer's number. As he waited to be connected, he thought again about Joey Grant and the hornet's nest he stirred up in Dugganville when he'd sent him up there to keep an eye on the girl and her lawyer. The man had totally botched the whole situation and had just been released on bail in Dugganville, facing assault charges. As far as he knew, the idiot hadn't implicated him in any of it, but the cops were certainly sniffing around in that direction. He made a mental note to deal with the situation as soon as he checked in with his lawyer.

After a few minutes with the front desk receptionist at the law firm, he was connected. Lacroix asked, "Are we done with these bastards downtown?"

His lawyer replied, "I've made it quite clear to them, any further harassment will lead to very expensive litigation."

Lacroix thought about the ongoing investigations into the three murders out on the island and then Remy D's apparent suicide. *They'll have no other reason now not to pin the shootings on Dellahousaye. He was overcome with his grief and anxiety after killing these three people and took his own life to escape the inevitable arrest and conviction for the murders.*

The shooter he'd contracted through a distant third party, had made tidy work of the hit. The fact that Remy knew the man from his father's past dealings must have been quite a surprise when he showed up at his door. Lacroix smiled at the thought.

The other loose end with the Griffith's restaurants seemed to be wrapped up now with the exception of Joey Grant, which he would deal with quickly. He had another investor ready to take him out of the rest of the damn mess.

With Remy out of the way now, he also had a clear route, particularly with the backing of New York, to take full control of almost all of Asa Dellahousaye's business. The thought of the power and wealth that lay ahead was exhilarating.

It may be time now to move back to New Orleans, he thought. *Let things settle here in South Carolina for a while.*

Asa D had moved much of their operation there a few years ago. He liked the climate and location better. *It's time to get back home,* he thought again.

When Alex got back to his office, he was not surprised to hear there were no further developments in the Dellahousaye twin's kidnapping, or on the body count that was now being investigated at the two homes of Remy Dellahousaye. He sat in Will Power's office, waiting for him to get off the call from Washington.

Sharron Fairfield walked in and sat at the other chair across from Powers.

"Just saw the police report on Hanna's client," Fairfield said softly, not wanting to interrupt her partner's phone call.

"She doesn't think it was an accident," Alex replied.

"The police have nothing more to go on... a kid runs through a crowd on the sidewalk, bumps a woman out into the path of a car."

"You're not buying that, right?" Alex asked.

"No, it's got Lacroix written all over it."

Powers ended his call and put the receiver back on the hook. "Nothing more from the forensics team yet at either Dellahousaye's beach house or from this morning in his den."

Alex said, "We can put Lacroix at the beach house at some point with prints from past visits, but nothing during the time of the shootings."

"Right," Powers said. "We'll probably find his DNA on Jillian Dellahousaye when the autopsy reports come back, but it's apparently no secret they were having an affair."

"And nothing more on the security system," Fairfield said, answering her own question.

Powers stood and turned to look out the window over the cityscape of Charleston. "No lead in tracking the Dellahousaye ransom money either," he said.

"I'm still trying to sort through the twins switching places," Alex said. "What the hell is that all about, and why didn't the real Ida D come forward when her sister was taken?"

"She did finally tell her parents," Fairfield answered.

Powers looked back. "We need to go see the twin again to see if any of her memory is coming back."

"They may release her from the hospital before we can get over there," Fairfield said. "I spoke with the hospital a few minutes ago."

Powers said, "Alex, Sharron and I will call and tell them we're coming over and to hold the Dellahousaye girl until we can speak with her again. Why don't you stay here and keep on top of the crime scene reports coming in?"

"No problem."

Back in his cubicle, Alex scrolled through messages on his phone. There was nothing that couldn't wait. He put thoughts of the Dellahousayes and Xander Lacroix aside for a moment to consider how best to help Hanna with her son.

He was heartbroken for her to have this to deal with now along with everything else she was dealing with. The death of her client, likely at the direction of Lacroix, made his temper flare again. *We need to take this bastard out!*

He was also deeply concerned for Jonathan. He knew personally how devastating a pain med addiction could be.

When he was with them at Hanna's apartment earlier, they had talked through the rehab process. They all agreed the first step was finding a doctor to quickly see Jonathan, assess his situation and recommend the best path going forward. He had given Hanna his doctor's contact information. The man had been very helpful for him over the past years with his own addictions.

He was also concerned there had been no further discussion of wedding plans, and certainly nothing more on her relocating to DC. Of course, they had both been overwhelmed with other issues and priorities these past few days, but he had a nagging doubt about Hanna ever giving up her life here in South Carolina, even for a short while until he could get reassigned.

He knew there was a real possibility his posting at the DC FBI offices would stretch much longer than he was being led to believe. He really had no control and no seniority to press his case as a new rookie with the Bureau. His greatest fear was Hanna staying here in Charleston and his assignment stretching into multiple years. *How likely was it she would wait for him?* he thought. *How would they keep their relationship together?*

Chapter Seventy-nine

Hanna left her son in the apartment and walked down the stairs to her office. Her legs felt heavy and stiff, and she held the handrail to steady herself. Seeing her son so helpless and afflicted now with an addiction that had raced out of control was devastating. The fact he had come to her for help was a promising sign, but she knew the road ahead would be difficult.

She walked into her office and sat heavily in the chair behind her desk. The first thing she saw was the file folder for Christy Griffith open in front of her, several pages of notes and documents spread out.

The scene on the street in front of the coffee shop played out again in her mind. The sound of the truck hitting the woman, glass breaking, and the image of her flying like a rag doll through the air were horrifying. She closed her eyes and buried her face in her hands to try to block out the images.

Alex had left with a promise to be back for dinner and to continue to help her with Jonathan. She knew she had to call the number for Alex's doctor to try to get her son in as quickly as possible. She pulled the note paper with the number from her pocket and placed it on her desk.

Alex had been there for her again, she thought. *Where would I be these past years without him?*

She had been so caught up in the crazy events of the past couple of days, she'd given little thought to their engagement, a wedding... a move to DC. When he proposed to her the other night at the party out on Pawleys Island, she had seen a light begin to shine at the end of a very long and dark tunnel that she had been struggling to pass through since the early times when her first marriage began to come apart at the seams. There had been so much stress and heartbreak in those years. More recently, her therapist had begun to help her deal with the anxiety and sleepless nights, but Alex was the one person she could count on through all of it.

Special Agent Alex Frank.

When he talked to her a year ago about leaving the Charleston Police Department and applying for a job with the Bureau, she understood his motivations to take his career in law enforcement to the next level. They both acknowledged at the time there could be complications in their personal relationship. She had been careful not to discourage his ambitions, though the thought of losing him weighed heavily on her.

They were at a turning point now she hoped they would never face. She had to decide what was most important in her own life... and in a new life with Alex.

She noticed the phone number for the doctor scrawled on the note in front of her. She reached for her phone and dialed the number.

Joey Grant waited for his car to be released at the salvage yard outside Dugganville. His lawyer had come up from Charleston and finally got him out on bail an hour ago. His head was still throbbing from the blows he'd taken the night before in the old shrimper's house. The lawyer woman had come out of nowhere and nearly taken his head off with a cast iron skillet.

His anger burned hot as he thought back on the events of the night. He was sure Lacroix would not be happy about any of this. He knew he would have to make this right if he wanted any chance to keep working for him.

Hanna stood from behind her desk to go back up to the apartment to check on her son. She had an appointment at the doctor for him scheduled for first thing in the morning. The office made a special effort to get him in right away.

As she approached the door to the hallway, a woman stepped into view. It was a face she thought she would never see again, or at least hoped she never would.

Grace Holloway had once been her closest friend. They met through their husbands who worked at the same law firm. Over the years, Grace had become almost like a sister to her, a welcome refuge after losing her brother years earlier in the plane crash.

Everything between them came suddenly to an end when Hanna discovered the woman had been having an affair with her husband, Ben, and had been part of the plot that led to his death.

Grace had been sentenced to ten years in prison and yet, here she was standing in front of her now just a few years after being sent away to the state penitentiary. Her face had aged noticeably. Her hair was longer, nearly to her shoulders and all gray now, no longer colored each month at an expensive salon. She was dressed simply in jeans and a white blouse, brown leather sandals on bare feet; a far different ensemble from her past days of high fashion.

Hanna didn't say anything, but just stood there as the memories and anger surged back.

"Hanna..."

Hanna just stared back.

"I'm sorry to surprise you like this..."

"Sorry?"

"Hanna, please..."

"You need to leave," she finally said, pushing past her.

Grace reached for her arm and stopped her. "I just need a moment."

Hanna turned and pulled her arm away. "There's nothing you can say, so let's not even start." Without waiting for a reply, she headed down the hall and up the stairs to her apartment.

There was no response from Grace Holloway.

Chapter Eighty

Ophelia dressed in clothes her sister brought from the apartment downtown. She lay back in the hospital bed with shorts on now to keep pressure off the painful wounds on her leg. She was waiting to be released and was looking forward to getting back to her own place to continue her recovery.

Her primary doctor came in, looking down at a patient chart in his hands. She and her sister shared the news of their identity switch and he now knew who he was really treating, though he had been clearly unhappy about their deception. He looked up. "Morning, Ophelia. You're looking better. Ready to head home?"

"Absolutely."

"Just want to take one more look." He turned a page over on her chart. "The FBI office called to ask that we keep you long enough for them to go through a few more questions they're following up on. They'll be down shortly."

She took a deep breath as she thought about another round of questioning with the much too serious FBI team. Her sister came in the door.

"Hey doctor," Ida said.

"Good morning," the man replied, looking up from his notes.

"Can we get O out of here today?" she asked, coming over and standing beside her sister.

"Yes, probably after lunch. As I was telling Ophelia, the FBI will be over soon to go through a few more questions."

Ida looked down at her sister who was shaking her head. "We need to help them find whoever did this to you, O."

"I know, but I just want to get out of here. No offense, Doctor."

"None taken." He placed the chart down and came around to look at the bandages on her leg. "I'm going to have the nurses dress this one more time. You have some serious lacerations that will take some time to heal properly. I want you to see your doctor every couple of days to have this checked and re-dressed. Some of the stitches can come out next week."

He began gently pulling back the tape holding the bandages that stretched from above her left knee down to her ankle.

Ophelia winced at the pain as she heard her sister ask, "Any idea what caused this?"

"If I didn't know better," the doctor said, "I'd say you got chewed on by a big shark. The cuts and lacerations are consistent with other shark attacks I've treated."

"Shark!" Ophelia cried out in surprise, looking up at her sister. As she started to ask, *how could a shark....?,* her mind began to focus on a sudden and frightening recollection of cold water, big waves washing over her, a large boat nearby... then, the dark shadow of the shark coming at her under the water.

She closed her eyes and the images came into sharp focus. She remembered the deadly encounter in full detail, the overwhelming fear, the searing pain when the shark pulled her under. "Oh, God..."

She felt Ida's hand on her shoulder. "I told Daddy I could sense you were being held somewhere out on the water," Ida said.

"I was trying to get away from the boat. They had me captive on a big boat. I was so sick, I had to get away. I think they were going to kill me!"

Special Agents Foster and Fairfield listened to Ophelia recount her story of her attempted escape from the fishing boat offshore from Charleston.

Foster said, "We got the tip from your father you may have been held out on the ocean. We found a stolen fishing boat abandoned, but with blood trace that has now been matched back to Ophelia."

"A stolen boat?" Ida asked. "I told my father about the boat. I know it's strange, but there are times the two us can feel each other's emotions, even sense what we're thinking."

Agent Fairfield replied, "We're still investigating the boat theft and other evidence we've found onboard. Nothing yet that would lead us to your kidnappers."

As Ophelia listened, it was all coming back to her now in frightening detail, beginning even with her abduction on the trail back from the beach. She remembered the long terrifying ride in the trunk of the car, her captivity in an old shack in the woods, the mask over the face of her captor, attempts to escape... *and then more... a phone call.*

"Ophelia?" It was her sister's voice.

She looked up at Ida. She stared back at the all too familiar face of her sister as the images and memories flooded back. *Oh god... what have I done?*

Jordan Hayes sat in the small reception area of the offices of the Federal Bureau of Investigation in Charleston. He reached to hold the cup of coffee he'd brought with him with both hands to control the shaking. He could feel his heart beating fast in his chest. He looked out the windows across the front of the room to try to calm himself.

A door opened to his right and the woman who had greeted him at the reception desk earlier, said, "Mr. Hayes, come with me please."

He stood to follow her through the door. As he walked along behind her, his conflicting thoughts and doubts about being here screamed in his head. He knew his father and grandfather would be furious. He also knew he could no longer live with the guilt of his possible role in Ida Dellahousaye's abduction.

Even more, he was haunted by the thought he would somehow be implicated for not coming forward earlier and even face arrest and jail time.

As the woman led him into a small conference room along the wall, he tried to convince himself again he was doing the right thing.

Alex was surprised when he got the call from up front that the grandson of former Senator Jordan Hayes had come to their offices to speak to the team investigating the Dellahousaye kidnapping. He knew Hayes was dating the abducted twin and was aware of all the information he had provided these past few days during the investigation. He was also aware of the firestorm of media frenzy the kid had endured as the press dubbed him *a person of interest* in the girl's disappearance. Alex had no idea where they'd come up with that, other than it made for good headlines and higher ratings.

When Alex had first seen the youngest Hayes being interviewed on camera, he had to laugh thinking about the father and grandfather's frantic reaction back in Washington as they continued to mount the campaign for the father to fill the vacated Senate seat in South Carolina. Knowing the former Senator Hayes' involvement with Asa Dellahousaye's attempts to expand his gambling empire in the state, it gave Alex some secret pleasure in the family's turmoil.

He walked into the conference room and saw the younger Hayes standing by the window on the far wall, looking out across the city.

"Mr. Hayes," Alex began, startling the man who turned now to face him. I'm Special Agent Alex Frank. I understand you have some additional information to share."

Hayes stared back for a moment, the nervousness and trepidation clear on his face. "Yes.... yessir."

"Please have a seat."

They both sat facing each other across the table. Alex watched as Hayes took a sip from his coffee cup, struggling not to spill as his hands were shaking noticeably.

"I'm very busy, Mr. Hayes," Alex said. "What can I help you with?"

Hayes began, tentatively. "You know of my relationship with Ida Della-housaye?"

"Yes, I'm very familiar with all of that," Alex replied. "You apparently have some more information to share?"

Hayes nodded, seemingly trying to shape his response. "There is something else..."

"Something you've kept from us?" Alex accused.

Hayes stuttered in trying to respond. "Something I feel now could be important."

"Now?"

"I'm sorry," Hayes said. "I've been thinking about everything that led up to Ida's abduction and something started to bother me. I should have come forward earlier."

"And what would that be?" Alex asked, trying to appear calm but his senses on full alert.

"I received a call about a week before we all left on spring break."

"A call from who?"

Hayes took another shaky sip from his coffee then placed the cup down in front of him. "A woman called to ask about our plans for the break."

"A woman?"

"Ida's stepmother."

"Jillian Dellahousaye?" Alex replied, squinting in surprise. "Why would she call you and not Ida?"

"I don't know, sir," Hayes said, his voice quivering. "I guess I thought she was just checking up on her."

Alex sat back, taking in what he was hearing. "Had Jillian called you before to *check up* on Ida?"

Hayes didn't hesitate this time. "No sir."

"What did she say, specifically."

"She said she was worried about us going to some crazy place for spring break. I think she mentioned Daytona or Panama City. I told her some of our friends from school were renting a house on the beach, far from all the normal college spring break mess."

"What else?" Alex asked.

"Well, she seemed pleased to hear that and then asked more about where the house was and who was going. I guess that was it."

Alex's mind was racing with the implications of this new revelation. "So, you told her right where you and Ida would be for your vacation?"

"Yes sir."

"And did you hear from her again?"

"No."

Alex continued, "You're aware Jillian Dellahousaye has been murdered?"

He watched as Hayes squirmed in his seat and took another drink from his coffee.

"Yes, I've seen the news. It's horrible... and now Ida's father..."

"An apparent suicide," Alex said, watching as Hayes nodded. "Is there anything else, Jordan?"

"No... no, I just felt someone should know about this. I can't imagine Ida's stepmother would have anything to do with her abduction, but..."

"Any other reason why you think she called you?" Alex asked again.

Hayes hesitated.

"This is the right time to tell us everything, Jordan."

"Please, I don't want this to get blown out of proportion, but..."

"But, what?" Alex said, leaning in.

"My father called and asked if I would speak with Jillian... as a favor."

"A favor?" Alex repeated.

"My family knows some of the Dellahousayes."

"Yes, I'm well aware."

"Again," Hayes continued, "this is all probably nothing. I guess Jillian didn't want her stepdaughter to know she was checking on her and didn't know who else to call."

Alex stood, a signal the meeting was over, and Hayes stood to face him. Alex reached across the table and the two men shook hands. "Thank you for coming in," Alex said.

Hayes replied, "I'm just happy Ida is back safe."

His response caught Alex off guard. "You don't know about Ophelia and Ida?"

A look of confusion came across Hayes' face. "What about them?"

Alex decided to let the twins fill the boyfriend in about their deception.

Alex escorted Hayes to the exit, then returned to his cubicle. As he sat at his desk, he kept thinking through what he had just learned. Why would Jillian Dellahousaye be calling the boyfriend and not just asking her stepdaughter, or even the sister, where she was going for spring break. He had no idea of the relationship Jillian had with the twins, but it certainly seemed odd. *And why was she going through Hayes' father in Washington? To get the kid's telephone number, obviously, but again, why not just call Ida and find out what her plans were?*

And now, Jillian Dellahousaye was dead and could never help answer these questions.

Alex rubbed his eyes, trying to sort through all the clutter in this case. He would need to fill his partners in before he called Washington and the office of Jordan Hayes, Jr., to get some answers.

Chapter Eighty-one

Ophelia lay back onto her hospital pillows propped up against the wall. She was feeling the exhaustion begin to overwhelm her again. She looked back at the faces of Agents Foster and Fairfield standing beside her bed. Her sister, Ida, was sitting against the far wall.

She had just shared all she could recall now of her abduction at the beach, her captivity in the remote shack and then out on the water, the veiled identity of her captors, her attempted escapes... the shark attack.

The two FBI agents had listened carefully, interrupting at times to ask clarifying questions. Recounting it all now out loud had drained her. The fear and, at times, numbing terror she'd experienced returned with clear focus.

There was one memory, though, she did not share. The thought of it again triggered a sick feeling in her gut. She looked down the bed at her sister. *What was I thinking?*

Sharron Fairfield excused herself when her cell phone buzzed. They were just finishing listening to the now remembered account of the Dellahousaye twin's abduction. As she walked out into the hall of the hospital wing, she kept thinking about all she had just heard. She could see it was Alex Frank calling.

"Alex."

She listened as Alex shared the details of his just completed interview with the twin's boyfriend, Jordan Hayes, and the strange call from the girl's stepmother. "Jillian?" she said in surprise when he had finished. "What do you make of that?" she asked.

Alex said, *"I'm trying to sort that out myself."*

"We just finished a very interesting session with Ophelia." She shared all they had just heard as the twin's memory was now clearing about her difficult ordeal.

When Fairfield had finished, she heard Alex ask, *"But no real clue on who was involved?"*

"No, she said her captors always wore Halloween masks, though she did say one of them had a familiar voice or accent... Cajun, she said."

"Cajun!" Alex replied. *"New Orleans... Lacroix?"*

"Exactly," Fairfield said. "We definitely need to have another discussion with Mr. Lacroix. I wonder if he has any knowledge or involvement with his girlfriend Jillian Dellahousaye's call to Jordan Hayes?"

Ophelia rode in the passenger seat beside her sister as they drove back to her apartment downtown. She looked out the window at the scenes of Charleston passing by, the old historic homes, the shaded streets, the people on their way to the next events in their *normal* lives.

Now that many of the details of her abduction were back clear in her memory, she tried to press down the chilling fact she had yet to share with anyone, even her sister.

Her thoughts were interrupted by Ida's voice. "I still can't imagine what you've been through. How did you ever...?"

Ophelia traded a glance with her sister before Ida looked back at the road ahead. She didn't answer the question hanging in the air. *How did I ever?*

The twin's mother, Brenda, had taken the call from Ida who shared all her twin was now remembering about the kidnapping.

As she sat on the couch in her hotel room, looking out at the bright blue sky of another beautiful Carolina day, she was thinking now about the horrifying ordeal her daughter had endured.

There was some solace in Ophelia's safe return and prognosis for a full recovery, but the twin's revelation in their near lifelong charade of switching identities continued to gnaw at her. *What else are they keeping from us?* she thought.

She had a flight booked back to Atlanta this evening after dinner. It was time to get back, she mused, putting her questions about the twins aside. *Back to what? A husband who could care less if I returned... a life full of pretentious friends and acquaintances who will dump me in a minute when my wealthy and socially prominent spouse finally pulls the trigger on our divorce.*

And where will I go next? she thought. *Remy is gone, my daughters have been deceiving me most of their lives. Maybe that's partly why I've never embraced them as I should have after the adoption. God knows!*

Ida cringed when the *love couple* met them at the door of Ophelia's apartment. It was mid-afternoon and they were both already stoned and barely coherent. The two of them had come down to the hospital yesterday for a short visit. Neither she, nor her sister had yet to reveal *the switch*.

Josh leaned in and hugged her sister. His eyelids were nearly closed from the weed. "Ida, we're so happy you're back. O has just been a mess since you went missing."

Ida thought guiltily about her trysts with the couple while her sister was away, held captive. She was haunted now by thoughts of the affair both twins had pursued with her father's man, Vincent, now laying in a morgue somewhere.

Susanna hugged both her sister and Josh together, her own lids also at half-mast. "We've been so worried," she said.

All Ida could think is how little it had slowed their partying and sex escapades.

Ida watched as Ophelia pushed through and sagged down into the couch, her bare legs now revealing the heavy bandages.

Josh was the first to notice. "Ida, what the hell?"

"Honey, what happened?" Susanna said in alarm, rushing over to the couch.

Ida, thought, *Enough already.* "Josh, Susanna, you both need to sit down. O and I have a few things we need to share with you."

She looked back at her sister who offered a slim smile, shaking her head.

Josh and Susanna had, of course, been stunned by the news of *the switch.* Ophelia tried to explain the deception though she feared they were both so high, they were not really comprehending what she'd just shared.

Ophelia watched as Josh looked over at Ida. "So, it's been you with us these past few days? Far out!"

Susanna just looked on with a dull, pot-induced stare.

Josh stood and walked over to Ida, suddenly plopping down in her lap. "You're a wild child, just like your sister," he said, trying to nuzzle her neck.

Ida pushed him away and he fell down onto the floor. He looked back up at her in surprise. "I always thought it would be awesome to do both of you with me and Susanna."

"In your dreams," Ida answered back and then stood and walked to the door. "I'll leave the three of you to get *reacquainted.*"

Ophelia tried to get up, but her bad leg wouldn't respond. "You don't need to go."

"I'll call you later," Ida replied, then slipped out the door.

Josh got up and came over to sit on the other side of her. He and Susanna both laid their heads on her shoulders. Josh rubbed her thigh above the dressings for her wounds. "Welcome back, baby."

She pushed his hand away, tired and disgusted now with the whole arrangement. As she finally managed to get to her feet, she said. "I think it's time for a break."

"A break?" Susanna replied.

Ophelia came to a sudden decision. "I think it's time the two of you made other plans." All she could think about now is time alone to think through all that had happened... *how she would ever tell Ida and the others what really happened.*

Chapter Eighty-two

Hanna sat across the table from her son, Jonathan, in a long and narrow restaurant two blocks from her office. They had just ordered some lunch, and both sipped from the chilled glasses of iced tea and lemonade on the table in front of them. Jonathan had been encouraged they would be able to get in to see a doctor so quickly in the morning.

Now that she knew about his addiction, she noticed the subtle changes in his demeanor, his reaction to things. His usually bright attitude and presence were clearly dulled by the drugs. Her heart sank as she thought about what he had been through and what might lie ahead.

Then, her thoughts returned to the surprise visit of her former friend, Grace. The shock of it lingered and she was trying to figure out how she received such an early release from prison. She hadn't been following the woman's case since she was sent away, but apparently appeals or parole hearings must have been underway for some time. She wondered if Grace's husband, Phillip, was somehow involved. She couldn't imagine the two of them getting back together after all Grace had been involved in, but who could possibly understand Phillip Holloway and where his twisted brain may lie.

She was so shocked at Grace's sudden appearance, her only reaction had been to throw her out, to get away from her and hopefully never see her again, for good this time. *The nerve of the woman to think she could just apologize*, Hanna thought.

She tried not to let her thoughts drift back to the many years, the good years she had with her former friend. They shared everything together, were nearly inseparable, until it all had come out. She remembered the night Grace was led away to the police cruiser parked in front of her old house on the Battery, the shock she still felt in discovering the woman's treachery.

Her thoughts were interrupted when Jonathan asked, "Mom, you okay?"

"Sorry, just thinking about something else."

Alex waited outside the home of Xander Lacroix for his partners to arrive. He watched as their sedan pulled to the curb and Foster and Fairfield got out to join him.

Fairfield said, "Well, let's see if the man is home or not. I'm sure he'll be surprised to see us again."

They walked through the gate and up the walk to the front porch. Will Foster rang the doorbell. In a few moments, the door opened, and a large man stood in the doorway. Foster held up his credentials.

"I know who you are," the man replied, though Alex didn't recall seeing him before.

"We need a few minutes with Mr. Lacroix," Foster said. "Is he home?"

The man nodded, then said, "Wait here." He closed the door, leaving them on the porch.

Alex turned and looked down the heavily shaded street in both directions, fine homes nestled into the trees, exotic cars parked along the curbs and up in the driveways. He had been thinking through all they knew about Lacroix, his business dealings with Remy Dellahousaye, the deceased father of Christy Griffith who had now met a similar fate, his affair with Jillian Dellahousaye. *And what does he know about Jillian's interest in her stepdaughter's spring break leading up to her kidnapping?*

He heard the door opening and turned back. The looming man was there again.

"Mr. Lacroix is busy. He says to call his lawyer."

Alex looked at the faces of his partners as they exchanged glances. Foster said, "Mr. Lacroix can meet with us now or we'll come back with a warrant."

"I said he was busy," the man answered with a slow and firm cadence and then slammed the door closed.

When Hanna got back to her office, Jonathan went up to the apartment to call his girlfriend, Elizabeth. She sat at her desk and immediately saw a small envelope with her first name written in the familiar handwriting of Grace Holloway. Her first instinct was to throw it in the trash without even opening the envelope, even run it through her shredder without reading it. Her curiosity got the best of her.

Hanna thumbed open the note and unfolded a single page of stationery with a message on just the front. She took a deep breath and began to read.

Hanna,

There are no words to express my remorse for all that's happened, so I won't even try. I've had a lot of time, as you can imagine, to think about all of this. I wake every day with a guilt so overwhelming, I can barely manage. I think back on how badly I've betrayed you, how devastating it's been for you with the loss of Ben and all that happened. Even though I've been released, I will never be free of the guilt and shame.

I will not ask for your forgiveness and by no means do I deserve it. I only want you to know that I wish only the best for you and Jonathan. I understand you're engaged now and I'm so thrilled for you and Alex.

I'm not sure where I'll settle yet, but I know it won't be back here in Charleston. I will need to get away for a fresh start, somewhere, to try to make something positive happen in my life.

All the best,

Grace

Hanna looked up and closed her eyes, trying to press back memories of dark times, terrible tragedy, stunning betrayals.

She read the note again, then folded the paper and ran it through the shredder on the floor beneath her desk.

Alex left Foster and Fairfield to drive his own car by Hanna's office before he would rejoin them at the FBI offices. They agreed they would need a subpoena to get Lacroix back down for further questioning. Fairfield was already on the phone to a judge's office as she got in the car to leave.

He pressed the number for Hanna's cell as he waited for a light to change. He heard her voice come on the line.

"You'll never believe who just came by to see me?"

He tried to focus on her question, thoughts of Xander Lacroix and Jillian Dellahousaye still troubling him. "Tell me."

"My old friend, Grace."

"You can't be serious? How in hell did she get out of prison?"

"I don't know. It was a very brief discussion."

"I can imagine. What did she want?" Alex asked.

"I didn't give her the chance."

He braked again as traffic slowed for another light.

"But she left a note... some nonsense about remorse."

"The woman has some nerve," Alex said. "She can rot in hell with your other so-called *friend*, that realtor out on Pawley's Island."

"Don't remind me," he heard Hanna reply.

"I have a few minutes," Alex said. "Thought I'd stop by and see how you and Jonathan are doing."

"We got in to see your doctor first thing in the morning."

"Good, good."

"Jonathan is really encouraged to get started on his recovery. Thank you for your help with this."

"We'll be there for him. It's going to take some time."

"I have a client meeting in a few minutes I really need to take. It's across town. I need to get going."

"Okay, dinner then," Alex said. "I'll call you as soon as I can get away tonight. We've got another angle to track down on the Dellahousaye kidnapping. I'll tell you about it tonight."

Hanna placed a couple of file folders in her bag and found her car keys in the clutter on her desk. She called Molly up front to tell her she was leaving for her appointment. Walking out the back door of the old house, she clicked the key fob to unlock the door of her Honda. She heard the familiar beep and click as the door unlocked. She came around the side of the car, opened the door and threw her bag on the seat beside her.

As she turned back to put the key in the ignition, the passenger-side door opened, catching her by surprise. Before she could react, the huge bulk of the man from the night before in Dugganville fell down into the seat beside her. She cried out instinctively, and then fell back against her seat as a black handgun was suddenly inches from her face.

"Not a word, Counselor," the man hissed. "Give me your cell phone."

Hanna reached slowly into her bag and then handed him the phone. She watched as he rolled the window down and threw it into the bushes nearby.

Alex's phone buzzed on the console of his car. He saw the call screen ID for Hanna's assistant, Molly.

"Molly, what's up?"

Instantly, from the panic in her voice, he could tell there was something terribly wrong.

"*Alex! They've taken Hanna!*"

"What!" He pulled over into a parking space and stopped the car.

"*She was going to an appointment, and I had something she needed to take with her. When I came out the back door, I saw her leaving. A man was in the front seat with a gun to her head! Alex!*"

He felt his breath catch in his chest. His mind was racing, trying to think what needed to happen. "Did you call 911?" he asked in desperation.

"*No, I'm sorry... I thought I should call you first.*"

"It's okay." Alex felt helpless, uncertain what to do. "Any idea who it was?" he asked.

"*No, I don't know. Oh Alex...*"

"Let me call this in," he said, "get a bulletin out for her car." He didn't wait for her to respond, ending the call and then pressing 911.

The dispatcher, who he knew from his time with the Department, assured him she would get the All-Points Bulletin out immediately for Hanna's car and keep him posted as well.

His next call was to Sheriff Pepper Stokes in Dugganville. His heart sank when the old sheriff confirmed the mob goon had been released on bail earlier in the day.

"I should have called to alert you, Alex, sorry. We had a terrible car wreck with fatalities up here and I've been out most of the day."

"It's okay, Pepper."

He called his office. Sharron Fairfield was back in the FBI offices working on the court order to get Lacroix back downtown for more questioning.

"They've taken Hanna!"

"They what?" Fairfield said in shock. *"Who?"*

"Joey Grant, the man who went after Hanna and my father last night up in Dugganville... he was released earlier today."

"Lacroix's man?" he heard Will Foster ask over the speakerphone downtown.

"He must have come back to get Hanna. Who else could it be?"

"What can we do?" Foster asked.

"Charleston PD has an APB out for her car." He paused, his thoughts racing. "I'm going back to Lacroix's!"

He ended the call as both Foster and Fairfield started to protest.

Hanna gripped the steering wheel firmly with both hands. She could feel the muzzle of the gun in her side as she drove. The man had been giving her directions as they made their way through town. Otherwise, he hadn't said a word.

She had no idea where he was taking her or what he had in mind when they got there, but the panic and dread she'd been fighting much of the past two years was back in full force now. *No one knows where I am. No one will even be looking for me!*

Alex had been only a short distance away from Xander Lacroix's house when he decided to go back. He raced down streets, honking for cars to get out of the way when traffic slowed. His heart was racing, thoughts of Hanna at the mercy of these scumbags again infuriating and terrifying at the same time.

His tires screeched when he braked to pull into the drive at Lacroix's house. He was out of the car and running before he even turned the car off. Not wanting to screw with the guy at the front door again, he ran around the side of the house along the drive. He saw Lacroix's big car parked in the back. There was a small porch to a back door. He ran up and began pounding on the glass, trying the lock, but it was secure.

"Lacroix, open the door!"

He took his gun out of the holster on his belt to smash the window. He saw Lacroix's man coming down the hall to the door, waving his hands frantically.

Through the door, Alex heard the man's muted protest. "We told you to call Mr. Lacroix's lawyer! You need to leave now!"

Alex raised his gun and pointed it at the man's chest through the upper glass of the door. "Open the damn door, now!"

Then he saw the shadowed form of Xander Lacroix coming down the same hall. As he got closer, Alex could see the furious look on his face.

"Lacroix, open this door, now!" he yelled.

Lacroix pushed his man out of the way, unlocked the door and pulled it open. "Have you lost your mind?"

Alex shoved his gun back in the holster and rushed at Lacroix, grabbing him with both hands by the shirt and pushing him back into the house. The other man grabbed him around the throat with his forearm and tried to pull him away. The three of them crashed into the far wall and Lacroix went down in a heap. Alex fell on him and went for his throat this time while the bodyguard continued to try to pull him off.

Lacroix's face was flushed red with anger. "Are you crazy...?"

"Where is she?" Alex demanded.

"What in hell... are you talking about?" Lacroix managed as the struggle continued.

Alex pulled back his right hand and was about to smash Lacroix in the face when a crushing blow across the back of his head paralyzed him. The intense pain faded quickly as he lost control of all muscle reflex. His last conscious thought as he turned enough to see the lead-filled blackjack in the hand of his attacker was, *Hanna!*

Chapter Eighty-three

Ida knew her sister had pulled herself back to the present reality of who she was, where she was and what had happened and yet, she was still acting strangely, distant and confused.

Josh and Susanna packed the few belongings they had and left a few minutes ago. *Good riddance!* Ida thought.

Ophelia came out of the kitchen, limping noticeably on her bad leg. She had a bottle of wine and two glasses in her hands.

"You need to take it easy with all the meds you're on," Ida warned.

"Just need to take the edge off, sister." She set the glasses on the coffee table in front of the couch and poured two full glasses. Without offering one to Ida, she took a long drink, swallowing more than half the glass as she sat back on the couch.

"O, take it easy!"

Ida went over and sat beside her sister, putting her arm around her back. "It's okay. You're home and safe."

Ophelia put the wine glass down and fell back into the cushions of the couch, breathing heavily.

"O, really, it's okay," Ida pleaded. She watched as her sister shook her head, her eyes pressed shut.

"O?"

Jordan Hayes knew this wouldn't go well. He listened as the phone continued to ring. He was driving back to Clemson after visiting the Dellahousaye twins, then the FBI. Finally, he heard his father's voice come on the line.

"What is it, Jordan? I'm right in the middle of something."

He hesitated, then gave his father the full account of his trip to the FBI office in Charleston.

"You did what?" he heard screamed back at him as he held the phone away from his ear. *"Have you lost your mind?"*

Jordan gathered his courage as best he could. "I don't know what Jillian had to do with Ida's kidnapping, but I want no part in this and I'm not going to prison for some damn favor you needed to honor!"

"Jordan, that's enough!"

Half the bottle of wine was gone, and Ida hadn't touched her glass. Ophelia had been pacing and mumbling something unintelligible, continuing to fill her own glass. Ida had not been able to get her to calm down. She moved over to get in her sister's path and grabbed her by both arms. "O, please! Let's sit down and talk about this."

Ophelia stared back, shaking her head, tears forming in her eyes. Ida felt her grow limp in her grasp and she led her over to sit down again.

"I didn't know where else to go... what I could do," Ophelia whimpered, the tears flowing down her cheeks now.

Ida took her sister's face in her hands to get her to focus. "Tell me what's wrong."

Ophelia sighed, a deep moan coming now as she pulled away and fell back into the cushions looking up to the ceiling. "I didn't think anyone would get hurt."

"Who? What are you talking about?"

"Jillian and Daddy are dead, and Ida is hurt so badly."

Ida shook her head in confusion. "I'm not hurt, I'm right here." She watched as Ophelia looked back at her. "I'm right here, O. I'm fine." A strange expression, a mix of fear and bewilderment came across her sister's face.

"I'm so sorry," Ophelia said. "I had nowhere else to turn... no other choice."

Ida leaned in close to her sister's face. "Calm down and tell me what this is all about."

Ophelia seemed to calm some as their eyes locked. She started rocking back and forward, slowly. Her eyes closed and she took a deep breath. Ida could feel the fear and anxiety that was gripping her sister.

When she looked back, Ida saw a bit of clarity returning.

Ophelia reached over and took Ida's hands in hers. "It was Jillian's idea."

"Jillian?"

"We met for dinner. We got together a lot because we were both here in Charleston." She wiped at her eyes. "We were drinking, and we stayed late, drinking some more. Jillian was going to get cut-off, too."

"Cut-off?" Ida said, trying to sort through the ramblings.

"Daddy was through with both of us," Ophelia said, sniffing. He was going to divorce Jillian and he'd told me he'd had enough."

"Enough of what?" Ida asked.

"Of me, my life, Josh and Susanna..."

Ida said, "I'm sorry, but I'm not following."

Ophelia took a deep breath and looked straight into Ida's eyes. "It was Jillian's idea... to stage the kidnapping."

"What!" Ida gasped.

"She wanted me to help and we would split the money, get a new start."

Ida leaned back, incredulous. "You did what?"

"It couldn't be me. Daddy would never pay to get me back. Jillian had it all worked out."

"Sister...?"

"As the time got closer," Ophelia continued, "I couldn't let you go through that. I called to switch for your spring break... and then, I just got lost in the whole thing, like I always do."

Ida still couldn't believe what she was hearing. "Who actually abducted you? Who was holding you?"

"Our friend, Vincent, Daddy's guy... we brought him in for a share of the money. He knew some people he paid to do it."

"Vincent is also dead, O!" Ida said.

"I know, I know! Ophelia wailed. "I don't know what happened."

CHAPTER EIGHTY-THREE

"If Vincent arranged all this, why did they treat you so poorly?"

Ophelia struggled with the question for a moment, then said, "If I hadn't kept trying to escape... I was you, Ida. I didn't know. I didn't remember. I thought it was real and they were going to kill me!"

"Oh, honey!" Ida groaned, leaning over to hug her sister.

Chapter Eighty-four

Hanna pulled into the drive of a big house along a shaded street a couple blocks back from her old house on the Battery.

"Around back," her captor said in a low, determined voice.

She drove slowly up the packed gravel drive and around into a large parking area in front of a garage with three doors, two other cars parked outside. Her heart leapt and then the panic returned when she recognized the FBI car Alex had been driving.

"Over there," the man said, pointing to a spot to the side of the garage.

She put the car in *Park* and looked over at the face of the man she had sent to the hospital the previous night, hoping to never see him again.

"We're going to make this right, Counselor," she heard him say.

She was determined not to show her fear. She wouldn't let this maniac get any satisfaction in the terror that was gripping her. *Where are you, Alex?*

Alex shook his head, raised himself up on all fours and tried to collect his jumbled thoughts. He looked down at a polished wood floor. A drop of blood fell from the side of his head and made a tiny splash beneath him. The pain in the back of his head was excruciating to the point he felt like he might pass out again. Behind him, he heard voices as he lost his balance and fell back to the floor, his face landing in the blood. He couldn't lift himself and felt his body fail to respond to any attempts to get back up.

Hanna walked down the hall in front of the man who still held a gun to the back of her head. The thought of the gun exploding into her brain was terrifying and she could barely put one foot in front of the other.

Ahead, she saw the face of Xander Lacroix step out from a doorway, a crazy and maniacal look on his face.

"What the hell are you thinking?" he yelled out.

Hanna winced as he raced toward her, then past. She turned and watched him push her captor hard up against the wall, slapping him twice, then grabbing his gun away.

"Boss, I knew you'd want to make this right."

"You are a complete idiot!" Lacroix yelled, inches from his face.

Lacroix turned back to her. His expression was still unhinged. He came to her and grabbed her arm, pulling her behind him through the door. As they came into what appeared to be a plush office, she gasped when she saw Alex laying on the floor, his face sideways in a pool of blood. "Alex!" she screamed.

She was pushed hard from behind and fell to the floor beside him. She inched her face close to his and saw his eyes open, dazed and uncomprehending. "Alex, I'm here. Please get up!"

He struggled to lift his head, then sunk down almost lifeless. She turned back and saw Lacroix standing next to the man who took her and another who stood behind them. Lacroix had the gun now, pointed at the floor. He looked down at her with more hate in his eyes than she had ever seen in a living soul.

Lacroix closed the distance between them and knelt beside her. He pulled the gun up and held it to the side of Alex's head.

Hanna felt the full panic of their situation and lunged at him. "Nooo!"

Lacroix swept a powerful arm up and threw her back down on the floor. He stood, towering over them. Seeming to gather himself, he said, "I want them both gone... now! Get them out of here and I swear to god, nowhere they'll ever be found."

Hanna felt herself grabbed under her arms and roughly pulled to her feet. Alex still lay prone on the floor beside her. She swung her elbow hard and caught the man lifting her squarely in the jaw. He fell back, yelling in pain and anger. She turned and dove on him, scratching at his face and falling on top of him. Other hands pulled at her as she lashed out in fury. Then, her arms were pinned behind her and she was pulled away. She sank to her knees in exhaustion and defeat.

Her ears were ringing, and she was overcome from her struggle to save Alex, but she heard Xander Lacroix say, "Get them out of here, now!"

Hanna watched as Alex was pulled to a sitting position against the wall of Lacroix's den. His face was a mask of blood and his expression was still dazed. Her hands had been bound by plastic zip ties behind her back that cut into her wrists as she struggled to stand and go to Alex.

Lacroix had left the room a few minutes ago and his two men had been working feverishly to get both her and Alex ready to leave the house.

The man who had taken her, the man Lacroix had called *Joey*, stood in front of her, his face leaning down just inches from hers. Softly, but with great menace, he said, "You and I are going to have some fun before I feed you to the gators." His breath was foul, and he smelled of sweat and... hate. As he reached to pull her toward the door, she kicked out with all her strength and caught him square on the knee cap. His eyes opened wide in surprise and pain. She knew he would be back on her in an instant, her hands bound, her fate clearly at his mercy, but she didn't care at this point.

The other man came over and slapped her hard across the side of her face. She fell to the ground, Alex beside her again, his eyes trying to gain purchase. With all her will, she struggled to her knees, trying to find the strength to go at them again.

She heard shouting and people running around her... more shouting and then a gunshot rang out. She flinched and fell prone, her face against the floor, her arms pinned behind her. Three more gunshots exploded nearby, and she closed her eyes, expecting the next to blow the side of her head away.

And then there was a calm silence for just a moment, the smell of cordite from the gunfire heavy in the air. Hanna lay there, totally exhausted and defeated, waiting for the final moment of her life.

She felt a soft hand on the side of her face. She flinched at first and then looked up.

Instead of the fury of Xander Lacroix or his man, Joey, she saw the totally unexpected and so welcoming face of Sharron Fairfield.

"It's okay, Hanna," Fairfield said, leaning close to her face. "Everything's okay."

Hanna slumped to the floor, all her emotions flowing now in a jumble of fear and relief. She looked over and saw Will Foster kneeling beside the still lifeless body of Alex. *Oh God, please, no!*

Chapter Eighty-five

Skipper Frank came up unexpectantly behind Hanna and kissed her on the cheek. She turned and smiled back at the big lumbering shrimper.

"Thanks for having us over for this shindig," he said, his eyes glazed already from a few too many shots of Kentucky bourbon and beer chasers. His wife, Ella, stood by his side, shaking her head in mock disgust at her husband, her eyes and flushed face betraying her own early intoxication.

"In all my years," Skipper continued, "ain't never been over to the big city of Atlanta. Too many Yuppies and BMW's for my liking."

Hanna turned and kissed him back on the cheek. "I'm glad you both could come." She hugged Ella.

The woman stepped back and said, "You doin' okay, honey?"

Hanna looked over and wanted to answer, but all the fears and doubts she'd been struggling with came rushing back.

Ella Moore Frank pulled her close in a powerful embrace. The heavy scent of the woman's perfume and the smell of the whiskey were nearly overpowering.

She let herself fall into the woman's arms, a safe refuge.

Skipper Frank said, "Your old man must have run quite a place to get a turnout like this."

She looked over at him and smiled as they all stood together in an elegant and expansive ballroom on the top floor of one of Atlanta's most prominent hotels. Two walls of the room were all windows looking out over the spectacular skyline of the city, the sun now low to the west. Long bars with servers were set-up in all four corners. The reception had only started thirty minutes earlier and the room was already near capacity with invited colleagues, clients, government officials, friends and family.

Allen Moss was finally retiring, and Hanna was here, with mixed feelings, to commemorate the occasion.

Hanna felt a hand on her shoulder and turned to see her father's second wife, Martha, standing behind her, dressed elegantly in a sparkling green dress, her hair adorned beautifully in flowing swirls on top of her still youthful face.

"Hanna, you look lovely tonight," Martha said, leaning in to give her an *air kiss* on the cheek.

"Martha," Hanna replied, trying her best to muster some goodwill for the woman. "Congratulations, you were finally able to get the old fool to call it a day."

"Oh, it wasn't me, dear. His cardiologist finally talked some sense into him."

Hanna knew this to be true and was so thankful her father was finally agreeing to step aside and live out the rest of whatever was left of his tentative hold on life to something other than the seemingly trivial travails of his many wealthy clients.

"Well, anyway," Hanna said. "I'm happy for both of you. Allen tells me you plan to travel."

"We leave for Greece tomorrow," Martha said, an excited light in her eyes.

"I've heard it's lovely," Hanna responded, her thoughts drifting to the fact she'd rarely made time in her past for travel.

A raucous round of applause broke her musings and she turned to see her father walking up to an elevated platform and small podium with a microphone at the front of the room.

Well into his seventies, the man still looked vital and strong, despite numerous trips to the cardiac ICU and repeated threats to his life on this planet, including a self-piloted plane crash that he and Hanna had both survived.

"Thank you! Thank you!" Moss yelled out to the crowd, holding his crystal glass of whiskey on ice up to silence everyone.

As the crowd turned their attention to him and the conversations stopped to listen to the retiring Managing Partner of the revered Atlanta law firm of Moss Kramer, Hanna's father stood silent for a moment, looking out over the assembled guests. He was dressed beautifully in an amazing coordinated and colorful ensemble of sport coat, shirt and tie. Hanna was sure Martha had been involved in the wardrobe decisions. His face seemed confident and strong, all challenges of heart and mind behind him now.

"I'll keep this brief," he finally began. "I've been around here long enough." The crowd all laughed, as expected, the long-extended term of his career a well-known fact.

Hanna listened as her father waded through the thankyous and appreciation for all in attendance and his final thoughts and guidance to all who would stay on beyond him. She looked out over the crowd. Some of the faces were familiar to her, long-time associates of her father and their spouses, a few distant aunts and uncles and cousins. Most in attendance she didn't know, *thankfully so*, she thought to herself.

She lifted her wine glass to her mouth and drank what was left, looking now to make her way back to the bar.

A strong arm grabbed her around the middle from behind. She turned and saw the smiling face of her fiancé, Alex Frank, the *G-man*, as her father continued to call him.

"Hello, beautiful," he said, dressed smartly in a dark blue suit and red tie, his graying hair cut and brushed back neatly.

Hanna fell into him and felt the warm and welcoming feel of his arms around her. "I can't tell you how much I appreciate you making time to come down here. This would all be intolerable without you."

"And you even invited the Skipper and Ella," he said, a broad grin on his face.

"Reinforcements!" she replied. "Low Country reinforcements to keep us sane."

"They're having a big time in the big city," Alex said, "as if they need any reason to party."

Hanna pulled him closer. "You're really feeling okay? I didn't think you could make the trip."

"I wouldn't have missed it."

"When are you going back on *active duty*?" she asked.

He hesitated, looking out over the crowd, then back to her, "There are a few complications."

"Complications?" she echoed, sensing the uncertainty in his voice.

Alex continued, "The Bureau has a few issues with my *Rambo* assault on Lacroix's house when I was trying to find you."

Hanna was surprised. "Why haven't you told me about this?"

He pulled her close, his cheek next to hers. "I'll work it out."

Hanna pushed back. "They should give you a commendation. You took Lacroix and his men down."

Alex smiled back, skeptically, and said, "Actually, Will and Sharron took them down. I was lying in a pool of my own blood, about to take the *deep sleep*."

Hanna shuddered, shaking her head at the gruesome memory. She pulled him close again. "Please, don't remind me. Do you really have enough on Lacroix this time?"

"Plenty," Alex said. "One of his goons turned on him and got us the recorder Christy Griffith found. We've also got a solid case now on the murders out at Remy D's house. Our new star witness puts Lacroix out at the house at the time of the murders."

"What about Remy?" Hanna asked. "It wasn't really a suicide?"

"Still working on that." He noticed Hanna's empty wine glass. "Come on, I'll buy you a drink."

Her father had finished his remarks and was accepting congratulations from a large group assembled around the podium. She caught his eye as they passed, and he smiled back.

As Alex led her through the packed crowd, Hanna saw her son, Jonathan, standing with his girlfriend talking to some of the cousins in attendance. He nodded as they passed, his face and expression appearing more normal following his early rehab and time working with Alex's doctor on his pain med dependence.

Alex ordered another glass of Cabernet for her and a beer for himself. They stepped away from the bar.

"Thank you for inviting them, too." Alex said as they found a place to stand near one of the walls of windows.

"Who?"

"Foster and Fairfield."

"They're starting to feel like family," she joked.

Hanna looked across the room and saw the two FBI agents together with attractive dates, standing in one corner of the room, glasses full and smiles on their faces. She was particularly glad to see the immaculately dressed and beautiful, Special Agent Sharron Fairfield, standing next to a ridiculously attractive man, her escort from Charleston for the evening.

She turned back to Alex. "I saw the latest news update this morning on the Dellahousaye kidnapping. Will one of the twins really go to jail?"

"Hard to say," Alex said. "She's got an amazing legal team and a platoon of doctors who will support her psychological challenges."

"She can certainly afford it now," Hanna said. "The news report said the twins will split most of their father's estate."

Alex shook his head. "The five-million-dollar ransom seems like nothing in comparison."

"Have you tracked down the money yet?" Hanna asked.

"Ophelia is cooperating. The money has been returned to her father's estate, so she'll get part of it anyway. Both of her partners in crime are dead, so no issues there. We're still trying to track down who they hired to actually abduct the girl, people close to Remy's man, Vincent, from what the Dellahousaye girl told us."

They both looked back at Alex's colleagues standing with their dates. Alex said, "We should go over and say hello."

"You go ahead," Hanna replied. "I'll stop over after I get a few minutes with my father." She watched him walk away, knowing they still had to have *the talk.* She still hadn't given him an answer on moving with him to DC. He wasn't pressing her, but they needed to get this resolved and move on, one way or the other. She was frustrated in not being able to come to a decision and she continued to push back discussing it with him.

She looked down at the engagement ring on her finger and then back to Alex as he was being introduced to Will and Sharron's dates. Any discussion of wedding plans had been put aside, which was also troubling. Again, Alex wasn't pushing her on any of this, but she knew he would have to go back to DC at any time.

"Hey kid."

She turned to see her father standing beside her. She pulled him close in a tight hug and whispered into his ear, "Congratulations, Allen."

He smiled back and they touched glasses in a toast to his retirement.

"Off to Greece tomorrow, I hear," she said.

He nodded and a thin smile spread across his face. "Martha is on a mission to get me out of town and away from the firm as soon as possible."

"She's doing a great job of it," Hanna said. "Are you really ready to give it up?"

"My heart surgeon tells me I don't have a choice."

"But, you're feeling okay?"

"I'm fine... just slowing down a bit."

"You *should* be slowing down!" she said and hugged him again. "I'm really happy for you and even Martha. I know we have a history, but I have to admit she really is good for you."

"She's been great," her father said. "And so have you. Thank you for agreeing to at least considering coming back to the firm when I'm finally gone."

"I'll be an old woman by then," she replied, smiling.

"Right," he said, then looked back intently. "I love you dear. I hope you and Alex have a great life together. I'm very happy for you."

She heard him but was having trouble acknowledging that the future was all so assured. "Thanks, *Daddy*," she finally said.

Alex turned when he felt Hanna's hand on his arm. He kissed her on the cheek and then introduced her to his colleague's guests. Handshakes were exchanged and a few pleasantries before Hanna leaned in and quietly said,

"Can we have a minute?"

He excused them and walked with Hanna across the room where they stood together looking out over the view of endless office towers, condominiums and hotels washed in the last light of the day. She placed her arm through his and continued to look out over the city.

"I can't go with you," she said, suddenly.

They finally turned to face each other. He had heard what she said but didn't respond. He could see a sad despair in her expression. He reached for her hand, the diamond on her ring finger held up between them.

"I'm sorry," she said, "but I can't leave."

He had been worried this was coming but had not pressed her on anything about the move or even a wedding.

"You're sure?" he finally asked.

She moved close and they hugged each other, her face pressed against his shoulder. "There's just too much right now," she continued. "If it was just work, I would try to make arrangements for the clinic to continue while I was away."

"Then what?" he asked.

"Jonathan is going into the rehab facility next week, the one in Charleston we've been talking about. I need to be there for him through all of that and when he comes out."

Alex listened and tried to make himself understand, but he felt his feet slipping out from under him, the plans he had, their future together. His mind was racing with reasons why he should try to talk her out of it, make her understand they could make it work.

"Alex?"

He looked into her eyes and saw tears welling up. He blinked as his own tears began and he reached up to wipe them away. He tried to push away his doubts and fears about their future. "We'll make this work.... I understand. We'll make it work."

The moment was interrupted when Alex was slapped on the back by his father.

"Why the long faces?" the Skipper asked. "Thought this was a celebration."

Ella came up and stood beside Hanna, putting her arm through hers. "What is it dear?" she asked.

Alex watched Hanna's face as she turned to his father's wife. She also wiped at her tears, then said, "We were just saying how happy we are to be together, to have each other." She smiled back at him.

We'll make it work.

THE END

A note from author, Michael Lindley...

Thank you for reading **THE SISTER TAKEN**! I truly appreciate your time with my stories.

The suspense and danger for Hanna and Alex continue in Book #5, **THE HARBOR STORMS**, when they face their most dangerous challenge yet when the murder of a friend and associate leads them to a plot that threatens to be one of the most devastating terrorist attacks in US history.

```
To keep reading THE HARBOR STORMS  go to Michael Lindley's
online store to buy direct at store.michaellindleynovels.com.
```

About the Author

Michael Lindley is an Amazon #1 bestselling author of mystery and suspense novels. His *"Hanna and Alex"* Low Country series has been a frequent #1 bestseller on Amazon in that genre.

His previous books include the "Troubled Waters" novels of historical mystery and suspense begins with the Amazon #1 bestseller, *THE EMMALEE AFFAIRS*.

"I've always been drawn to stories that are built around an idyllic time and place as much as the characters who grace these locations. As the heroes and villains come to life in my favorite stories, facing life's challenges of love and betrayal and great danger, I also enjoy coming to deeply understand the setting for the story and how it shapes the characters and the conflicts they face.

I've also loved books that combine a mix of past and present, allowing me to know a place and the people who live there in both a compelling historical context, as well as in present-day. I try to capture all of this in the books I write and the stories I bring to life."

Copy the Bookfunnel link below to sign up for my *"Behind The Scenes"* newsletter to receive announcements and special offers on new releases

and other special sales, and we will also send you a FREE eBook copy of the "*Hanna and Alex*" intro novella, *BEGIN AT THE END.*

You can connect with me on:

🜨 https://store.michaellindleynovels.com

Subscribe to my newsletter:

✉ https://dl.bookfunnel.com/syy533ngqn

Also by Michael Lindley

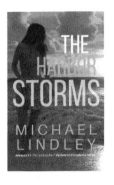

THE HARBOR STORMS

To keep reading **THE HARBOR STORMS**, go to Michael Lindley's online store to buy direct at store.michaellindleynovels.com.

Made in the USA
Columbia, SC
08 June 2025

59085384R00170